P9-CMX-410

"Grace, Emma is my daughter. I can't abandon her now that her mother is gone."

"Aidan, you're not being fair. How long have I waited to have a baby in my life, to share every bit of the experience with you? And now this... this child that will only serve to remind me every single day of my life that my husband has been unfaithful." Grace balled her hands into fists. "You should have been honest with me."

Aidan rushed to the side of the bed and knelt in front of her. "I should have. I know that. And I have no other explanation other than my own stupidity, my need to not have you angry at me. But now there is a child in our lives who just lost her mother, and who will be going through a terrible time. I can't leave her to deal with that without me. I...I can't."

His eyes implored her to understand. "I realize that this is a lot for you to accept, but Emma needs me...needs us."

Dear Reader,

Writing to you at this moment in time is both pleasant and sad. As some of you may know, the Harlequin Superromance line will be ending June 2018. Working for Harlequin has been a dream come true for me. It's been a wonderful experience to bring my characters to life with the help of the Harlequin editors in Toronto.

As I wrote this book, I was reminded of how easily life can change and how much of our lives are affected by the actions and thoughts of others. This is particularly true for Grace and Aidan Fellowes, deeply in love and happily married until an event outside their day-to-day lives changes everything. This story is not only about a couple's commitment to their marriage, but also about the importance of empathy. If Aidan and Grace hadn't been able to empathize with each other, and with Emma, the little girl who entered their lives, the story would have been over before it began. Empathy, whether for your spouse, a friend or a colleague, is the key ingredient needed to strengthen relationships and the first step in acceptance of a situation beyond our control.

It is with fond memories and an open heart that I offer you *Bringing Emma Home*.

I love to hear from my readers. I can be reached on Twitter, @Stella_MacLean, on Facebook at Facebook.com/StellaMacleanRomanceAuthor or through my website at StellaMaclean.com.

Sincerely,

Stella MacLean

STELLA MacLEAN

—

Bringing Emma Home

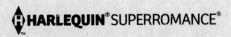

If you purchased this book without a cover you should be aware that this book is stolen property. It was reported as "unsold and destroyed" to the publisher, and neither the author nor the publisher has received any payment for this "stripped book."

Recycling programs for this product may not exist in your area.

ISBN-13: 978-1-335-44924-5

Bringing Emma Home

Copyright © 2018 by Ruth MacLean

All rights reserved. Except for use in any review, the reproduction or utilization of this work in whole or in part in any form by any electronic, mechanical or other means, now known or hereafter invented, including xerography, photocopying and recording, or in any information storage or retrieval system, is forbidden without the written permission of the publisher, Harlequin Enterprises Limited, 22 Adelaide St. West, 40th Floor, Toronto, Ontario M5H 4E3, Canada.

This is a work of fiction. Names, characters, places and incidents are either the product of the author's imagination or are used fictitiously, and any resemblance to actual persons, living or dead, business establishments, events or locales is entirely coincidental.

This edition published by arrangement with Harlequin Books S.A.

For questions and comments about the quality of this book, please contact us at CustomerService@Harlequin.com.

® and TM are trademarks of Harlequin Enterprises Limited or its corporate affiliates. Trademarks indicated with ® are registered in the United States Patent and Trademark Office, the Canadian Intellectual Property Office and in other countries.

Printed in U.S.A.

HARLEQUIN®
www.Harlequin.com

Stella MacLean loves creating contemporary romances in which the characters find love and fulfillment while learning to live in the moment. She draws her story ideas from her life as a wife, mother, grandmother and friend, and from her professional background as a nurse and accountant. Stella loves to travel and spend time with friends, and she is an avid gardener, taking great pleasure from digging in the dirt and watching seeds she has planted add beauty and grace to her gardens.

Books by Stella MacLean

HARLEQUIN SUPERROMANCE

Life in Eden Harbor

The Doctor Returns
To Protect Her Son
Sweet on Peggy

Heart of My Heart
Baby in Her Arms
A Child Changes Everything
The Christmas Inn
Unexpected Attraction

Visit the Author Profile page at Harlequin.com for more titles.

This book is dedicated to those in a marriage who have faced challenges in their relationship and found the courage and determination to work through those challenges to a deeper, more committed relationship. You are the real heroes.

CHAPTER ONE

GRACE FELLOWES REMEMBERED the exact moment her life changed forever. She'd been sitting in her high-school math class trying to work on a calculus problem when Aidan Fellowes slid into the desk next to her and smiled that smile of his that made her heart lift and turn over in her chest. She remembered feeling light-headed and dizzy, his smile fueling her breathlessness.

She tried not to blush—not a cool thing to do. Yet every bone in her body, every part of her being was alive to him, to the way his eyes focused on her and the way her body warmed, despite the fact he hadn't touched her.

She remembered when their eyes met, when he took the pencil from her fingers and showed her how to solve the problem. She remembered the fall leaves raining down around them, offering a crackling melody under their feet as they crossed the school parking lot to his Jeep. As they reached his vehicle, he took her hand, and from that moment, there was no one else for her but him.

Now, sitting in their bedroom in a solitary wingback chair, with the beginning tendrils of early light slipping around the bedroom drapes, her love for her husband was even stronger than it had been eighteen years ago when they first met. Glancing across the room to where Aidan lay sprawled on the bed, her gaze followed the line of his cheek as he slept, the easy movement of his chest as he breathed deeply, and she considered climbing back into bed with him.

Her fingers trembled as they traced the edge of her wedding band and diamond solitaire while the anxious ache brought on by the past held her in the chair, unable to go to him. They had been married for ten years and really focused on getting pregnant for nearly seven years, which meant that Aidan had left a lot of the out-of-town travel to visit clients to her brother, Lucas Barton. They were partners in a computer engineering firm they'd started when they'd both graduated from university.

Yet despite the sacrifices, despite how hard she and Aidan had tried, how much testing they'd gone through, she had to face the fact that she would not give birth to a baby she could hold and love with all her heart.

As their last failed chance to have a baby of their own crushed her dream of becoming pregnant, she finally decided to broach the topic of adopting a baby. Last night she'd cooked Aidan's favorite meal—shrimp and grits—and made his favorite dessert, chocolate cake. She'd spent days preparing the meal and rehearsing what she'd say.

She'd been so excited after dinner, unable to stop repeating the story of Cecilia and Dave, her friends, and their new baby boy, James Patrick Adair. When she mentioned that she'd put a call in to the same adoption lawyer their friends used, she'd waited for Aidan to respond, to say anything that gave her hope he might be willing to adopt. He hadn't.

Later, when they'd gone to bed, Aidan had turned away from her, leaving her disappointed and feeling completely alone. More than anything, she'd wanted him to hold her, to tell her that they would see the lawyer about an adoption as soon as his schedule allowed. She would have gladly accepted his need to put off that appointment for a bit because of his busy work life. She would even have accepted his asking to think about it awhile, plan for the changes adoption might mean. Anything to feel that there was still a chance for a baby to complete their life together.

What hurt even more was that he hadn't made love to her, hadn't tried to soothe her feelings of emptiness. Back when they were trying so desperately to get pregnant, their lovemaking had become more mandatory than spontaneous. But since they'd stopped trying, they'd rediscovered the joy of making love in their king-size bed.

She glanced around the room, remembering how happy she'd been when they bought this home with its four bedrooms—bedrooms she'd hoped to fill with their children. Her gaze returned to Aidan's face, relaxed in sleep, and she felt even more determined to encourage him to talk about adoption.

He stirred and her heart soared. She rose and went to the bed, sat beside him, soaking in his scent, smoothing the tufts of his glossy auburn hair mussed by the pillow. "Are you awake?" she whispered.

"Hmm." He reached up, his fingers trailing through her blond hair, tantalizing her with his touch, the feel of his skin on hers, the very presence of him filling her with joy.

He moved the sheets back, his arm reaching out to surround her. "Get in here, woman. I'm not ready to get up just yet, and you don't need to sit in the cool air," he said, his voice deep, his smoldering look banishing everything but her need for him.

She snuggled in, pulling the sheet over her half-naked body. "What were you doing up so early?" he asked, kissing her chin, his hands smoothing the hair from her face. "You're not up checking your temperature, are you?" He gave her an inquiring glance. "I thought we were done with that." He pushed a pillow under his shoulders, pulling her tighter into his embrace and kissing her, a long, slow kiss that melted every bone in her body.

"We are," she said, her throat feeling blocked while the memories played around her mind—the hope, the effort, the beautifully decorated nursery, the agony of loss… all of it for nothing. What should have been happy, wonderful years of starting a family had become the most desolate time of her life.

He tucked her close to his side, his lips brushing her forehead. "This is hard for you, and for me, but the doctors had to tell us the truth. We have to accept that. We've got to move on."

"I know. But weren't you excited about my news last night?" she asked, stroking his chin, watching to see how he'd respond. Maybe after a night's sleep he was ready to talk about when they could see the adoption lawyer.

He sighed. "We need to really think about this a little more. After what we've been through, it's a huge decision."

"I realize that." She continued to gently touch his face, feeling the light stubble there. He didn't pull away as he had last night. "But the adoption lawyer has made such a big difference in Cecilia and Dave's life. I want to talk to him. I decided to call his office to see if we could get an appointment…if you're willing to go with me."

"What was his name again?"

"Sterling Martin. I told you all of this last night," she said, feeling frustrated but trying to hide it. "His office is just off King Street. He specializes in private adoptions. Cecilia and Dave are so happy with their new baby. James P is such a perfect child."

Aidan's fingers trailed along her collarbone, something he did whenever they talked about having a child. "Honey, I know how important this is to you. To us. But just this once, can we wake up and think about something else? Like maybe a vacation to Europe. We always said we wanted to go. Remember? All those times we watched our friends take off on vacation to some place interesting while we stayed home because of your worries about what could happen if you conceived while we were out of the country."

His words stung. She understood his feelings and, at times, had shared them. But he didn't understand how much she needed a baby. Her arms ached every time one of her friends had a baby. Then, when Cecilia and Dave had adopted, Grace finally felt hopeful over the possibility she and Aidan might, too. He simply needed more time to think about it, and she was willing to wait. "Sure. Why don't I make breakfast for us? I promise not to talk about adoption."

"That's my girl. All I really want to do is spend time with you. Just you. Would that be okay?"

"I would love that," she said, recognizing the expression on his face. He wasn't going to talk about a child right now. It was up to her to accept that and have a pleasant breakfast with him. But that didn't mean she was giving up. Not a chance.

Suddenly, she brightened. She knew what she'd do. She would invite Cecilia and Dave to dinner, maybe a good Southern barbecue evening. Cecilia's praise for Sterling Martin would carry more sway than anything Grace herself could say at this point. Aiden had a great deal of respect for Cecilia, one of the computer engineers in his firm.

He rubbed her shoulder, his fingers circling the skin over her collarbone—a clear sign that Aidan had something on his mind, something he wasn't ready to share with her. "What is it, honey?"

He sighed. "Just thinking that it would be nice if you came with me today. I have a client I have to see in downtown Charleston. But I want you with me." He held her closer, running his lips along her hairline, driving her crazy with need. "Once I'm finished, we could have lunch, take a carriage ride around historic Charleston, buy something for your garden at one of the stalls at the market. We've often talked about going into the city and spending time wandering the shops. Why don't we do it today? I want you with me," he repeated slowly, his gaze searching her face, coming to rest on her lips.

"Oh, Aidan, I want that, too, but I promised Cecilia that we'd meet for lunch." She looked into his hazel-green eyes, seeing the disappointment. Trying to soften the blow, she whispered, "I wish you'd come by and see this little baby. You will not be able to resist him."

THE OLD GUILT swirled around Aidan's mind. He didn't want to talk about babies or adoption or anything related to that today. He wanted his wife to pay attention to him and only him, to focus on their relationship. That was all he'd wanted for the past seven years: her undivided attention on him and their love for each other. Was that so much to ask?

He'd done everything she wanted, raced home when she called him, tried to console her when each attempt to conceive failed. But at times it hardly seemed worth it. Their marriage had become a marathon of waiting, hoping and frantic lovemaking, all to try to have a baby.

He didn't want to remember the one time he'd slipped up, but that weekend entered his mind, as it had a few minutes ago. It had happened five years ago and was long over. He'd hooked up with a woman, a client whose business was in Spartanburg. He'd never heard from her again after that one weekend, and didn't intend to renew any contact. All the same, he felt guilty about how much he had enjoyed having a woman's attention focused solely on him. He scrubbed his face with his hands to hide the memory of how that weekend had felt. Sighing, he turned to Grace. "Are you sure you can't come with me?"

"I'd have to call and cancel lunch with Cecilia, and I want to see James again." Grace sighed as she snuggled closer to him.

He soaked in her smile, felt the old pull of attraction that had been there between them since the day they'd met in high school.

His eyes focused on hers, he saw the glint of desire there, and his mind raced over the possibilities. She was everything he'd ever wanted in a woman, a wife. There had to be some way to convince her to come to Charleston with him. "Why don't I book a suite at the Planters Inn? We could go out to dinner, or order room service, a bottle of wine…just the two of us. We haven't stayed downtown in Charleston in years. What do you say?"

"A night in Charleston?" she asked.

"Or two nights, if you'd like. Beautiful surroundings, all the amenities. Think fluffy robes, nothing on under them. Pure luxury in a suite all to ourselves. Me reaching for you," he whispered in her ear, hearing her breath quicken as his body hardened.

He kissed her lips, felt her body curve into his. His blood hot, his body arching toward hers, he felt her immediate response as if it was imprinted into his consciousness.

"I would do anything for you, Aidan Caldwell Fellowes," she said, her lips on his throat, her breath searing his skin.

"And me for you," he whispered, pulling her under him as his lips sought the soft skin between her breasts.

Her quick intake of breath was all he needed. He continued to kiss her skin, moving his tongue along the space between her breasts. "If you come with me to Charleston, I promise you the best time you've ever had, Mrs. Fellowes." He raised his gaze to hers. "You will not regret a minute of the time you spend with me."

She sighed, her hands stroking his face, her skin flushed pink.

He eased his hands over her tummy, down

along her hips, hugging her body against his. "What do you say?"

She looked deep into his eyes, her lips parted, her hair spread across the pillow. "You never cease to amaze me, Aidan," she whispered, her fingers continuing their course over his cheek, down his neck.

"How so?" he asked, loving this game, this moment when she would succumb to him. It had always been that way. He would entice her with something, a dinner out, a trip, a night in, just the two of them. Until recently, Grace had always gone along with his plans. And now, with the whole issue of a baby settled, he wanted them to go back to the beginning, back to the way things were.

"I agree we need to get away, time to ourselves. It would be really nice to spend a couple days in Charleston. You win, my love. I'll cancel my lunch date."

He kissed her, cradling her head in his hands. "Thank you. You won't regret going with me. Besides, how can you resist the chance to have me all to yourself?" he teased, aware of the times he'd wanted her to go away with him when he'd be gone for days without her, and she'd remained at home, either for a doctor's appointment, redecorating the baby's room or a quilting event.

"Aidan, I love you," she whispered as her body writhed under his caress, a groan of pleasure escaping her lips.

"And I love you," he murmured against her skin.

Two hours later, he and Grace arrived in Charleston. "Why don't I drop you some-where along King Street, give you a little time to shop? And before you say anything about the cost, I want you to buy whatever you want. Promise me you'll do that," he said.

She smiled at him, her body still humming from the time they'd spent in bed making love. It was as if everything that had stood between them, all the pain and uncertainty of the past few years, had slipped away. It was as if they were back to the way they'd been when they first got married.

Aidan was so right about what they needed—the time together without anyone interfering. She smiled at the memory of those early morning hours. As they'd packed to leave, joking and talking with each other the way they once had, she was certain they would work everything out.

She was confident that this trip was meant

to be. The next couple of days together would work its magic on them. She'd never stayed at the Planters Inn, but she'd heard about it from a friend who had spent her wedding night in one of its beautiful suites. Grace had helped her plan her big day and had seen the photos of the inn, all gold and cream with deep hues of blue and roses everywhere. She couldn't imagine a more perfect place for a getaway. "I promise to buy whatever I see that I like," she offered, stroking his arm.

"Perfect. I'll call you the second I'm out of my meeting and we'll go for a late lunch," he said, navigating the tight lanes of traffic leading toward Broad Street, the hallmark of Charleston civility.

"I wish we'd planned to do this with Lucas and Maria. She's such a great shopper, and we always have a good time together. I was never so happy as when Lucas arrived back from a business trip to Spartanburg to tell me he'd met the woman of his dreams. Do you think they'll get married? I mean, Lucas talks about her all the time, and I want him to be as happy as we are."

"Lucas and Maria are not on my mind at all. They have their life and we have ours," he said, his gaze direct, a small furrow forming between his eyes as he turned to her. "All I want is to let the world go away and you and I focus on us," he said as he maneuvered the large SUV into a narrow parking spot.

"Okay. No more talk about anyone or anything but us," she said. She didn't want anything to ruin their minivacation. Reaching across the wide console, she squeezed his hand where it rested on the steering wheel. "I can't wait for you to be finished. You're right. We need to get away. Starting today, we'll plan to do something like this once a month. We deserve time alone together, don't we?"

"Exactly. Why can't we just take off, act like a pair of teenagers in love? The way we used to do," he said, his smile intimate, wrapping around her, signaling that whatever was bothering him had gone.

She kissed him quickly. "After I'm done shopping, I'll call a cab and go to the inn. I'll check in and be waiting for you. Just for you, I'm going to buy something really sexy to wear tonight." She kissed him again before she reached for the door handle. "You'd better be ready," she teased, seeing the love in his eyes. Her body tingled. "I'll order a bottle of champagne."

He pulled her to him and kissed her, his

mouth moving over hers in a way that made her weak with desire. "I can't wait, woman." His smile radiated happiness as his lips brushed hers. "I'll see you later. We'll order room service and you can model your latest purchase...before I remove it."

FIVE HOURS LATER, Aidan lay sprawled on the bed, Grace in his arms, the sheets crumpled around them, his need for her completely sated.

"You are the most beautiful woman in the world," he said, his throat filled with emotion as unexpected tears tingled behind his lids. He hadn't felt this way for a very long time. He'd come to the inn and been met at the door of their suite by his wife dressed in a skimpy lace item that covered just enough and hinted at a lot more. He'd fallen into bed with her, and they'd had the best afternoon of lovemaking he could remember.

Slowly he kissed her lips, his fingers caressing her cheek. "I've never loved anyone the way I love you."

She returned his kiss. "I love you, too, so much," she whispered, her gaze on him and only him.

"I've missed this," he said, his heart filled to overflowing.

"What do you mean?" She toyed with the hair on his chest.

"The way we made love, the closeness, the sheer excitement of simply enjoying each other."

She pulled back a little. "But we've always—"

He placed his fingers gently over her lips to silence her. "Not like this. Not with this intensity and simply for the sheer pleasure of being with each other."

Her gaze never left his face, and he saw the shimmer of unshed tears in her eyes.

"I don't mean to say we haven't made love to each other these past years, but there was always the other—"

"We've been over this before," she said, her voice soft with a tinge of hurt.

Aidan wished he'd said nothing. "I'm sorry. This has been fantastic, and I shouldn't have said anything. It's just that I feel like I have you back. The Grace I married and have loved for so long. That's all I meant. That's all I've ever wanted."

"Me, too," she said, her voice wistful.

"Then let's not think about anything other

than ourselves for the next two days. If I have my way, we won't leave this room. We won't need to." He leaned up on one elbow and smiled at her. "I don't ever want to leave this bed, but I am a little hungry. Why don't I order room service? Another bottle of champagne, even?" He winked at her.

Grace chuckled. "You think you'll get me a little tipsy and have your way with me again?"

"I've already had my way with you. Or did I leave such a poor impression that you didn't notice?" he asked, kissing her again, feeling the heat rise, the tremble of her lips against his.

"I noticed," she whispered, her hands moving over his chest, feeding his desire.

He held her close, his mouth claiming hers, his hands spreading across her back, moving down her body, her answering intake of breath music to his ears. "Yes," he whispered against her lips. "We will put food on hold for a while longer—"

The chime of his cell phone startled him. "What was that?"

"I thought you turned your phone off," she said leaning across him, her breasts skimming his chest. "I'll do it for you. No more interruptions."

He let her slide across him, enjoying the feel of her body on his. "Whoever is calling can wait."

Grace picked up the phone and turned it off. "There. You don't know how much pleasure I get from turning off your phone. Do you realize that it's always on? That we're always at the mercy of that piece of plastic?" she asked, sliding her body down his, making his breath quicken as her fingers trembled over his heated skin.

"You can turn my phone off anytime, Mrs. Fellowes, if this is what you intend to do while it's off," he said, his hands reaching for her shoulders, his body arching toward hers.

"This and a whole lot more," she murmured as her gaze met his, the love in her eyes fueling his need for her. He stretched out in the bed, luxuriating in her touch, anticipating every move her body made along his.

The room phone blared.

Grace sighed and shifted to lie next to him. "What is going on?"

"It must be important, or maybe it's the inn wondering if we need anything. Either way," he said, reaching for the sleek black phone on the bedside table, "I'll take care of it and we can get back to..." He looked into her eyes, saw her excitement and almost didn't pick up the phone. "I'll get this over as fast as I can."

He grabbed the phone.

"Aidan, it's Nancy. Sorry to interrupt, but I've had an urgent call from a lawyer in Spartanburg. He insists on talking to you now. He's on the other line to be transferred to you."

"Did he say what he wanted?"

"No. Just that he needed to talk to you as soon as possible. There seems to be some sort of emergency."

He exchanged surprised glances with Grace. "But Lucas looks after our clients in Spartanburg. Did you tell him that?"

"I did, but he said it's a personal matter, that he needs to speak to you directly."

"Okay, put him on," Aidan said with a sigh, pulling Grace closer as he settled in to hear what the man had to say.

"Hello, is this Aidan Fellowes?" a deep, gruff voice inquired.

"It is. What is so urgent that you need to speak to me today? I'll be back in the office on Monday and we can talk then."

"I'm afraid that won't work. I have to ask you a few questions," the man said.

"Who is this?" Aidan said, annoyed at the man's presumption that he could dictate to him.

The phone was silent for a few moments. "It's Larry Knowles. I'm the attorney for Deidre MacPherson."

"I'm sorry," Aidan said, his mind scrambling over the possibilities. Deidre had never attempted to contact him after their long-ago weekend together. "Why are you calling me? I have no connection to that person."

"Ms. MacPherson was killed in an automobile accident on Thursday. According to her will, you are sole beneficiary of her estate with the proviso that you become the legal guardian of her daughter, Emma."

Aidan swung his legs over the side of the bed and sat up. "You've got the wrong person. This is a mistake."

"Not according to what I'm reading here." He could hear the rustle of pages and a short pause. "She states that you are Emma's father. She wants you to be her daughter's guardian and to adopt her as soon as possible. When you do, you will receive the total of her estate worth over five million dollars. Her will is very clear on this point. Did you have no idea that she'd done this?"

It wasn't possible. He couldn't be the father of Deidre's child. They'd spent a weekend together. Nothing more. He'd tried unsuccessfully for years to get his wife pregnant. What was the likelihood that he'd fathered a child with another woman?

This story had to be a lie. Obviously, Deidre had decided to make him responsible for a child he'd never met and couldn't possibly have fathered. He took a deep breath. "I have no idea what you're talking about. I think this conversation has gone far enough," he said forcefully, his eyes meeting Grace's anxious expression as she snuggled under his arm, the gentle touch of her hand offering him her support.

"No. It hasn't. Not until you agree…" More paper shuffling. "I have here a document, a DNA test that Ms. MacPherson had done on her child and you. You are the father of Emma Leigh MacPherson. We need to talk. When can you be in Spartanburg, Mr. Fellowes?"

"There has to be a mistake. I don't know what you're talking about," Aidan said, the lie slipping so easily off his tongue.

Aidan's stomach rose against his chest as

his mind raced over the words this man had spoken. Something was wrong. This couldn't be happening. It had been years ago, another lifetime, and none of it had meant anything to him. Grace knew nothing about that weekend, had never questioned any of his business trips.

His wife was a Christian who believed that the truth was a guiding principle in life. He believed it, too. He hadn't wanted to lie to her about that weekend, and so had pleaded a heavy workload in Spartanburg.

He didn't want to lie to her now, but he had no choice. If she found out that he'd fathered a child while they were trying to get pregnant, she would be devastated. He had no doubt that she would leave him. He couldn't let that happen. Not over a mistake he had always regretted.

It had nothing to do with their life now. Grace's happiness meant everything to him. He glanced furtively at his wife, seeing a look of confusion on her face, wishing he could end the call and it would all simply go away.

"What is going on?" she asked, sitting up straighter, slipping away from his side.

He had to do something to save the situation before he was forced to use words that would cause Grace to be suspicious. "Look, Mr. Knowles. We can discuss this on Monday. I'm sure there is some misunderstanding. We'll clear it up then."

"That won't work. This child, your daughter, is living with her nanny, but arrangements need to be made for her. There is no immediate family, and if you don't take the little girl, other arrangements will have to be made. I need to see you tomorrow. I'll be in my office. What time can you be here?"

"I can't drop everything just because you want to meet," Aidan said, trying to make sense of this, but even more, trying to absorb that he was supposedly the father of a child he'd never known existed.

He scrubbed his face in disbelief. If this proved to be true, how was he going to tell Grace? He pressed the bridge of his nose, concentrating on regaining control of the situation. Whatever was going on with this Mr. Knowles, he would not let it spill over into his life with Grace.

CHAPTER TWO

AT THE SUDDEN change in Aidan's voice, a chill ran through Grace. Something was horribly, terribly wrong. She'd never seen Aidan look so awful, so confused and uncertain, in all the years she'd known him. "Honey, what is it?"

Grace watched his anxious expression as fear wrapped around her heart, blocking the air from her lungs. Had someone been hurt? Was it a friend? Someone at work? Lucas? Her body quaked at the thought. It couldn't be her brother, could it? The way Aidan's gaze moved around the room, never connecting with hers, was terrifying. Unable to help herself, she reached up to put her arms around his shoulders, needing to learn more with each passing minute. "What is going on, Aidan? What is it?"

Clutching the phone tighter to his ear, he turned away from her. "If you insist, I will be there tomorrow afternoon. Not a minute before.

Whatever is going on here, I'm as anxious as you to get to the bottom of this."

Relief whistled through her at his words, the strict business tone he used. From what he said, it was clear that no one was hurt or in trouble, at least, no one she knew. Yet the soft light from the window exposed the pallor of Aidan's skin. "What's wrong?" she whispered urgently.

"It's nothing, a misunderstanding that needs to be cleared up, that's all," he said, hanging up.

"What sort of misunderstanding?" she asked, as her nails bit into his shoulders.

"Someone died and I'm needed in Spartanburg tomorrow." His tone was matter-of-fact, his expression grim, adding to her concern. She'd never known Aidan to respond to someone's death with such anger. It was as if he didn't believe what he'd been told.

"That's awful. I'm sorry. But why did they call you? If it's about business, why didn't they call Lucas?"

He shook his head, still holding the phone as he rose from the bed and went to the window.

Grace went to him, wanting to comfort him. Taking his hand, she said, "Whatever is going on, I want to be there with you. Tell me who died."

"It's someone…I knew… A client."

"Someone you knew? In Spartanburg?"

Aidan turned away, moving closer to the heavily draped window, his shoulders slumped.

She waited. He didn't turn back to her, seek her out the way he did when something was bothering him. He'd been like that since the day they'd met. She could always rely on him to share his thoughts, whatever they were, good or bad.

"That was a call informing me about the death of Deidre MacPherson, the CEO of one of our major clients in Spartanburg. It seems I'm needed there urgently. Tomorrow at the latest." He scrubbed his face with his hands. The only sound in the room was that of his long, agitated sigh as he placed the phone on the table, staring at it as if it had bitten him.

The set of his shoulders, the way he didn't seem to see her or even be aware of her, made Grace realize that, for the first time in their marriage, he was lying to her. He was keeping something from her or he wouldn't be so evasive. He'd hidden things from her before, like a surprise birthday party or when he gave her diamond earrings on their tenth anniversary. But they were surprises, not lies.

And this was a lie. She didn't understand how she knew it was a lie. She'd never been suspicious of Aidan, had always trusted him completely. But now it was clear that there was something he was concealing, something so important to him that he was willing to lie to her about it. Her stomach lurched. "Aidan, what is going on? I'm your wife. You owe me an explanation."

"That was her lawyer. He needs to talk to me." Aidan glanced around, spotted his underwear and awkwardly pulled them on, all the while never once glancing in her direction.

"About what? And why you?" she insisted, though her heart pounded so hard in her ears she could barely hear.

"That woman, the one who died..." He searched the room for his shirt and pants. "She left her entire estate to me."

"Why? Why would a woman leave you her money?"

"Because—" Aidan grabbed his clothes and got dressed hurriedly. "Because she's crazy. She claims that she had a child. That the child is mine. I haven't seen her in five years. I have no idea why she thinks her child is mine." His look when he met her eyes was one of agony and despair.

Grace couldn't breathe. She reached out to the drapes to support her as her knees began to buckle. His words cascaded over her, blocking her thoughts, filling her with disbelief and panic. A strangled cry emerged. "What are you talking about?" There had to be a mistake. Aidan and she couldn't have children. All the testing proved that. She searched his face, seeking some sort of denial from him. "Tell me this isn't true. This can't be true. You can't have a baby."

"Grace, you need to sit down," he said as he came to her, pulled her into his arms and led her to the sofa near the fireplace. "Let me try to explain what I believe is going on."

"Did you have an affair with her?" she asked, her body shaking at the enormity of it all. Aidan in another woman's bed. Aidan making love to another woman, his hands, his body on hers. The intimacy of the act, the love he was capable of making to Grace offered to another woman. "Tell me the truth!" she demanded, feeling sick to her stomach with anguish.

"Grace! I'm sorry. Really sorry." He went

down on one knee in front of her, his eyes pleading, his voice filled with remorse.

"Five years ago?" She heard a scream and realized it was hers. "You had an affair five years ago when we were trying to have a baby?"

"Not an affair. Not really." He scrubbed his face with hands that shook. "You and I were going through a rough time."

Her mind fumbled over his words. Her husband, the man she loved, had had an affair with another woman. He'd broken a solemn vow to her, one he'd taken before God. This couldn't be true. But hadn't he just admitted to it? "When? When did you do this?"

"I... Back when I managed our clients in Spartanburg. Before Lucas took over."

"Is that why Lucas started going there? Is he aware of what is going on?"

"No. No one knows. It was just one weekend, and I've regretted it ever since." He stared at the ceiling, then back at her. "I've never regretted anything more in my whole life."

There were tears in his eyes, but it didn't matter. No amount of tears could change what he'd just admitted to. "Regretted it," she echoed. "You had sex with her and you *regretted it.*" She struggled to sort out her thoughts. This was all wrong.

"I swear I did not know she had a child. And I know it isn't mine. I wouldn't... couldn't."

"Stop! You just admitted to having sex with a woman who had a child. Your child."

"No! Not my child!"

"You lied to me all this time. I didn't lie to you. But you sure as hell lied to me. You had an affair with another woman." She pounded his chest, grabbed his hair and pulled as hard as she could. "You destroyed everything!"

He winced. His eyes didn't leave her face. "Grace, please stop. I don't want to upset you." He touched her bare leg.

"Upset me," she seethed. "You've more than upset me, you bastard." Suddenly she became aware that she was naked. Desperately wanting to cover herself, to feel whole and in control, she pushed his hand off her. "Get out of my way, Aidan. I'm getting dressed and getting out of here."

"Grace. No. Don't leave. Please let me try to explain. I realize that this is a huge shock for you. It's a shock to me, as well." Aidan reached for her again, but she pushed him away as she got off the sofa and moved across the room.

"A shock to you? Really?" she said, feeling the bitterness like a flush of acid seeping through her mind. Everything she loved and cherished had been swept from her life by his awful words.

He followed her as she moved around the room, gathering up her things. "I didn't mean it that way. I mean getting the call and not knowing what was happening—" He lowered his head. "I've totally screwed up."

For a fraction of a second, she almost went to him, to console him the way she always had.

But those days were dead and gone. She couldn't let him touch her when she knew that he'd had an affair with another woman, and had lied to her about something so personal, so destructive that she would never trust him again. "If this is *not* your child, a DNA test will prove you're not the father, won't it?"

His expression filled with anguish, he glanced away.

Angry and disbelieving, Grace tried to remain calm. Struggling to get into her skimpy sundress and high heels, she hopped on one foot as she fastened her watch on her wrist.

It seemed to be taking forever to get dressed. She just wanted to get out of here as soon as she could, away from the man who had destroyed her world.

A man, she now realized, she didn't really know at all. "This woman you had sex with had the DNA test done, didn't she?" She pointed at the phone, her voice rising. "That man. That lawyer wouldn't be calling you if there wasn't proof that you are the father of this woman's child."

"He says he has DNA proof. But I don't believe it. We, you and I, can't have children, and so this has to be some sort of awful mistake."

Grace struggled to put on her earrings and finally gave up, throwing them on the floor. Aidan grabbed them from where they landed on the plush cream carpet. "I gave these to you," he said, in a disbelieving tone. "They're your favorites."

"I don't want jewelry bought out of guilt," she said, striding into the bathroom. She combed her fingers through her hair, applied a little blush and gathered her cosmetics bag. She may just have been totally humiliated by her husband, but she was a Southern woman, and she would not leave the suite without looking in control and in charge.

In the bedroom, she shoved the remainder of her things into her suitcase. So many thoughts were crashing around her mind, each delivering yet another blow to her self-esteem. Her husband had had an affair and a child by another woman. "If this is true, it means that I'm the one who can't have children, doesn't it?"

"Grace, we've been over this dozens of times before. The doctors told us it was no one's fault that we couldn't have children. That some people simply can't conceive. Please don't do this."

"I have no choice. I've waited our entire marriage for a baby, and now I learn that you are a father."

"Grace, honey, I recognize this is hard for you. I wish I didn't have to bring it up," he said, his head lowered, his expression downcast.

"But you did and now I have to deal with it. How could you do this? To cheat on me, on us, is unbearable. And the fact that you didn't recognize how hard this would be for me, to know you had a child when I couldn't. You have destroyed everything."

"Please, Grace, don't say that. It's not over between us. It can't be. We love each other.

I've hurt you and I will make it up to you somehow. I should have told you about the weekend with Deidre, but I didn't want to hurt you over nothing. And it was nothing. Just a mindless fling because I was feeling so isolated and alone in our marriage. But that's no excuse. I broke the promise I made to you. Please understand I never meant to hurt you. You, of all people. I love you, Grace." His face was ashen, his eyes pleading.

"A mindless mistake showing your total disrespect for me, for our marriage, and I'm to believe that it's as simple as you making a mistake? How stupid do you think I am?"

"I don't think you're stupid. I'm the stupid one for ever having anything to do with the woman." Aidan stood still, misery an almost tangible aura around him.

"Well, it's too late now. You can't go back and undo what you did. And because of what you did, there is a child and you're the father. Is it a girl or a boy?" she asked, feeling nothing, as if her body were floating off somewhere, that none of this was real.

"It's a girl," he said, his voice flat, as if the realization hadn't yet dawned on him that he was a father.

"How old is she?" Grace demanded.

Aidan glanced around the room his hands shoved deep into his pockets. "I guess she'd be four or so."

"What do you intend to do about her?" Grace asked.

Aidan gave a long sigh. "I don't know. I figured it would get cleared up tomorrow."

"If you're so sure the child is not yours, maybe you should take our lawyer with you," Grace said, trying to sound reasonable and in control even as her heart crumpled in her chest.

Her husband had fathered a child with a woman he'd had a weekend hookup with. That hurt in the worst way possible. All those times they'd hurried to make love while she was ovulating, only to be disappointed. All those times…the heartbreak she'd had to face…while he'd sought the attentions of another woman.

"Grace, I need to learn what I can about the situation. Maybe you're right. Maybe I should take our lawyer, but first I'd like to see for myself what is going on." He rubbed his palms together. "I know it's asking a lot, but would you go with me to Spartanburg?"

She was halfway to the door when he said the words. She stopped and turned around so quickly her overnight bag banged into the back of her leg, delivering a stinging blow. "Me? You're asking me to go with you? You destroyed my faith in you, and now you want me to help you solve a problem all of your making."

"I have no right to ask this. And you have every right to refuse me."

"You got that right. For now, all I can think about is how you deceived me and slept with another woman while we were trying so hard to have a child of our own… Or, at least, I was trying," she said, her voice failing her as betrayal and anguish swept through her. Without warning, humiliation burned her throat. Her head swam. "I don't understand how you could have done this to me, to us," she cried. "But you did. You destroyed our marriage."

Instantly, he was at her side. "It was a stupid mistake. I was feeling as if the life we wanted together would never happen. I wanted a child so much. I wanted our life to be complete. I thought that you would be happy if only we could have a child. Then I started to feel trapped by all the doctor visits, the appointments, the expectations."

She stepped away, her back straight, her

eyes boring into him. "I don't want to hear your excuses. Not ever again."

"Grace, please listen to me. I was in Spartanburg working with a client, working hard and wishing I could be home with you, instead."

"A client? You mean this Deidre MacPherson person?" Grace asked, trying to decide how much longer she could stand to be near him, knowing what he'd done to her.

Aidan held her shoulders, his touch gentle and kind, the way he always behaved when he wanted her to understand something going on with his work Without warning, the time he'd come to her, telling her they'd have to mortgage their home in order to meet a loan payment flashed in front of her. The threat that they might lose their home had been one of the worst moments of her life. To lose her home meant she would lose the place she dreamed of raising their children.

"Yes, it was Deidre MacPherson's business. She had just landed a major contract and we were providing technical support. I had to stay over the weekend with my technicians to get the system up and running. We went out to celebrate and something happened. I never saw her again or had any form of contact. I swear—"

"I don't want to hear it!" She glared at him, gritting her teeth.

He stepped back. "I didn't mean to remind you... All I want you to know is that I have nothing to hide where she is concerned. And that includes whatever this lawyer has in mind for us. There is simply no way I am the father of that child, but this Larry Knowles isn't going to let it go. He has to do what his client laid out in her will."

The warmth of Aidan's body mingled with his cologne, filling her nostrils, and for a few pain-filled moments she wished they could simply forget everything that had happened and go back to bed. Feeling deflated and faced with the anguish in his eyes, she relented a little. "Oh, Aidan, you have ruined everything. Everything you and I ever wanted or needed is gone for good. I don't know you anymore."

"Please don't say that. I've gotten us into a terrible mess. And I will find a way out of it, if only you'll give me a little time to make things right," he said, his voice shaking.

Aidan looked into her eyes, into the depths of her, her heart and her soul. They had always had this connection, this one-to-one sensation whenever they spoke about those things close to their hearts. She wanted to reach out to him, to soothe him, but the agony of what he'd done left her feeling so betrayed and angry she could barely breathe. She couldn't touch him knowing that another woman had touched him, probably in much the same way. "I don't want to deal with this, any of this."

"Neither do I, but this man won't stop trying. And it might be better if we faced this head-on, like we would with any crisis in our lives. What do you think?" He held his breath. His gaze searched her face.

"What if we go and he has irrefutable proof that it's your child?"

Once again, his hands reached for hers. She hugged herself, not letting him touch her.

"Grace, that's not possible. The more I think about it, the less likely I think it is that it's true. In my experience, she was always meticulous in her dealings with people. If I was the father of her child, why didn't she tell me? I can't help but believe that she would have wanted me to know, to share the responsibility for the baby, the cost of her education, all the things that are needed to care for a child. I can't imagine that she wouldn't have insisted that I help out. What woman wouldn't?"

"What will we do if it is your child?" Grace asked, as she kept waiting to wake up from a bad dream, cry out and be cuddled by her husband, the way it had happened after other nightmares.

The thought that a child would come into their lives in such a destructive, personally tragic way was almost beyond believing. "If this child is yours, you've hurt an innocent child because of your careless behavior while destroying our marriage."

Aidan stood perfectly still. "I realize that, Grace. And I have no idea how I'll make it up to you, but I will. As for the little girl, we owe it to her to talk with this lawyer and see what proof he thinks he has that I'm her father."

If she was to keep her marriage as God intended, and rebuild the trust they'd always shared, she had to work her way through this horrible mess. But she couldn't do it without proof that Aidan was serious about making amends. "There is only one way I will consider being involved with you in this, and that is if you tell me everything. If I find out you've been lying to me about this woman, about your time with her, our marriage is over."

"I have told you the truth. And there is zero chance that this is my child. You and I have been trying to get pregnant for years, and every doctor we went to couldn't find the cause. I simply won't accept without further DNA tests, that I could have fathered a child so easily. Not after all the times you and I have made love, all the procedures we went through. It's as simple as that. From my point of view, this is a mistake on someone's part. I want to get it straightened out so that you and I can go ahead with adopting a child."

"Adopt a child? How can you even think of such a thing when our marriage is in so much trouble? Didn't you just tell me that you'd had an affair, that there might be a child from that affair? You think that this will simply be over by you admitting to what you did?" she asked, shocked and angry.

"I didn't mean right away. I meant after this is over."

"Aidan, this won't simply go away. The fact that you had an affair is bad enough. The thought that you had a child with this woman makes everything impossible. Can't you see that?"

She stood with her hand on the door, her head pounding, and watched her husband's face. A face she loved, had loved most of her life. And now, because of one phone call, it might all be over. "Well? Aren't you going to say something?"

"Grace, I'm begging you to go with me. You can't imagine how terrible I feel for the pain I've caused you. I want to make it up to you by being totally honest about all this. From now on, wherever this takes us, I want you with me."

She heard the sincerity in his voice, saw the expression of remorse on his face, and her determination to walk out slipped from her. Whatever he'd done, however much he'd hurt her, she was still his wife and she had to allow him to make this right. Maybe he couldn't, and she would have to live with that. But whatever came out of this, she didn't want to end up regretting what she'd done, how she'd behaved.

As she stared at him, memories of their life flashed before her eyes, all the good times they'd had together would end up being for nothing if she acted too rashly. Deep down inside she wanted to believe that, despite everything, they might still have a chance.

"I don't know if I can do this, any of it. You've hurt me in ways I could never have imagined. Right now I hate you, and I can't imagine ever getting over what I'm feeling."

"Grace, I'm so afraid," he said, his hands working at his sides.

"Would you be willing to go for marriage counseling?" she asked.

"Of course. All I want is you, Grace. I want us to find each other again, to feel what we've felt all these years."

She looked at the man she'd married ten years ago, at the light dusting of freckles on his cheeks, the way his eyes seemed to see straight through her. Was it possible she might have feelings for him again? That somehow their marriage would survive this? Love didn't die easily. She'd seen her parents' marriage and the trouble they'd gone through, the loss of faith when her dad's gambling problem had nearly bankrupted the family. She had to believe that her marriage would survive this, that marriage counseling might help them regain the trust they'd lost.

But she had no idea how. And if it turned out that Aidan had been unfaithful, it could be the final blow to their marriage, something that Grace would never get over. To a part of Grace, it was simply unbelievable that her husband could have fathered a child when they'd done everything to have one of their own. No one had said it was her fault that they couldn't conceive, but deep down, she blamed herself. Proving that Aidan hadn't had a child by this woman would help ease her guilt that she was responsible for their infertility. If this whole thing was behind them, as Aidan said, they could go to counseling, reaffirm their marriage vows and work with the adoption lawyer to find a baby.

Grace took a deep breath to ease the tension headache. "Okay. I will go with you, but that's all I'm willing to do."

He grabbed her, held her tight. "I love you, Grace. So much," he said, tears streaming down his cheeks, his shoulders shaking.

"We'll get through this," he whispered close to her ear. "There is nothing we can't do if we put our minds to it. I made a mistake, but I'm willing to make it up to you. As for the child, there is no way that little girl is mine. And I'll prove it by having the DNA testing redone in a reputable lab."

"I hope you're right," she said, her voice low as she looked into his eyes.

"This is one giant mistake on someone's

part, and I'll prove it." He put his arm around her shoulders and led her to the sofa, all the while feeling her resistance. "I should never have told you about Deidre the way I did. It was thoughtless and hurtful. There's nothing I can do to fix that, but if you'll go with me while we establish that I'm not the father, then we can work on us."

"It's not that simple, Aidan. I'm not going to go along with whatever you want. I've had enough of that. You don't really believe that this will be over so easily, do you?" she demanded, pushing his hands away.

"I don't know, but I want to see if I can start to make things right with you. Grace, I can't bear to lose you, and we will get through this. I'll make a reservation at an inn in Spartanburg, and after all this is behind us we will continue what we started here," he said. "That is, if you want to."

"I don't know what I want. The only thing I'm certain of is that this is a long way from over."

Aidan saw the misery in his wife's eyes and his heart contracted in his chest. How could he have done this to her? "Grace, I have been so damned stupid. You deserve better than what I've given you by way of explanation. I'm sorry about everything, but most of all I'm sorry for causing you such pain. Thank you for agreeing to come with me. And I promise you that we will figure this out. Just give us time."

She gave him a harsh look he'd never seen before. His stomach sank as he realized the monumental task ahead of him.

THE NEXT DAY, as they drove toward Spartanburg, would have been so pleasant if not for the impending meeting. Aidan had lain awake for hours wondering how the DNA test showed him to be the father. And if he was the father, why hadn't Deidre told him? As he thought about it, he couldn't help but wonder why, when she had no immediate family, she hadn't told him—if it were true. No woman would want to go through a birth and the raising of a child without some sort of family support.

And why had she done the test if she didn't plan to tell him? Had she had a relationship with another man and wanted to be certain that he couldn't claim the child? She was obviously a rich woman. Had a man she'd dated tried to say the daughter was his?

The lawyer hadn't said how old the little

girl was. Maybe she was too young to be his daughter. He knew the exact weekend he'd spent with Deidre, so if the child had been born more than nine months after that, she couldn't be his. Had Deidre appointed him guardian because she thought he would do what he could for her daughter, regardless of whether or not he was the father?

As he mulled it all over, he could not understand her motivations. No matter how he looked at it, he couldn't figure out why she would keep the paternity of her daughter a secret, yet name him as the child's father in her will. It made zero sense. Even if Deidre was trying to prevent another man from gaining custody of the child, there were more effective—and less destructive—ways to do so.

For now, he would concentrate on the road ahead and trying to ease Grace's concerns about what they'd face at the lawyer's office. "I booked us into the nicest inn around the area. Might as well enjoy being comfortable while we get this over with."

He glanced at her, at the way her golden hair fell around her cheeks, at her beautiful lips and the set of her chin. All features he was intimately acquainted with and loved about her. He squeezed her hand. "We're going to be fine. This will be settled easily. I'll have our lawyer look after the details of a second DNA test and then we'll head back home. When we get home I'd like us to plan a trip to Europe. We've talked about it, but now I think we should do it. We've earned our time away to explore all those places we learned about in school. What do you say?"

"Aidan, will you stop? We—if there is a *we* when this is over—have more important things to deal with."

"But all this doesn't change the fact that we deserve a wonderful trip away from here, from my business and all that it entails. I'm also offering you the shopping trip of a lifetime— anywhere in Europe you'd like to go. You'll have a chance to shop to your heart's content. Will you think about it?"

"Let's get this meeting over first," Grace said, her lips set in a firm line.

She didn't touch his arm as she often did when they were driving together. He missed her touch, the way it made him feel.

They drove into downtown Spartanburg to the address they had for the law office. It was an elegant older home just off the main street with a wide verandah and tall white columns flanking the entranceway. Upon entering the cool, open foyer, they were greeted by a woman wearing an impeccable navy suit. She smiled at them as she introduced herself and led them to a quiet, high-ceilinged room at the rear of the building. "Mr. Knowles will be with you momentarily. Is there anything I can get either of you? A coffee perhaps? Soft drink?"

"Nothing for me," Aidan said as Grace shook her head.

Aidan focused on the space to keep his mind from what was about to happen. The wood paneling and large window with teal satin drapes that looked out into the back garden dominated the room. There was no desk, only an antique table and chair placed along the wall near the window. The opposite wall contained a credenza that spanned its length. "This isn't your typical lawyer's office," Aidan said to overcome the hushed silence of the room.

"This must be one of those boutique law firms that specializes in estate work," Grace said, remaining where she'd stood since they walked into the room.

He came toward her, his arms aching to

wrap her in his embrace. "Are you okay? You were pretty quiet in the car."

She shrugged. "What did you expect from me under the circumstances?"

"I—I don't know. Maybe a word of encouragement?"

"Really? You wrecked my life. You insisted that I come here. What more can you ask of me?"

The door opened and a man entered, his navy tailored suit and gold tie a perfect accent for the room, his dark hair and mustache impeccable. "I'm Larry Knowles. So glad you could make it today," he said without shaking hands. "Shall we get started?" he asked, pointing to the two chairs across from the table. He smoothed his tie as he sat. "Mr. Fellowes, as I explained on the phone, you have been named by Ms. MacPherson to be guardian of her only daughter. She has left very clear instructions as to how this will be worked out."

"Please stop right there. My wife and I, for personal reasons, do not believe that I am the biological parent of this child. We want the DNA test done by a reputable lab of our choosing before we go any further with this discussion."

Larry Knowles sat back in his chair, a surprised look on his face. "DNA is conclusive proof as far as I'm aware."

"That's assuming that the samples gathered were handled correctly, and that the lab followed strict procedures. I am not aware as to how or where my DNA was collected, and if it was collected in such a way to establish it was mine. It certainly was done without my permission. How have you determined that the DNA used to establish paternity was, in fact, mine?" he asked, his gaze locked on this annoying man who seemed so confident.

"It's true that I cannot personally vouch for the authenticity of the sample. Of course, I'm relying on Ms. MacPherson's information," the lawyer said, showing his first moment of uncertainty.

"Then it only seems right to me, given how much is at stake, that the testing be done again. I'm sure there is lots of Ms. Mac-Pherson's DNA still present in her home, and I'm willing to provide a fresh sample for examination."

Larry Knowles looked straight at Aidan, started to say something, then stopped. He glanced quickly at Grace, then back to Aidan. "I have no reason whatsoever to doubt Deidre

MacPherson. She was a friend as well as a client. But I do see your point. My only wish is that you do it quickly as possible. Emma is living in her home with her nanny, and this needs to be resolved."

"What happens to Emma when it is proven that my husband isn't the father?" Grace asked.

"You have to understand that Deidre was absolutely positive that your husband was the father of her little girl. Having no close family she wanted to give her daughter to, she chose the biological father as guardian in the event Deidre didn't live to see her child grow to adulthood. If, for whatever reason, your husband doesn't take the child, she will be a ward of the state, which means that foster care will have to be arranged," the lawyer said.

"Are you certain there is no family for her?" Aidan asked. "None at all?"

"A cousin who is in her sixties." The lawyer glanced between them. "Look, I know this is a shock for both of you. And I understand you feel there has been a serious mistake made. If you'll give me the name of the lab you want to deal with, I will make arrangements for Emma to be tested along with you. But in the meantime, Deidre had one more request."

"What is it?" Aidan asked, suddenly afraid that it might be some sort of burial request since she had no family. He didn't want to put Grace through anything more than was necessary.

"Deidre put together a video of Emma's life over the past four years. It's simply a visual portrait of a little girl who was the light of her mother's life. They were very close and Emma is a beautiful little girl. Deidre wasn't certain how you'd respond to her last wishes and so she requested that you watch the video before you left my office. It won't take long."

He opened a drawer and brought out a laptop, setting it on the desk in front of Aidan and Grace. A few clicks and the screen glowed blue before the picture of a newborn appeared. "I'll leave you to watch the video and be back in a few minutes."

Unable to stop himself, Aidan leaned toward the screen. Slowly photos emerged, showing an infant asleep in her car seat, followed by her first steps and her wide smile, dressed in a Halloween teddy bear costume. A woman's voice, carefully modulated, yet warm and upbeat, filled the room.

"Is that Deidre speaking?" Grace asked.

A chill ran along his shoulders. It felt as if

Deidre were in the room. "Yes, I believe so…
It's been a while." He would have recognized
her voice anywhere. It was such a distinct mix
of Southern drawl and New England twang.

"The child is so sweet." Grace sighed.
"How lucky she was to have such a beautiful baby girl."

Slowly the images shifted to show the home
she lived in, the front steps and the street in
front of Deidre's house. There were closer
shots showing Emma's rosy complexion and
her glossy red curls. Aidan recognized the
backgrounds in the photos—all were places
around Deidre's home and office.

Grace took his hand. "Have you seen any
of these before?"

"No. Never," Aidan said as the video
showed Emma in a pink party dress, her
red curls framing her face. There was something so familiar about her, about the way
she cocked her head and smiled at the camera. Deidre could be heard in the background
wishing Emma a happy third birthday.

The camera panned close, so that Emma's
face filled the screen. Aidan stared for a minute, slowly becoming aware of something he
couldn't mistake for anything other than what
it was.

"Aidan. Look!" Grace cried. "She's got the same cleft in her chin as you have. And her smile. Oh, God. Aidan. Her smile is yours."

Aidan swallowed against the impact of the little girl's face. She did have his chin… "A lot of people have the same feature. Let's not jump to conclusions." Fear mixed with foreboding clutched his heart. He moved his chair closer to Grace's and pulled her hand into his lap. "This little girl is beautiful, but she could be anyone's little girl," he said, unable to grasp the truth of what he'd seen a few minutes ago.

The next photo was of Emma hugging a large teddy bear. Deidre's voice could be heard once again. "Aidan, if you're watching, it means I am gone. I need you to care for our daughter. I had the DNA testing done just a few months after Emma was born. There is no doubt that you're the father. Emma has your smile, your curls and that cute little cleft in her chin. My last wish is that you provide her with a loving home and care for her in my stead."

The next photo slid onto the screen, a close-up showing Emma laughing at the camera as she clutched another teddy bear, this time a black one with a big red bow, her round cheeks glowing. She moved up close to the camera. Close enough to see every feature on her tiny face. The smile was so endearing, the little girl so happy and carefree. This beautiful child was innocent and would pay the price if he denied her.

"She is your daughter and you are her father. Please love her with all your heart as I have. Please," Deidre pleaded.

Grace pulled her hand away. "You believe her, don't you," she said, her voice cold and distant.

Disbelief shook him. What if this little girl was his daughter? What would he do if she were? Even the thought, the possibility of a child opened something inside him, something he'd never really felt before. He looked at Grace, saw her anguish and put his arm around her shoulders.

Grace pushed him away.

There had to be some mistake. It was so unreal—the lawyer's call, the emotional trip here, the realization that there was a pretty good chance Deidre's daughter was also his. "Grace, we are going to have the DNA test redone. We'll pick a lab back in Charleston and I will pay whatever it takes to have the testing done as fast as possible. We won't jump to any conclusions until then." He cleared his throat. "This is so difficult for you, finding out that I had relations with Deidre. I've hurt you in ways I never intended...ever. But we'll work this out, somehow. You'll see."

Grace wrapped her arms around her middle and nodded at the screen. "Aidan, look at her. She is so much like you in her appearance and her smile. How could you think this isn't your child?" Her voice sounded choked with tears as she huddled in the corner of her chair.

"Grace, please, let's wait and see." As the video ended, despite his denials, he knew Emma was his daughter. He knew because the close-up shot revealed that Emma's left eye held the same tiny glint of a different color that his mother's had. A bit of pale yellow in the blue of the iris. A family trait. "Let's get that lawyer in here and then we can arrange the testing. After that, we'll go home and wait for the results."

He rose, waiting for his wife to stand, resisting the urge to take her in his arms and convince her that what had happened five years ago had been long over, even before it began. "I love you. My relationship with Deidre was wrong and a complete betrayal of you and of us. Whatever the tests show,

I want you to know that I have never loved anyone the way I love you."

Slowly Grace stood, being careful to stay away from him. Regardless of what he wanted, he knew she would not allow him to touch her. "My only hope is that you see your way clear to forgive me," he said.

Without looking at him, she said, "Aidan, I can't forgive you. Every part of my life has changed, all because you betrayed what we had together."

CHAPTER THREE

SEVERAL WEEKS LATER Grace placed a seafood casserole in the oven and set the timer. Her words in the lawyer's office had proven prophetic, because everything about her life had changed. The drive home had been a long, silent one with each mile forcing her to face the cold truth. She could think of little else but what Aidan had done with that woman— a woman who claimed that her child was his.

The easy closeness Grace and Aiden had shared had disappeared as if it never existed. She'd moved into the guest bedroom, too tired to sleep as her mind went over that day at the Planters Inn.

Meanwhile, Aidan behaved as if nothing had changed. He'd worked long hours, as he always did. Because of his behavior, Grace couldn't help but worry that maybe Deidre wasn't the only affair he'd had, that he might have spent the past few nights in the arms of another woman. She was embarrassed at how naive and foolish she'd been to never question anything her husband had told her. She'd even considered hiring a private detective to follow him, something she was deeply ashamed of, but she'd found herself doing all sorts of things she would never have dreamed of a month ago.

She'd given everything, every part of herself, to her marriage. She'd never once considered having an affair, and she despised the fact that her husband had felt the need to have one. Sure, it had been rough going through the tests, trying to have a baby. But he wasn't the only one wishing that it could be over while praying for a baby to make their life together complete.

What hurt most was that now she had to face the fact that he didn't want a baby nearly as much as she did. He could deny that, but it was true. He'd seen fit to have a fling with someone during the darkest period of her life, and he'd resisted talking to the adoption lawyer.

She'd begun to realize that all her plans for a happy life with Aidan that included children lay in ruins. A part of her was sure that there was nothing left between them.

She realized that most of her friends would

see her willingness to try to repair her marriage as degrading and pointless, given his infidelity. But despite these past few weeks, she knew Aidan to be a decent man.

To talk about adoption in the middle of this crisis was pure denial on her part. Yet she hadn't let go of that dream, that possibility of getting a child. She supposed, underneath it all, she needed to keep her life as normal as possible and to believe that she and Aidan had a chance to survive this if they worked hard enough.

So she'd made dinner. For them and two of their friends, Cecilia and Dave. As though everything was fine. As though Grace and Aidan were actually considering adoption. It was better than facing the evening alone, which was what she'd been doing since seeing the photos of Emma.

Aidan came up behind her and put his hands on her waist, something that had always made her lean back into his embrace. "Grace, I've finished setting the table. Anything else I can do?" he whispered close to her ear, sending tiny points of excitement hurtling down her body. She resisted the urge to lean into him and, instead, ran hot water into the sink in preparation for cleaning the frying pan and spatulas she'd used.

He continued to hold her gently yet securely. She was powerless to resist him. "Grace, I know how hard this has been for you, this waiting and wondering."

She turned in his arms and gazed into his eyes, his body's warmth drawing her closer. "If you really know how difficult this is for me, why haven't you stayed home with me during the evening? It's lonely here with no one to talk to about all this."

He bowed his head, his forehead touching hers. "I wish I had. Most of the time I sat in my office trying to face the truth about me, about what I'd done, how stupid I felt. Wherever my thoughts took me, one thing remained the same. This is my fault. I hurt you. I'm sorry. So sorry for what I did. I can't say it enough."

She wanted to resist him, make him pay for what he did to her, to them. But she needed his arms around her, needed to feel his body pressed into hers. She missed him so much, his lovemaking, his caring touch, the feeling that they would always be together. She put her arms around his neck and raised her face to his.

He reacted with a deep sigh of need, his lips touching hers, demanding and hot. She angled her body closer, feeling his erection against her tummy and writhing against it.

"Oh, Grace. I've missed you so much," he said against her mouth, his breath hot on her lips.

"Me, too," she whispered, pulling him closer, her need for him sweeping all other thoughts from her mind.

He picked her up. "We've got time," he said, holding her tight as they started for the bedroom.

"You're going to carry me upstairs?" she said, surprised. "You haven't done that in years."

"I may spend my days behind a desk but I can still carry my wife upstairs," he said, his embrace firm as he maneuvered through the living room toward the stairs just as the phone rang.

A mechanical voice blared from the phone on the hall table. "Call from Knowles Attorney at Law. Call from Knowles Attorney at Law."

He stopped. She slid from his arms. They stared at each other.

"You'd better take it," Grace said, her

voice strained, her heart doing a slow, hard pound in her chest. She watched her husband's face as he spoke with the lawyer, his eyes on hers as he listened.

"I understand. So it's conclusive." He fidgeted with the handheld unit, shifting his weight from one foot to the other, his eyes swerving around the room. "Thanks. Yes. Please fax the results to my office as soon as you can." He hung up, coming toward her, pulling her into his arms, his body pressed to hers. "The test results prove that Emma is my daughter. I can't believe this. I have a daughter... How could I have a daughter?"

A chill ran down Grace's spine. He said the words with a reverence she hadn't heard from him before. "You mean *you* have a daughter."

"I can't believe it," he said again, as if he hadn't heard her, his eyes shining with unshed tears. "But deep down, I knew by the spot of color in her left eye. I saw it. Mom had the same spot, the same yellow area in her iris."

Grace stepped out of his arms. "You were sure the day we saw the video, but you didn't tell me. You let me hope that there might be a chance that the DNA test was wrong. How could you?" she demanded.

He glanced at her, his expression gentle. "I wanted to protect you as long as I could. But, yes, I knew that Emma was my daughter. I don't know how it could have happened, but it did."

Anger flooded her at his selfish words. "How can you stand there and tell me you don't know how it happened?" All these nights, he hadn't been sitting in his office worried about her. He'd been thinking about his daughter and what that would mean to him. All the while, Grace had been home alone trying to make sense of what was going on and missing him with her whole heart.

"What do you mean?" he asked startled.

"Oh, for heaven's sake, Aidan. You made this happen by having sex with this woman. How can you stand there and pretend this was fate when you broke our marriage vows?" Grace demanded, so angry she could barely breathe. "Stop lying to yourself," she said as she stomped upstairs, anger filling her mind and soul with the stark realization that her marriage was over.

She turned at the top of the stairs to face him where he stood at the bottom looking up at her. "You had your fling and now you have your child. Congratulations." With that she went into the guest bedroom and slammed the door. Throwing herself on the bed she cried until there were no tears left.

THE NEXT MORNING, Grace awoke to the sound of the phone ringing, once again the stupid, mechanical voice announcing the caller, only this time, it was her friend Cecilia's name. Grace didn't have a clue whether they'd shown up last night or not. She hadn't been able to hear anything over her tears.

Her whole life had been tossed, and that was all she could think about. She assumed that Aidan had dealt with dinner, but she couldn't bring herself to care what he did. She owed her friends an apology, but she couldn't do it right now. Her head ached, her mouth was dry and her whole body felt numb.

She heard Aidan's voice, his consoling tone and his offer to have her call Cecilia back when she got up. But she wasn't getting up for a very long time. Her life in this house was over. The man she'd thought she knew didn't exist anymore. And instead, she was faced with the fact that her husband was completely absorbed with his present circumstances, leaving her to work out her feelings toward him alone, to cope with the loss of her dream all over again.

She heard Aidan come up the stairs and scrambled to bury herself under the covers. When the door opened she called out, "What do you want?"

He entered the room, standing next to the door. "We need to talk, Grace."

"You're the one with the secrets. Why don't you start?" she asked sarcastically. She was done trying to be the perfect, caring wife.

"Last night was difficult for you, and again, I'm sorry."

She wanted to stay buried beneath the duvet, but if he was going to stand there talking, she decided to face him, to not back down or allow any feelings she had left for him sway her. It wasn't as if she didn't have anything to say and better to get it over now. She sat up, bracing herself against the mound of pillows. "Aidan, if you'd behaved like my husband and not some philandering shell of a man, you wouldn't have to apologize. You have singlehandedly destroyed our marriage. I hope you're proud of what you've done."

She saw the hurt in his eyes, the way his hands shook as he held them against his face. "That was mean of me, but you deserved it,"

she said, swinging her feet over the side of
the bed while hugging the duvet close to her
body, realizing, as she looked at her feet, that
she was still dressed in the clothes she'd worn
yesterday.

"You're right. But we have to talk. I called
the lawyer this morning, and he wants to
know if we're going to be in Spartanburg
sometime this week to settle the estate."

"What do you want me to do about it? She's
your daughter. And her mother was your
lover," she said sarcastically.

"She is *our* daughter, and she's going to be
part of our lives. I want to talk this over with
you. I need to have your support on this."

"My support?" She gawked. "You think
after everything you've done that you're en-
titled to my support?"

"You're my wife, and you will be Emma's
mother."

"Aidan! Wake up! I am not Emma's mother
and I'm not your wife. You made sure of that."
She couldn't look at the sorrowful expression
on his face any longer. Instead, she focused
on the embroidered edge of the duvet.

"Grace, Emma is my daughter. I can't
abandon her now that her mother is gone."

"Aidan, you're not being fair. How long

have I waited to have a baby, to share every bit of the experience with you? And now there's this…this child, who will remind me every single day of my life that my husband has been unfaithful, appears and I'm supposed to be her stand-in mother?"

Grace balled her fingers into fists. "You should have been honest with me. About the affair and about this child. You knew the truth when we were at the lawyer's office. And again you didn't respect me enough to tell me the truth."

Aidan rushed to the side of the bed and knelt in front of her. "I should have. I know that. And I have no explanation other than my own stupidity, my need not to have you angry at me. But now there is a child in our lives who just lost her mother and who will be going through a terrible time. I can't leave her to deal with that without me. I—I can't."

His gaze implored her to understand. "I realize that this is a lot for you to understand and accept, but Emma needs me…needs us." He took her hand in his, his fingers gently stroking the soft skin of her wrist. "I can't imagine what life will be like for Emma now that her mother is gone. She's only four and she is going to be alone if we don't help her."

"Why do you keep saying *we*?" Grace asked, feeling her throat tighten.

"If you'd come with me, you'd have a chance to see her and offer your caring and support. Grace, you're the most loving and kind person on the planet. And there is a little girl in need of everything you have to offer. Don't pass up the chance to help her because of the mistakes I made. Don't make her life more miserable because of something I did. I will do anything you ask if you will come to Spartanburg with me."

Grace looked into his eyes and saw the truth of his words. He wanted to go to his daughter, and she wanted him to go. Despite her hurt and her fear of how this child would change their lives, she wanted him to go to his little girl. She wanted the little girl to have all the support and understanding possible. But Grace could not go there with him. Couldn't act as if nothing had happened, as if her life hadn't been tossed in the garbage by the man who claimed to love her.

Yet, he had a point; there was a child who needed all the support she could give. "Why do you need me? There must be other people to help out. People she already knows. People who love her. What about Deidre's friends?"

"I don't know who Deidre's friends are, but the only way I can find out is to go back to Spartanburg."

That he would be unfaithful to her after all they'd been through, after all the time they'd loved each other—it still was inconceivable that he would have been with someone else.

And he had the audacity to expect her to be supportive of him while he went to visit his daughter.

"Everything I thought we were working toward, every dream we'd had about a family ended last evening. I'm the one who can't conceive. I am the one who is infertile. Even if we could reconcile, I would never be able to give you a child." She struggled to keep the ugly tears in check. "You can't expect me to go along as if nothing has changed between us."

Aidan sighed deeply. "I promise you, Grace, that if you go with me, I will do whatever you ask where we are concerned. I don't pretend to understand how you feel, but I will respect any decision you make once you've seen Emma. It's clear we need time to work on our problems. I won't deny that. But I also want you to see this little girl."

"Why are you so fixated on this, Aidan?

A few days won't matter. You're a complete stranger to this child. You could simply upset her. What good would that do?"

"I hope that doesn't happen, but if it does, I'll find a way to deal with it," Aidan said, his eyes not meeting hers.

Suddenly she felt a cold sensation around her heart. She was alone in all this misery. Aidan didn't understand what he was asking of her or he would never have asked it. He would have known how painful it would be for her to face the child he'd conceived with another woman.

But, most of all, she felt alone because he had a whole new focus in his life. He had a daughter, and his eagerness to see her made Grace feel invisible…unimportant.

Yet deep down, a part of her longed to see this child—a little girl who, through no fault of her own, had been thrust into their lives. What would it be like if, somehow, they could work things out between them and Aidan took over his little girl's life? How would holidays, like Christmas or Easter, be if Emma was with them, was an integral part of their lives? It was so easy to imagine those moments, moments Grace had already dreamed of, lived for all these years.

She'd dreamed of feeling moments of pure joy with her child. With Emma in their lives, there would be wonderful events—the miracle of Christmas and the Christ child being real and present in their lives.

There was a little girl who, regardless of how it had come about, would become a part of their lives…if only they could resolve their differences. Grace struggled with fear and so many other emotions. How could she mother another woman's child when that child would trigger suspicions about her husband's behavior? Grace would always wonder what he was doing, what he was really feeling, whenever she looked at the child he'd had with someone else. Grace had been living that way these past few weeks, and it had been unbearable. "Aidan, if we are going together to see Emma, I need you to tell me that that you aren't hiding anything more from me."

He nodded his head vigorously, his face tight with anxiety.

"Are you sure you're telling me everything about your relationship with Deidre? How am I to believe that you weren't in touch with her these past four years? Because it just doesn't make sense to me. What woman would spend the money to prove who the father of her child was without ever telling him about it?"

"I have no idea why Deidre did what she did. But I swear to you, I had no contact with her."

"And you and Deidre haven't been seeing each other?"

"Grace, I have not seen Deidre since those two days five years ago. I've done a lot of things wrong, but I want to get this right. What I said last night about Emma being my child is only partly true. You're my wife. I love you. And this is *our* child. I can't help but believe that your faith in God had something to do with this child entering our lives."

"What? You're not making sense."

"We love each other. We've tried everything to have a baby. And I'm really sorry that Deidre died. She was essentially a good person, but her passing has given us the gift we've been dreaming of for years. It may not have happened in quite the way either of us wanted, but it is a chance for us to start our family."

She had always been a practicing Christian. She believed in God's will and his plan for her and her life. Could it be that Aidan was right?

Was this how God worked in their lives? She wasn't sure. "Do you think it is possible?"

He nodded. "I do."

Seeing the anguish on his face, Grace clasped his hand, her love for him reawaking within her. This was a very difficult situation, and they would be a long time working through it, but if they could... She leaned across the bed to touch him and tried to forget her fears and her suspicions.

If they were going to make their marriage work once again, she had to accept what had happened. If, in the end, they couldn't work things out, she had to be certain that she'd done what she could to save her marriage. "I'll go with you to see Emma."

He kissed her hand, a long sigh escaping his lips. "You will not regret this. I promise you that we will do this together."

CHAPTER FOUR

THEY PACKED A few things and started out of town just as the sun began to warm the air. Grace couldn't help but feel anxious. As much as she wanted to support Aidan and Emma, she was still in shock over what had occurred in such a short time. Doubt and betrayal continued to circle her thoughts, refusing to leave regardless of how she tried to think of God's will.

She felt suspended, dislocated, since the lawyer had called. The news that Aidan would now be responsible for his daughter didn't seem to be real, despite her earlier hope. "How are we going to make this all work?" she asked.

"To be honest, I'm still trying to figure out why Deidre didn't tell me."

"Maybe she never intended that you find out."

"But why? All those meetings we held to discuss the operational issues of her company back five years ago, I thought I knew her. At least a little bit. I never pictured her as someone who would hide such important information from anyone, let alone me."

"What do you mean by that?" Grace asked, feeling uneasy.

He glanced over at her. "I mean that she seemed so upright, so honest and caring. I'm surprised, that's all."

"How can you call her upright and honest? She went to bed with another woman's husband. How can you defend that behavior?"

"Sorry that didn't come out the way I intended. I meant in relation to her work."

His supportive words for this woman were disconcerting. She searched for something to focus on as her stomach rose into her throat. "Did you make a reservation for us for tonight?"

"No. I didn't think of it. But we can do that easily when we get there."

Aidan drove carefully through the city streets toward the highway leading out of town toward Spartanburg. "Grace, I have been so busy building up my company, making plans for us, for when we have a family, that I didn't take in what it would really mean to have a child in our lives. But now that this little girl needs us, it's as if we're being given a chance to have what we always dreamed of. I want to be there for her."

A part of her didn't really care how he felt, but she tried to sound interested if only to keep the conversation going. "You have a lot to think about if you're going to give her a good home, so much planning needs to be done."

He squeezed her hand. "Thank you."

He sighed and smiled at her, making her heart do a funny flip-flop in her chest. She wanted to go home, to pretend none of this was happening, to go back to the way things had been before that first phone call from Larry Knowles.

"It's just that there is so much to think about—"

He squeezed her hand a little tighter. "Stop worrying. We'll figure it all out together. We'll see how Emma is doing when we get to the house. The nanny will be there and probably a couple of Deidre's closest friends."

"Do you know where Deidre lives… I mean, lived?" Grace asked, wondering how he would have known if he hadn't seen her since the end of the affair over five years ago.

"She might have moved since you were last here."

He gripped the wheel, his eyes skirting hers. "Mr. Knowles told me she lived in the same house as when I knew her."

Reality crashed down on Grace, billowing around her like an unwanted mist. Memories of those lonely nights when she'd waited for Aidan to come home, to make love to her, praying that this time there would be a baby for them. Believing his absence meant he was building a future for their family.

She had awoken this morning hoping it was all a terrible dream, not real. Just before the pain rushed her, reminding her of the loss of trust, the ache of knowing her husband had slept with another woman.

She believed in marriage, had been raised in a home where vows of any kind were taken seriously, and none more than the marriage vow. She wanted to take him back and put her whole heart into forgetting the past. They had married right out of college and had had their share of disagreements like any couple, but never something like this.

Her hurt, her soul-deep wounds prevented her from forgetting anything. And she doubted they would allow her to forgive.

There were so many questions and so few answers. Why had Deidre chosen not to tell Aidan about Emma when she was alive? Wouldn't she have wanted her daughter to be close to her dad and his family? Why had she left everything to Aidan on the condition that he accept Emma into his life and become her dad?

Grace couldn't imagine any woman who would have behaved that way. She certainly wouldn't have. She would have insisted that the child's father share in the responsibility for caring for and raising it. She would want her daughter to have all the love and support possible, regardless of how she felt about the father. So how could Deidre not be in touch with Aidan and still expect him to step in as parent?

None of this made any sense...

"Grace, honey, time to wake up," Aidan said softly.

"What?" she asked, suddenly awake. After not sleeping for days, the smooth motion of the car had lulled her to sleep. Sitting up straight, she glanced out the window at the quiet boulevard basking in the midmorning sun. "Should I put Deidre's address into the GPS?"

"No. We're only a few minutes away from her house."

It was humiliating to realize that her husband had been to Deidre's home. Had they made love in her bedroom? Grace's stomach sank, pressing into her backbone. Of course they had. They wouldn't have needed to hide out in a hotel room to carry on their affair when Deidre's home was available and waiting.

Grace closed her eyes, trying to resist the image of her husband and Deidre making love in the home she was about to enter. A sharp ache close to her heart made her grit her teeth. She couldn't wait to get away from the place. The ache of betrayal reminded her of what had gone on without her knowing. "We…we need a reservation for tonight."

"I'll look after that once we've seen Emma. I'm worried about how she'll react to us appearing in her life right now…" He turned right onto a tree-lined street, weaving through the many twists and turns of a roadway designed to slow traffic around homes whose gabled entrances, brick exteriors and long, elegant windows spoke of wealth and prestige.

Grace shrank into the seat, suddenly wishing she hadn't come with Aidan. She didn't want to see this house, this place where her husband had made love to another woman—a woman he hadn't admitted having a fling with until circumstances forced him to do so. The car slowed as Aidan pulled into a driveway surrounded by a hedge that protected the house from the street, the massive gardens sweeping toward the entrance, flashing bright red and yellow flowers of all sizes and shapes. Following the curve of the driveway, they stopped in front of a massive dark wood door.

"We're here," Aidan said, turning off the engine. "Are you okay?" he asked, turning to her his eyes filled with concern. "I realize that this isn't easy for you," he murmured, taking her hand in his and kissing her fingers. "If you'd rather, I can go in first, if it would make it easier for you…"

Her heart hammered against her rib cage. Could she go in there? Could she face a little girl who was about to be part of their life? If they stayed married, of course.

She glanced around, hoping to see other vehicles along the circular drive. There weren't any. It had been several weeks since Deidre's passing, and yet Grace had expected to see evidence that people were still coming to check on a little girl who had lost her mommy. Where were all this woman's friends? Or didn't she have any?

The tragic way Deidre had died should have meant that her friends were taking turns caring for her daughter. She took a deep breath. "I'm not sure I can do this. Go into the house where you slept with another woman. It's not fair."

"It's all right if you can't. You've come this far with me, more than I expected or deserved."

At least he acknowledged her perspective. No, she couldn't go inside. Yet…she was drawn to see this little girl, this child who was dealing with so much. "Let's get this over. Maybe the nanny isn't home. Maybe she took Emma to friends' or to the library," Grace said, the knot in her stomach hardening.

Without a word, Aidan came around to her door, opened it and took her hand in that reassuring way of his. Suddenly she felt faint. "I'm not sure I can do this, Aidan."

He squeezed her fingers. "You can. I'm right here if you need me." He took her hand and led her to the imposing front door, his fingers pressing the doorbell as his eyes held hers. "This will all be okay. I promise you. *We'll* be okay."

The door opened and a tall woman with dark hair and penetrating brown eyes greeted them. "You must be Aidan Fellowes. I recognize you from the photo. Come on in," she offered, leading the way into the formal living room to the right of the entrance hall.

"I am, and this is my wife, Grace," Aidan said, his arm coming around Grace's shoulders.

The woman's expression was one of kindness. "I'm Emma's nanny, Lisa Gomez. I've cared for Emma since she was born."

She pointed to the sofa opposite the fireplace. "I'm aware of Deidre's intentions concerning Emma, and I want you to know I approve of them. A child should be with her father in a situation like this. Emma has a lovely photo of you, Mr. Fellowes."

Grace sat on the edge of the sofa her mind reeling. *A photo of Aidan?* She turned to Lisa. "You have a photo of my husband. Why?"

Lisa glanced quizzically at Aidan before she answered. "He is Emma's father. Deidre wanted Emma to be able to recognize her father. Deidre's company worked closely with his company, and I'm sure they stayed in touch through work, although she never said as much."

Lisa raised her eyebrows, her gaze resting on Grace's face, a look of understanding dawning on her face. "I'm terribly sorry, Mrs. Fellowes. I don't know why, but I thought Aidan was single when he and Deidre met…"

Aidan had sworn he hadn't been involved in Deidre's business after the affair. He'd claimed Lucas looked after anything Deidre's company needed. Was that the truth? Had her husband been here since that weekend? Was she the only one who didn't know what was going on? Had Aidan and Lucas both hidden the truth from her? Lucas wouldn't do that, of that she was certain.

Tears burned Grace's eyes. She fought to regain her equilibrium, deciding to say nothing more to this woman. Her hands clammy, her breath coming in short gasps, she struggled to stay in this room and listen to what was being said. Her eyes sought the door. Her body tensed as she placed her feet firmly on the floor in front of her. "Could I see the photo of my husband?"

"That's not necessary," Aidan said.

"I'd like to see the photo of *my* husband,"

she said, suspicion writhing through her at Aidan's objection.

Lisa left the room and came back a few minutes later, holding the framed photo out to Grace. "Deidre wanted Emma to understand that she had a dad who didn't live with them. Deidre wanted her to see what her dad looked like."

Grace searched the photo for clues as to where it had been taken...a park somewhere. She didn't recognize the photo or the place, but the smile on Aidan's face was playful and open. How could he have been looking that way if their relationship was a quick hookup, a fling, as he'd described it? And why had they been in a park she didn't recognize? "I thought you had no role in Emma's life, that you knew nothing about her until the lawyer called," she said, seething.

"I swear to you I didn't," Aidan said, his smile forced as he glanced across at Lisa. "You've never met me before, have you, Ms. Gomez?"

"That's correct. I knew you by the photo only. But I assumed she was in touch with you over her arrangements, Mr. Fellowes," Lisa said, a small frown forming.

Aidan shook his head emphatically.

"After her dad passed away last March, Deidre decided that, since there really weren't any close family connections, she wanted to provide Emma with a sense of belonging," Lisa said, her gaze one of disbelief as she continued to stare at Aidan. "I can't imagine that she didn't tell you what she was doing. Once Deidre made a decision, she stuck to it. Because of that, I assumed you knew about Emma and that one day you would show up here. Deidre didn't say that, exactly, but I am pretty sure she intended to find you and encourage you to be involved in Emma's life."

Aidan clutched Grace's hand, a look of dread in his dark eyes. "I never heard one word from Deidre after that weekend. I swear to you, I didn't know any of this."

Cold anger crystallized Grace's thoughts. "Then tell me why she made all those plans. It doesn't make sense to me, and it clearly doesn't make sense to Lisa, the woman who was closest to the situation."

"Grace, I'm telling you, I am as much in the dark as you are."

"Aidan, please don't lie to me. Did she ever try to contact you about Emma before this?" Grace asked, her quiet tone belying her inner anger.

"I wasn't in touch with Deidre after those two days. I had no reason to go near her. I knew it was a mistake, and I wanted to get away from all of it as fast as possible."

Grace felt hot tears on her cheeks and was mortified that a stranger was able to witness her pain, her embarrassment She looked her husband over carefully, searching his expression for any indication he was not telling her the truth. Despite his protests, she couldn't imagine having a child and not being part of its life.

How could her husband, who claimed to love children, who had willingly been involved in trying to have a baby with her, not have been part of Emma's life? The Aidan she knew would not have been able to stay away from his only daughter.

In Aidan's business, he was often away overnight visiting one of the many clients his company had across the southeastern United States. He called her every night from his cell phone, which meant that he could be anywhere and she wouldn't be able to verify his location even if she wanted to. And she hadn't wanted to. She'd trusted him to tell her the truth.

Now she had to face reality. How could

she be sure that he hadn't made regular trips to see his daughter? He could have stayed somewhere in Spartanburg and met with Deidre and Emma without anyone knowing. He could have easily kept his whereabouts from everyone, including her brother, Lucas. Her thoughts ran the gamut from wanting to believe her husband to realizing what he said was probably not true. With a sinking heart she said, "And you never once came to see Deidre or Emma?"

"I swear to you, Grace. I wasn't aware of any of this."

She couldn't look at him anymore, not when she was swamped by fear that she had put her faith in a man who had intentionally deceived her. "I simply can't accept that Deidre, who had no family, wouldn't have sought you out, and arranged for you to be a part of Emma's life. After all, how long could Deidre continue to show her daughter your photo without the child wanting to see you?" She pushed the hair off her face in resignation. "And I'm sure that, like any mother, Deidre would do anything she could to make her daughter happy, and sooner rather than later, it would have meant getting in touch with you."

Aidan looked at her as if she'd struck him. "Grace, please, this is difficult for everyone."

"Mrs. Fellowes, I only want what is best for Emma. But I realize the two of you might need a chance to talk this over. The accident and its aftermath has been a shock for everyone. I have to go now to pick up Emma from kindergarten. If you'd like, I can take her to the playground on the way home, give you both a little time to talk this out." Lisa glanced from one to the other.

"Yes, please do that. Give us a half hour or so." Aidan cleared his throat. "Then bring Emma home. We'd like to meet her."

Grace watched warily as Lisa left the house. Everything felt surreal, out of place. Fighting her fear, she turned to her husband, praying for him to say the words that would make everything in her life right again.

CHAPTER FIVE

EXHAUSTION BURNED BEHIND Aidan's eyes. It had been a difficult drive here, and even though he knew he would have to explain so many things to Grace, he hadn't expected her to be so hostile. Sure she was angry and hurt, but she had to know he was telling the truth. He'd always told her the truth, shared everything with her—until his involvement with Deidre. Shame had forced him to hide what he did. Shame and the belief that nothing would come of the two days he'd spent with Deidre. That his secret would never harm the one woman he loved.

He reached out for Grace's hand, entwining his fingers with hers. "I'm so sorry about all this. But I've always been honest with you."

"Not about this," Grace said, pulling her hand away.

The loss of her touch chilled him to his core. What could he say that would convince Grace of his sincerity? "I made a mistake, and it will never happen again. We will find a way through all of this if we put aside our feelings for a little bit and concentrate on Emma. We need to make plans for how we will manage to take Emma back with us." He touched her cheek. She turned away. "Grace, I know we can work this out," he pleaded, his stomach aching with dread.

She moved away from him, distrust clear in her eyes. "How can we? Deidre chose you to be the custodial parent for Emma, even though she didn't discuss it with you beforehand. But Emma represents your lies and the way you broke your vows. Aidan, there are two of us in this marriage. We are not supposed to have secrets, hidden lives."

"We don't!"

"That's what you want me to believe," she said, and Aidan couldn't miss the harsh tone in her voice, so unlike his wife.

Feeling at a complete loss as to what to say or do, he slumped in the chair. "How can I convince you that I had nothing to do with Deidre these past five years?"

She sighed as she stared around the room as if looking for a way out. "I—I wish there was a way you could convince me."

He wanted to reach out to her, to take her

in his arms, but the look on her face told him his touch would not be welcome. "Grace, I wish there was, too. But there are other considerations. There is a child who will be here soon, who has no idea why you and I are in her home. Don't you think we need to concentrate on her and what she'll need?"

"I'm not responsible for what happened here, and I'm not responsible for your daughter. You are, and you have to do whatever you need to do," Grace said, her voice low and controlled, her eyes dark pools in stark contrast to her pale skin.

Despite his sorrow over Grace's behavior, Aidan wanted to soothe his wife but had no idea how to do it. She'd always been his mainstay, the one person he could rely upon. "Grace, I don't want to do this without you. You're my wife and I love you. I have to figure out how to handle this. I have to find a way to be a father to Emma when I don't even know her. I will have to decide how we should live, whether she comes home with us right now or I stay here for a while to see what arrangements need to be made about Deidre's estate, the dissolution of assets and what I'm expected to do."

He scrubbed his hands together as his mind worked through the possible issues surrounding Deidre's death and estate. Interspersed were thoughts of Emma, of what the next few hours and days would be like for his daughter. "I've never been a parent. It was always just an idea to me, not something with a practical application."

"Said like a true computer engineer," Grace said, her tone furious.

Shocked he turned to her. "Grace, what's the matter? We're in an emergency situation and have a lot to think about in a very short time. I need your help."

Grace stood, her hands clenched at her sides as she stared at him. "Did you hear yourself? Did you hear how selfish you sound?"

"What? I'm trying to figure out what to do. I can't do that without your help. I need you, Grace."

She glared at him. "You never once talked about me, about how I feel, about what this will do to our lives together. All you can think about is doing what Deidre wants. She's dead. She's not coming back. And yet you didn't, for one minute, stop and consider what I'm going through, did you? All you want from me is my help. You want me to make this better for you."

She scraped her hair off her face and blotted

her cheeks with her fingers, her voice shaking. "I'm just as important in this situation as you are, as Emma is. You need to consider my feelings, talk things out with me. But instead of that, you go on and on about what *you're* going to do."

He stared at her face, at the anger in her eyes. How had he gotten this so wrong? "Grace, I didn't mean it that way. I'm so used to assessing a situation and deciding the best course of action to solve the problem. It's how I think."

Grace picked up her purse and slung it over her shoulder. "This is not a situation, Aidan. This is real life, where people you claim to love are in pain. Emma is going to miss her mother for a very long time. You are not going to have your lovely well-ordered life where every problem has a solution anymore. You will have to face each issue with your daughter with your heart not your head. But most of all, I will not have you making decisions without me having a say in how we do things. This is my life, my marriage, and I will no longer be told what decision *you've* made and simply go along with it."

Shocked and suddenly terrified, by her words, her accusations of his selfishness ringing in his ears, Aidan jumped up. "What have I done? I'm as upset about all this as you are. I deal with it differently, mostly by focusing on what can be done, but that in no way means I don't want your input on this."

"You don't get it, do you?"

"Get what?" he asked, confused and really, really scared in a way he hadn't experienced since he got the news that Deidre had passed away.

"You and I need to go home and talk this over between the two of us before we make a decision that will change our lives forever. Lisa is clearly concerned for Emma. She will look after her as long as needed. A few weeks or a few months won't make any difference. There's no rush to sell the house. Emma may need to be left in her kindergarten to give her a chance to get over the loss of her mother before she faces any other changes."

"Children adapt," he said defensively.

"I'm sure she will, given time, love and caring. Meanwhile, if this is to work out for everyone involved, we need to go home, talk this all over and decide how *we* will cope with having a child dropped into the middle of *our* lives."

"Dropped into the middle of our lives? Is

that how you see this, as somehow something done to us? It may have been, but we're the adults here. We understand what's at stake." How could Grace even consider leaving a little girl who had just lost her mother alone? This wasn't like her, not at all. "Grace, I can't leave Emma here without her family. We are her family now. I can't do it, and neither can you. You love children. And this little girl lost her mother. We may have to move in here for a while, but in the end, she will be coming home with us."

Grace's eyes radiated a mix of anxiety and anger. "You're not listening to me. This is too fast, way too fast. My life has been destroyed. I'm barely able to cope as it is. I need time to work this out. We both do if we are to stay together. It's too much too soon. I need to…" She eased away from him. "I can't stay here and watch you decide things based on what you want. There are three of us in this, three people's feelings to consider. Ignoring what I want, my opinion and ideas, isn't right. Life doesn't work that way, Aidan."

"But I want you to be with me when I meet her." Was she suggesting that they simply walk away? Where had all of this gone so wrong? "When we got in the car this morning, I never imagined that we'd be coming here only to leave again."

"I'm supposed to do what you want while you ignore what your behavior did to me, is that it?" Grace said, the disbelief in her voice tearing at him.

"But there is so much that has to be done as soon as possible," he protested.

"Not until we talk about this. I mean it, Aidan."

"What do you want me to do?" he asked, exasperated by her attitude. "This is my child. You can't really want me to walk away. It's just that right now you're hurt and upset. You'll feel differently when you see Emma."

She focused her gaze on him with a look he knew so well—desperation and hope mixed together. "Okay. Before she gets back here let's run through the possibilities."

"Which are?" he asked, suddenly aware that he had never considered that there might be a different answer than the one he'd constructed from Deidre's request.

"Emma is a little girl who has only known the life she's living right now. How can we assume that moving her to our place, taking her away from everything that is familiar is going to make her life better? What if she has family here who could take her? An aunt and uncle, maybe? I have to believe that Deidre chose you because she believed you'd do what was best for her daughter. And that's what you and I have to consider. Have you considered that if we decide not to take her, there will have to be other options for her care?"

Shock sparked through him. "Grace, not for a minute have I considered not taking her. I thought you understood that. We've waited all our married lives for a chance to have children. Now we have that chance."

Grace closed her eyes for a few moments, her body trembling. "Aidan, there is more than one answer here. There has to be. I'm not ready to take on the care of that little girl so soon. There has to be a way to work this out so that we have time to adjust to what all of this means." She looked straight at him, her expression one of determination. "If you're not willing to do that, I have no other option but to leave you here to work things out on your own."

"Leaving? You can't. I mean you wouldn't leave a child who needed you." He struggled to accept that Grace might leave. "Grace, I'll make a reservation for us at a hotel where we can stay while we work out how to do this.

If you like, we'll wait to meet Emma later. I'll leave a note for Lisa, and that way she'll know how to find us. I'm sure that if you think about this, you'll come to realize that being with us in our home is the best answer for Emma."

The look in Grace's eyes was one of deep regret as she spoke slowly. "I can't do this right now because what I feel matters. I need time to come to grips with what has happened to you and to me, to our marriage. Yes, Emma's care is important, but so is the state of our marriage and my feelings. I will not make a snap decision about something that will affect the rest of my life. If you won't see things my way, try to understand how much I need time to think about this... I'm going home." She looked into his eyes, holding his gaze. "I want you to come with me, but that's up to you."

"No. Grace, please don't."

"Aidan," she whispered, her voice thick. "It's better this way. I don't want to fight with you, but I can't decide to take custody of this child this quickly."

By her resolute expression, he knew he'd lost. "Grace, I wish you'd stay. We could get to know Emma a little, see how much she needs us to care for her, to give her love and stability in her life," he said, making one last attempt to convince her.

"I wish I could, too. But I can't do this, not this way." She held out her hands for the car keys. "I'm sure you can rent a vehicle if you need one."

He watched her walk toward the door, his heart pounding in his chest, his eyes filling with tears. Loss, desperation cascaded over him as he followed her, intending to reach out to her one last time.

As Grace opened the door, she turned to him, her eyes meeting his. "I guess it's too late to ask you to see things my way."

He swallowed, feeling haggard and worn-out. His gaze shifted from hers while his jumbled thoughts sought a response that would make Grace stay.

Yet it was clear from the expression on her face that Grace's mind was made up. He touched her shoulder, wanting to pull her into his arms, but knew the warning signs—the stiff set of her shoulders, the fingers clenched on the strap of her purse. Grace would not allow him to embrace her. "You have a safe drive, and call me when you get home, will you?" he asked, feeling awkward and out of place.

"Of course." As she fumbled with the strap of her purse, her eyes remained fixed on the far corner of the room. Without another word, she left the house.

CHAPTER SIX

HER HANDS SHAKING, Grace struggled to put her home address into the GPS. She had no idea how to get out of the city to the highway. Her only clear idea was that she had to get away from here.

She wanted Aidan to come running out the door, get into the car with her and agree to leave for home with her. She might have been willing to meet Emma, to stay overnight and drive home tomorrow while they talked. But none of that was possible given Aidan's attitude. He had to have understood how she felt, and yet he refused to take her feelings into consideration.

Her destination finally loaded into the GPS, she eased out of the driveway, her eyes searching the windows of Deidre's house for any sign of her husband. There was none. He had decided to remain inside the house, not even coming out to the car to make sure she was okay to drive.

Gripping the wheel, she started down the driveway, her head aching and her heart hurting so badly she cried out, her gasp of agony filling the car.

Concentrate. You can't make it home if you don't.

Maybe she should check into a hotel and wait until tomorrow to leave. It would be easier, and by morning, she might be able to get Aidan to see reason. Her heart lifted at the idea, then came crashing down. Their last few moments together had proven that her influence over her husband paled in the face of his concern for his newly discovered daughter.

Besides, she couldn't fight with him any longer. She needed to get home, to talk to her brother. He'd be able to offer suggestions about what to do, how to get Aidan to see the truth. Their marriage had been through enough between the stress of fertility testing and Aidan's confession of his affair. To think that he was suddenly willing to risk the fragile remains of their relationship in order to raise another woman's child, a child he claimed he had no involvement with, hurt her to the core.

As she listened to the soothing female voice directing her through town to the highway she had a horrible sinking feeling that this would not turn out well, not because Aidan didn't want to fix it—she was pretty sure he did—but because she didn't know if she could go through another round of loss.

Their inability to conceive a child had been so devastating. But facing the cruel truth that Aidan could father a child meant the devastation was on her. She was inadequate; she had been the cause of their unhappiness all along. All these years, all the times they'd tried for a baby, she'd been the reason they couldn't have a family. A sob shook her.

Focus. Focus on the moment.

As she reached the highway, she instructed the phone to dial her brother's number and he answered on the first ring. "Where are you? I called the house to talk to Aidan when he didn't show at work. What's going on?"

"I'm on my way home from Spartanburg," she said, feeling relieved at the sound of her brother's voice.

"What? Why were you in Spartanburg? Where's Aidan? I need to talk to him."

She did her best to remain calm while she told Lucas what had happened and about the DNA results.

"I had no idea that he'd had an affair…and

now a child? What in hell is going on with Aidan?" Lucas asked.

Had Aidan not told Lucas anything? She hadn't talked to her brother because she hadn't seen him since all this happened. But Aidan talked to Lucas every day.

"You can see why I had to leave. He had an affair and now he's obsessed with the child from that relationship. All the times I tried to get him to understand how important a child was to me, how much I wanted to be a mother. Suddenly he's completely determined to be a father to a child he claims he's never met. It's as if she's all that matters."

"Gracie, you know that's not true. Aidan loves you. He always has. Sure, he made a mistake, and he is definitely making one now, but you need to give him a little time to sort things out. I'm sure once he has a chance to see what being responsible for this little girl means, he'll be back to you, begging you to help him figure out the best plan. I agree with you. This is all too sudden."

Grace moved into the left lane, accelerating as she passed a transport truck. She was driving way too fast but she didn't care. She had to get home. "I'm not so sure. He is completely determined to bring Emma home with him, to be her daddy and provide her with a good home. He hasn't given me, or what I need, a thought since we arrived at Deidre's house. It's as if I don't exist. Lucas, I'm afraid."

"Of what?"

"That Aidan has been involved in Emma's life all along. He denies it, but I can't believe him. And the photo the nanny had was so upsetting. Aidan said he didn't know about it, but I can't believe that he didn't. It was a photo taken in a park I didn't recognize. Someone had to have taken it, and by the smile on his face, it was someone he cared about. On top of that, the nanny said that Deidre wanted Emma to know what her father looked like. That's why the photo was there. But what if it was more than that? Lucas, I can't face this. I can't. He has blocked any attempts to see an adoption lawyer, and until this, he seemed okay with not having children. I've given Aiden everything I have to give, and I'm still on the outside of his life."

"Take it easy. Remember you're driving and it's not safe for you to be worrying and distracted behind the wheel."

She began to cry softly, feeling the warmth of the tears as they coursed down her cheeks.

She eased her foot off the accelerator a little. The blare of a horn sounded as the car behind her pulled out and passed her. "If he has hidden other things from me, my marriage is over. I might be able to forgive him for the affair, but if he's been seeing her and his child all this time, I can't forgive him for that."

"Sis, you're upset. But please just drive carefully and make it back here in one piece. I'll be waiting for you and we'll talk. Okay?" he said, his voice filled with concern and compassion.

"Okay." Talking to her brother made her feel a little better than she had when she left Aidan. But Lucas made everyone feel safe, listened to everyone's woes and always seemed to have the right answer. When they were growing up, she had often sought his advice. "Thanks. What would I do without you? I'm so glad you were on the other end of the line when I called."

"Me, too. See you in a few hours. And call me if you need to. You hear?"

"I will. I promise." Lucas had always been there for her, and he was Aidan's best friend. If anyone would know what was going on in Aidan's head, her brother would. Just knowing Lucas was waiting for her made the drive so much easier. She felt calm enough to concentrate on her driving as the road unwound in a long ribbonlike arc of asphalt.

Hours later, having listened to an audio book for the remainder of the trip, she pulled into her driveway, to the home she'd shared with Aidan. As she pressed the remote to open the garage door, she fought back loneliness so profound her breath felt trapped in her throat. For one fleeting moment, she doubted her decision to walk out on Aidan.

Maybe if she had stayed, encouraged him to talk about how they would care for Emma together, put aside her hurt feelings, they could have made some decisions. Then she recalled his mulish expression. No, there wouldn't have been any discussion or compromise. Aidan would make up his mind, the way he always did.

And that, more than some of the other problems before them, seemed to point to the end of her marriage.

AIDAN WATCHED THE car pull away and his heart turned over in his chest. He didn't want Grace to leave. He should have gone out to beg her to stay, but he hadn't because… because he didn't know what to say to her.

He'd felt this way so many times before when they'd been trying to have a baby. Grace had been so intent on getting pregnant that everything else in their lives was forgotten. They'd stopped talking about anything other than having a baby. Their time together had become charged with waiting to see if Grace had a positive pregnancy test.

When Grace had wanted to take Emma's custody slowly, to consider all the aspects of what it meant to take her, he'd been surprised. Having witnessed her obsession with having a baby, he'd assumed that Grace would be as willing as he was to take the little girl into their lives as soon as they possibly could.

His wife wanted a child, and Emma needed parents. To him it was a gift from God, the answer to their prayers.

Yet when Grace had protested, his first instinct had been to defend his position, his plan. He'd been hurt that Grace didn't seem to feel as he did about Emma. Yet he knew he needed Grace more now than he ever had in his entire life.

He'd screwed everything up. But one thing he was thankful for: he'd held his tongue. When she accused him of being selfish, he'd almost said something about her selfish obsession these past years. If he'd said that, there would be no chance that she would ever listen to him again.

But Grace had been right about one thing. They needed to talk this out together, and he had to take it easy, let her express her fear and reservations about assuming custody of Emma. He had a few reservations of his own, including how they would cope with a child who was old enough to realize that her mother was gone, but too young to understand why her life would have to change.

As he watched Grace drive away he wanted to run after her, tell her how much he loved her and that she was right. They needed to sort out their feelings and expectations before they made a decision about Emma. And that meant they needed time alone together to prepare for what lay ahead.

Yet he couldn't find the motivation to walk out on his daughter. She faced the long days and nights without her mother. It was so important that Emma have people around her who loved her while she learned to cope with her new circumstances.

His heart heavy, he turned toward the window to see the brake lights glow red as Grace pulled out of the driveway. He knew his wife would call Lucas to seek his advice. When she told him what Aidan had done, Lucas would be angry, and rightfully so. Aidan doubted that Lucas would understand his point of view, and he couldn't blame him.

Aidan glanced around the room, remembering the two nights he'd spent in this house when he and Deidre had been together. Deidre had used birth control, something she'd been very emphatic about. How had the birth control failed? Deidre had loved details, had reveled in getting everything right.

Another idea skirted the edge of his mind. He couldn't imagine someone like Deidre taking any chances with her personal life. Yet she had insisted that they work in her home, a home equipped with all the technology to do so. Had she intentionally misled him? Had she chosen him to be the father of her child, invited him into her home, intending to get pregnant, keep the child and continue on with her life? Had her father's death made her realize that if she passed away, Emma would be alone? His mind ran over the possibilities as his eyes took in the space that appeared unchanged from five years ago.

Focused on his thoughts, he was about to head to the kitchen for a glass of water when the door from the garage opened. Lisa walked in carrying a pink Dora the Explorer backpack while Emma followed holding a huge brown bear, the one in the video. His heart soared as he looked at his daughter. She was even more beautiful than the photos he'd seen. Uncertain about how to approach the little girl staring at him, he smiled, trying to put her at ease.

Lisa put the backpack on the end of the kitchen counter. "Emma, do you know who this is?" she asked, her gaze sweeping from Aidan to Emma.

Emma promptly popped her thumb into her mouth and reached for Lisa's hand.

Lisa patted Emma's curls soothingly as she spoke. "He's come to see you."

His chest tight, he knelt in front of his little girl and held out his arms. "Hi, Emma, I'm your dad," he said.

Emma stopped sucking her thumb and stared at him, her eyes filling with glossy tears. "No! Mommy. I want Mommy."

He edged closer. "I'm so sorry," he said softly, despite his disappointment. His little girl needed him, and he would be here for her. "Come, let me hold you," he whispered, marveling at how natural it felt to be here with his daughter.

"No! Mommy!" Emma screamed, her arms reaching for Lisa as tears flowed down her tiny face.

"Aidan, I'm sorry about this. It's all pretty new for Emma," Lisa said, picking her up and snuggling her close as Emma continued to sob, her face pressed into Lisa's chest.

Helpless to figure out what to say or do, Aidan watched in dread as Emma stared at him, her eyes dark with fear. He was a stranger to his only child, his daughter. She didn't want anything to do with him. He hadn't expected this. He'd assumed that she would recognize him from the photo, remember what her mother had said, and would want him to hold her.

He struggled to stem the flood of fear circling his heart. He was in over his head. He had no idea what he was doing or how to do it. He'd never considered that Emma would react this way. How would he ever manage to care for his daughter if this behavior continued? He glanced at Lisa, seeking her support.

"Aidan, please don't worry. Emma has been very upset since…you know. She'll be better soon. You'll see."

He didn't see at all. He hadn't been around kids very much, and he had no idea how to deal with them. Now, with his daughter so upset, he didn't have a clue how to reach out to her. Yet he knew he had to if he was going to be her dad. Instinctively, he backed away, keeping the smile on his face, his heart heavy with disappointment. "Emma. Your daddy is going to wait in the living room. Is that okay?"

Emma, her face buried in Lisa's neck, didn't respond.

CHAPTER SEVEN

EXHAUSTED AND WORRIED, Grace pulled into the garage. It was so good to be home, but so awful to be going into the house she and Aidan shared and to acknowledge he wasn't here. As angry and hurt as she'd been leaving Spartanburg, facing the house alone somehow made the trouble between her and her husband a fact and, in a very clear way, more real to her. Loss and loneliness trapped her where she was.

Never in her wildest dreams had she ever imagined she'd be faced with her marriage in tatters, and suspicion and distrust toward the man she'd loved. His infidelity changed everything she'd believed about her marriage and her husband. Glancing around the garage, Aidan's tools hanging over his workbench, she couldn't help but wonder what else he might have done while working out here on a Saturday afternoon, who he might have called, knowing he wouldn't be overheard.

If she needed any proof of how much her marriage was in trouble, she had only to look at what happened a few hours ago. The Aidan she knew would never have allowed her to leave Spartanburg, not without following her, if only to say goodbye and to reassure her that he would miss her. She was so accustomed to his presence in her life that she felt empty...drained.

She grabbed her overnight bag from the backseat and started toward the door leading into the house. Just as she unlocked it, she heard her brother's truck pull into the driveway. Relief flooded her. She raced out to him. "I'm so glad to see you, Lucas," she said, wrapping her arms around his neck and hugging him close.

"That husband of yours needs his butt kicked," he said, patting her shoulders as she clung to him. He wiped her hair from her face as he put his arm around her waist and walked with her into the house. "I'm glad you got home safely."

"Me, too," she said, watching as he put her overnight bag on the floor by the cupboard and moved to the counter where he ran water and filled the coffeepot. She watched her brother, her affection for him lifting her spirits. He was the best brother anyone could have wished for. Leaning against the counter as he moved about her kitchen, finding cups and getting cream out of the fridge, she unwound a little. Whatever came next, her brother would be here for her.

"Sis, despite how dumb Aidan is behaving, it's going to be okay," he said, pouring two cups of coffee and passing one to her. "Things seem pretty awful right now, but you and Aidan have been through lots of stuff together. This won't be any different." He put cream and sugar in his cup and offered her both.

"Just cream for me," she said.

"You've given up sugar in your coffee?" he asked.

"Yeah. I saw a program on the ill effects of too much sugar and decided to cut back," she said distractedly as she placed her hands firmly around her cup, sipping slowly.

Lucas's gaze assessed her. "You've had a rotten time of it, haven't you?"

Her hands began to shake at his words. The cup clattered onto the counter, coffee spilling over the edge. "I don't know what to do."

"I'm so sorry, sis," Lucas said, his voice filled with sorrow. "What can I do?"

"Help me understand what is going on."

"I'm still convinced that Aidan will come to his senses and realize what a total jerk he's been."

"But that doesn't change how awful I feel, how mixed up I am," Grace said as she edged onto one of the navy-blue leather stools at the kitchen island. She'd put so many hours of planning into this space when they were remodeling their home.

The off-white cabinetry had been suggested by the interior decorator and she'd loved the look of it. Aidan had insisted on an extra-large fridge with lots of freezer space so he could buy whatever amounts he needed for the meals he liked to cook. Unable to stop her eyes from moving from one beautiful part of her kitchen to the other, a flood of memories overtook her. "Remember the time Aidan cooked all those ribs for the staff, using both ovens? And the huge mess afterward?" she said.

"I do. He invited the whole office and did most of the work. It was a great party, and everyone appreciated being here."

"It wouldn't have been so messy if Aidan hadn't spilled a platter of ribs. I can still see the two of you trying to get the gooey, sticky juice stuff off the ceramic tiles," Grace said.

"You were a good sport about that. Most women would have thrown a hissy fit and called for a cleaning service."

"There are so many good memories here, Lucas. But right now, I can't imagine how we're going to work out our problems, especially when Aidan doesn't think there are any. He brushed me off when I asked about this Deidre person. It's as though he thinks I'm simply overreacting and that I'll get over the affair and accept his way of doing things with Emma."

"Do you want me to talk to him? Get him to see what he's done?"

"I don't know what good that would do. The affair was five years ago, and he says it meant nothing, which sickens me. How could it mean nothing when there is a child? You should have seen how totally focused he was on his plans for Emma... I still can't figure how he's going to manage a little girl who has just lost her mother. He's never been a parent. He's never had to look after anyone before. And what if he causes Emma serious emotional issues by forcing her to leave everything she is familiar with so soon after her mother's death? All to satisfy his need to be a parent."

"It's that serious, is it?" Lucas asked, sitting on the stool next to her.

"Worse. He's not listening. It's as if he is trying to make up for something…"

Lucas took her hand in his. "I cannot picture how it must have felt for him to find out he has a daughter. But Aidan's always been so cool under pressure, so able to manage everything. You said he spent most evenings after he found out about Emma in his office. Maybe he was trying, in Aidan fashion, to come to terms with what it meant to suddenly find that he's a father."

"And after his infidelity, am I supposed to sit around and wait for him to come to me, to be the person who supports *his* decision?" she asked, feeling her throat tighten.

"Don't say that. Think back to the day you had the car accident. Remember? Instead of rushing in and staying by your side, he first arranged to have the surgeon meet him in emergency where he grilled him about how the procedure would be done."

She couldn't help but smile. "Yeah, he arrived in my room, the surgeon trailing behind him, the surgery time set. When he finally felt everything was under control, he sat at my bedside with the most anxious look in his eyes."

"See? You simply have to trust Aidan. He'll work this out." He patted her hand before getting up to freshen their coffees. Passing her mug to her, he said, "I realize that it doesn't help you deal with his betrayal, but right now you need to think about you. You've been through so much in such a short time. Why don't you just take a long, hot bath, read something? Get some rest. Give this a little time. Your husband tends to act first and seek other people's opinions later."

"But this is different. This is me. His wife. First, I find out he's had an affair and a child. Then I find out he hasn't got time for my feelings."

"Have you considered the possibility that this whole thing is as big an adjustment for him as it is for you?"

"What? Adjustment? He's anxious to take over with Emma. That hardly sounds like he's having trouble adjusting."

"Think about it. Aidan's an only child. He never had anyone in his life totally dependent on him—until Emma. That has to cause him all kinds of anxiety regardless of how he appears to be behaving."

"I can't let myself care how this is affecting him when he doesn't care how it's affecting me. As far as I'm concerned, I don't know where we go from here, and I wonder if all the pain is worth it."

"Only you and Aidan can work on that. But if you feel you need to give him more time to sort things out, for the two of you to figure out what you want, then you'd better tell him that."

He came around the island and hugged her tight. "Sis, one of the principal traits of a Barton is to let our hurt feelings rule our thinking. I'm proof of that. Maria has helped me see how easily I can be hurt, then withdraw to lick my wounds. For my money, that's what you're doing now."

"You think I should go back to Spartanburg?"

"I think you should do whatever it is that makes you happy. You and Aidan have been happy and will be again, but not until you work out your differences. Listen to Aidan. Find out what he's going through. I'm betting you're both going through a lot of the same stuff."

"But he's ready to jump into fatherhood without so much as a word of how it will work with Emma, a child he knows nothing about. He is so stubborn," she said.

"That's part of what you can help Aidan with. You understand what a huge change this is for Emma as well as for both of you." He touched her cheek. "You're not a quitter. Talk to Aidan again. Tell him how you really feel…"

He looked into her eyes and she saw how much her brother cared. She wasn't in a strange city trying to cope with a little girl who had been traumatized. She really didn't understand what her husband was going through right now, and she never would if she didn't get in touch with him again. They had so many issues to work on, but none of it would matter if they couldn't talk to each other.

"Okay. I guess it wouldn't hurt for me to make the first move. I'll stay here tonight, then head back tomorrow morning."

"As a show of support, I'll take your car and gas it up before I head over to my condo. Maria is anxious to hear how you and Aidan are doing."

"That's so sweet. Visited any jewelry stores

lately?" she teased, feeling a little better, not quite so desperate.

"I'm not telling you, Ms. Matchmaker," he said, laughing as he went out the back door.

She watched him leave, thankful she had a brother and aware of how much she depended on him for advice. Aidan didn't have the option of relying on a brother or sister, something she hadn't taken into account in this situation. She would remember that the next time they talked...if they talked.

Should she call him now? Her stomach clenched at the thought.

After an hour of indecision, Grace dialed Aidan's cell phone. He answered on the first ring. "I'm so sorry, darling, for everything," he said, his voice warm, caressing her senses. "I felt so awful when you left here. I wanted to beg you to come back."

"Why didn't you?" she asked, knowing full well that she probably would have stayed if he'd done that.

"I don't know. I don't understand what is going on with me. When I met Emma she screamed, didn't want me near her. All I could think about was that you'd have done a much better job than I did. You would have known instinctively what to do."

Feeling closer to Aidan than she had since all of this began, she held the phone tighter. "Aidan, why did you have an affair?"

She heard his sudden intake of breath and waited to see if he'd answer her.

"I want to tell you the truth, but are you sure you want to hear what I have to say?"

"Yes. I am." Her knees threatening to give out on her, she sat down on the sofa.

"Okay, but what I have to say is going to sound totally selfish." He cleared his throat. "I'm sure you weren't aware of this, but I seldom felt you were hearing me about anything other than trying to get pregnant."

"That's not fair! I always listened to you."

Aidan didn't say a word for a few minutes. "Do you have any idea how many times I tried to get you to go on vacation? And each time you'd insist that you couldn't go because you had to be near your gynecologist."

"What can I say? Yes, I wanted to be pregnant, and I was afraid of being very far from my doctor. Why was a vacation so important?"

"Because I wanted you to focus your attention on me, on us and our marriage."

"I did. Having a baby was important to both of us."

"Yes. But many times I felt as if you weren't even aware of me except as the man who could get you pregnant."

There was a long pause while hurt rained down on her. "You really felt I ignored you except when we were—no. That's not true!" she screamed at him. "You wanted a baby, didn't you? Why are you only now telling me about how you felt?" she demanded, trying to gain control.

"Because I didn't think you'd listen to me. Every time I tried to talk about something else, something we might do or an idea for my business, you didn't seem very interested. At first I didn't mind so much, but as the years went on and things got so intense, so desperate, I felt as if what I wanted or needed really didn't matter."

"That's so unfair," she yelled at him. "You had your work. You had your life outside this house. I had nothing…nothing but the hope that we would finally conceive."

"And that's why I kept my feelings to myself. I didn't think that you'd be interested in how I felt unless it somehow related to getting pregnant. Do you have any idea how many times I simply wanted to hold you in my arms, to have you fall asleep in my arms, not from the effort of getting pregnant but because we loved each other and needed to hold each other close?"

Feeling the sincerity of his words across the connection, she began to see that maybe… "I was obsessed with getting pregnant. Is that what you're saying?"

He gave a huge sigh of relief. "Yes. After years of being together, the Grace I fell in love with seemed to have changed, and I didn't know how to deal with it. I was lonely, Grace. I needed my wife back."

"But that doesn't forgive what you did. You could have talked to me like you're talking now. We could have worked on getting a little balance in our marriage. You know I would not ignore you that way. You had to see that I needed you to share your feelings with me. Instead, you went to bed with another woman."

"An act that I am so sorry for. Believe me. You cannot imagine how sorry I am. I'd change it if I could."

"That's not possible. We both know that. And now there's a child," Grace said, her heart aching from the unfairness of life. "All I ever wanted was a baby."

"Me, too, Grace. Me, too," he whispered.

"And now you have one."

"No. *We* have one. We have a little girl, Grace."

"A little girl who came out of an affair you had," she said, her voice rising again.

"If Emma could have been your baby, I would have loved and cared for her, for you, for the rest of my life."

A moment of quiet fell between them. "Aidan, I wish I could tell you that with time and effort on your part, I might be able to forgive you. But I'm not sure if I'll ever be at that point, to feel it in my heart to forgive what you've done."

For a few moments, she feared that he might not answer, and it tore at her with a force she could never have imagined. What if she'd gone too far in what she'd said?

"Grace, I would like to be able to tell you that I will never hurt you again. But that's not possible. I've hurt you already. But I want you to believe that there isn't anything I wouldn't do to make this up to you. I haven't worked out exactly how to do that, but believe me, I'm going to try. I need you more than I could ever have imagined. Not just because of Emma, but because you're you. You make my life worthwhile."

A shudder ran through her at his words. "Oh, Aidan, if only none of this had happened," she whispered.

"But it did," he said, desolation tingeing his words.

CHAPTER EIGHT

ALTHOUGH SOME OF the things they'd talked
about last night were painful, Grace felt a little better this morning. The call had given her
hope that they might be able to work things
out between them.

Just as she finished tidying the bedroom
and placing clothes in the laundry hamper,
the phone rang. Aidan. She hadn't expected to
hear from him so soon. "How are you doing?
Did you get any rest?" she asked, falling into
her old habit of being concerned for him.

"I did a little, not much. I'm too worried
about how I'm going to cope with Emma."

Should she simply say what was on her
mind? After last night, it was worth a try. "I
thought that maybe if I drove to Spartanburg
today, we could talk about all this, maybe
work out a plan for Emma."

"I'd like that so much, darling. I really
believe we can solve this if we try. We can
get our life back on track. To be honest, I

spent part of the night thinking of ways to fix things, and so if you are willing to come here, I'd like to see you as soon as possible."

"How is Emma?" she asked.

"She cried when I came near her again last night. She wouldn't let me put her to bed. Pretty upsetting stuff, but like Lisa said, Emma has just lost her mom. Lisa suggested that I might consider having Emma see a child psychologist. I hadn't thought of that. For now, I'd like to see if I could gain her trust, have her be willing to spend time with me...with us."

Grace heard the uncertainty in his words and remembered her promise to herself to keep in mind that Aidan had no family member to confide in or rely upon the way she did. "Aidan, it will take time. She sees you as a stranger, and it will be a big change for her to see you as anything other than that. I'm sure it will eventually work out."

"If you're here with me, everything will be fine," he said, and she knew by his tone he expected her to reassure him that she would be there for him.

She suddenly felt shy and uncertain. She'd never behaved this way around Aidan, this new thing of holding back. She'd always rushed in to support him in whatever he was doing.

"When will you be here?" he asked, and she heard the loneliness in his voice.

His need for her drew her in. The familiarity of that role comforted her, despite their issues. She couldn't help herself, it seemed. "I'm ready to go now, so about two hours maybe."

He gave a protracted sigh. "I'll be waiting right here for you. Truthfully, I spent a miserable night last night without you."

"Me, too," she confessed.

"Grace, please drive carefully," he murmured in her ear.

"I will. I have to pack, then I can get on the road," she said, as she placed her pajamas in her suitcase.

As she hung up, she realized she would like Aidan to come home with her. Their conversation last night proved they could work on things together, and that lifted her spirits, made her believe they could put their marriage back together eventually. Just on that one subject they had so much to think about, to talk about, and it would be much easier to do it here in their home.

They needed to sit down with a counselor

to talk out their concerns about how Emma had come into their lives and how it had affected their marriage.

She climbed into the car, her mind focused on what lay ahead. She had so many doubts about all this. She wasn't sure she wanted the child of her husband's affair. What if she couldn't accept Emma into her life? She felt guilty for feeling that way, but she couldn't help it. And a part of her resented that he would simply assume that she would be okay with the child he'd fathered without her.

Given the way he was behaving, she wondered how to talk to him about her concern about raising another's woman's child and all that meant for her. How could she get him to see her point of view? If they were to get through this with their marriage intact, she and he both had to be totally honest about how they felt.

Hours later, she pulled into the driveway she'd left so hurriedly yesterday. Aidan met her at the door, his arms outstretched. "Oh, Grace. I've missed you so much. So much."

She walked into his embrace feeling his warmth, breathing in his scent. He held her tight as he rocked her back and forth.

"I missed you, too, Aidan. Last night was

the loneliest night of my life," she whispered into his cotton shirt, soaking in the newly scrubbed scent of his body. "Where did you stay last night?"

Still holding her tight, he led her into the house and along the hall to the kitchen. "I stayed here. Lisa thought it might help if I was around when Emma got up this morning. Lisa has gone shopping and Emma is at kindergarten. We've got the house to ourselves. Larry Knowles called to say he'd like to see me to start the process of working out the estate details. I want you to go with me," he said, drawing her into a kiss that made her knees weak with desire.

He smiled. "I've got coffee ready to go, and I went to the local bakery and got your favorite sandwich—Swiss cheese and ham with mayo and mustard." Without waiting for her reply, he moved to the counter and began making coffee, his back to her as he worked.

"I'm famished. Did you get yourself a sandwich, as well?" she asked, slipping into her old behavior of thinking about him first. Yet it felt so easy, so natural. She shrugged off her concern that he might expect things to go back to the way they were. That couldn't happen.

He got two plates out of the cupboard and put them on the island. "I did. I ate earlier. The lawyer appointment isn't until two o'clock, so we have time."

Grace watched her husband as she organized her thoughts, what she wanted to say. She knew how important Emma was to him, but she needed him to understand how she felt about it all. "Aidan, I think we need to be very clear on what we want to do."

He looked up from cutting her sandwich in half. "Of course we need to be clear. But I'm not sure if you mean it the way I do."

"I mean Emma is a little girl who has never lived anywhere but in this house. We live miles away, with a life that we've made for the two of us, a life that never included a child, despite our wishes. At the very least, we will have to childproof the house. We'd have to find a pediatrician, a dentist who is good with children—"

"But once she's over the worst of it, Emma will be fine. Children adapt easily," Aidan said, as he studied her. "You don't see it that way, do you?"

"What I see is a child who will need a lot of care and attention in a loving, familiar environment. That environment isn't our home where nothing is familiar to her. It's here with her nanny."

"But what about us? We have been waiting most of our marriage for a child. Now we have one," Aidan said, a bewildered look on his face.

"It's not just about having a child in our lives. It's about doing right for her and for us. That all takes planning and caring, Aidan. And so far we've done none of it."

"I don't understand," he said, his eyebrows drawn together as he poured the coffee and brought the cups and cream to the counter between them.

"This is a huge change for both of us. We'll have to make sacrifices to make sure that Emma is cared for and happy."

"But that's the whole point. We now have a child. We are a family," he said, leaning on the counter.

Grace couldn't look at her sandwich let alone take a bite. "Aidan, I'm not sure I can accept Emma as my child. I…I… She belongs to you and Deidre."

Aidan stared across the glossy surface of the counter at her. "She belongs with you and me. Deidre is gone. She is not coming back. She left her child in our care. Deidre wasn't part of our lives, but we've been given the gift. Something good has come out of Deidre's death. At least, that's how I see it."

Grace took a deep breath, preparing herself to offer up what she felt. Crossing her fingers that Aidan would listen, she said, "That's not how I see it. I need time to accept her into our lives. She is a part of you, and I respect that. But she's not a part of me. I can't have a child, and I'm afraid that having Emma with us would be a constant reminder of my inability to have a baby and of your infidelity."

Aidan blew out an impatient sigh. "Grace, how can I convince you that Deidre was never really part of my life? The only really good thing that came out of that relationship was Emma."

Her throat choking with tears, Grace tried to find the right words. "Aidan, I need time to sort this out. We need time together, to adjust to having a child in our lives so suddenly. Would it be possible to leave Emma here with Lisa while you and I go home and work this out?"

"Are you saying you don't want Emma?" he asked, frustration tingeing his words.

"That's not what I said at all. What I said was I need to be sure that taking Emma into our lives at the moment is the right thing for us. We have so many problems we need to work on. This is all so sudden, and I need to feel that we are doing the right thing. I need us to talk it all out, rather than jump in so fast."

"The right thing? This isn't about right or wrong. This is about my daughter, our daughter. Grace, you're overreacting to all this. Don't let what happened years ago influence how you feel about Emma. This is our life. We have a child. What we both have wanted all along."

"But what you did back then is now influencing everything in our life, in my life. You had an affair, which you didn't tell me about. You find out you have a daughter from that affair and I'm supposed to jump onboard without a moment's thought or hesitation. I'm your wife. I was your wife before Deidre and before this child. I need you to support me in this, to give me time to adjust."

"I don't know what to say. You want me to leave Emma here while we go home and work on you adjusting to having a child in our lives when we've waited years for this opportunity. I don't get it," he said.

"This child is not ours. She's yours and

Deidre's. Not mine. I can't simply ignore what you and Deidre did to my life, to my faith in you. It's this simple. Either I'm part of this decision or I'm not," she said, anger rising through her.

"Grace, I can't abandon Emma. And that's what it would feel like if I went home with you now. But if you stay here with me, I'm willing to spend time working through this with you, reassuring you in any way I can."

"I don't want reassurance. I want to be involved in deciding what is best for her and for us. Don't you see?" she asked, feeling miserable and alone. "If you'd been willing to adopt a baby, we'd be a family now. Taking Emma into our lives would be different, if we already had a child."

"Grace, where is this coming from? Are you afraid that I am taking Emma out of some sort of loyalty to Deidre?" he asked, his dark eyes intent on hers.

She shrugged in defeat. "What do you want me to say? We can't seem to talk about this without you presenting what you want and expecting me to go along with it."

"That's not true! I want you to be part of this, but I can't abandon my daughter."

She wondered if he'd heard any of the

words he'd just spoken or saw their effect on her. Probably not. Aidan wasn't ready to accept anyone else's ideas on this. How long that would last, she didn't know. Perhaps coming here was a mistake. "For the umpteenth time, I'm not asking you to abandon your child."

"Then what are you saying?" he asked.

"I want you to listen to my side of things. I failed you by not having our baby, and it's clear that you want your child. I've always wanted my own child, my baby. It didn't happen. We don't always get what we want, Aidan," she said, her voice failing her as sobs shook her whole body. Through her tears, she searched for her purse. "This was a mistake, my coming here. A mistake."

"DON'T SAY THAT, GRACE," Aidan pleaded, going to her and holding her while she cried. He'd been so glad to see her when she drove in the driveway. Last night's conversation had been so open and caring, yet so laden with things that neither could say. He'd been thrilled to have her return to him, and he'd foolishly believed they could agree to have Emma return home with them.

Holding her close, he whispered, "I never

meant to hurt you. I am as confused by all of this as you are. Not long ago I was running my business, we were having a little break in Charleston and life was good. And, yes, I didn't jump on the adoption thing right away because I felt we needed a little time to catch our breath, get our lives on track before we began the search for a child. It wasn't that I didn't want to adopt. I wanted us to take our time."

"And that's what I'm asking you to do now. What difference will a week make in Emma's life? Isn't a delay while we talk this out better than our marriage suffering and Emma being caught in the middle?"

He held her shoulders as his eyes searched her tearstained face. "Grace, I love you. I didn't realize that you felt this way. But you don't know how it felt last night to watch Emma, to feel that visceral connection to someone, someone who is totally dependent on me, what I do and how I do it. For the first time in my life, I'm confused, uncertain. And yet I've never felt this alive. Emma's a lovely little girl and I'm sure you will fall in love with her. Just wait until she gets home from kindergarten."

"I—I don't think that would be a good idea."

"Why not? She's a part of our lives."

"You don't get it, do you?" She glanced at him and the sadness in her expression crushed his heart. "You want us to include a little girl in our lives and to overcome the damage caused to our relationship by the fact you had an affair without being clear on what all this means to each of us."

"I guess I don't get it. I want to, but every time I say something it comes out all wrong," he said, feeling lost, adrift and afraid that he was about to lose her.

"I need to know that my feelings matter," she said in a matter-of-fact tone.

"They do!" Was that the problem? Was she feeling left out? She shouldn't feel that way. He wasn't leaving her out. "Your feelings have always mattered—"

"Let me finish. I need for us to take this slow, to talk this out together before we decide to take her home with us. This is a big decision for both of us. It will change our lives, our relationship, forever."

She couldn't be suggesting that he walk away from Emma, leave her here on her own without family, could she? "But Grace, Emma is my responsibility. I love her and I can't walk away from her."

Grace sighed. "I'm simply suggesting that you come home with me—Emma will be fine with Lisa for a little bit—and we work out a plan, look at our options. And if we decide to become parents, we find a kindergarten for Emma. We get our house ready for a little girl." She paused, then said slowly, "And we start proceedings to adopt her…if that's what we decide we want to do. In the meantime, she's safe and content here with Lisa."

He frowned in surprise. "Grace, there is no decision to be made about whether or not we take Emma. The decision is when and how," he said, his heart surging in his chest as he began to see what was going on here. Grace was worried over things that were easily fixed. "You and I and Emma will be a family. Together we will arrange for everything Emma needs. You will be a wonderful mom."

Grace's expression was despondent as she looked at him before turning away. "I am not Emma's mother. Her mother just died. If we're to be Emma's family, if that's the best resolution for all of us, you and I first have to be together on how we'll do it. If we're not, we'll only make *your* daughter unhappy. Is that what you want?"

Hurt, like a dull blade, jabbed at his heart. "I don't want anyone to be unhappy, especially not you," he said, feeling the situation slip out of his control. Where had he gone so wrong?

"Then come home with me. Call Mr. Knowles and reschedule your meeting." She took his hand in hers, her skin warm and inviting. "We have so much to consider. If we are to get through all of this, we need to go to counseling."

"Counseling isn't necessary if we love each other and want to be a family. Grace, don't do this to me. I already feel guilty that I had an affair and that I didn't know about Emma. I could have been here for her, but I wasn't. I can't make that right. But I… We've got a chance now to do what she needs."

"Your lack of involvement in Emma's life was Deidre's decision and out of your control."

He clutched her hand tighter. "That's true. And now I've got a chance to make it up to her by being with her. She's just a little girl. She's confused and missing her mom. I can help her. You can, too."

Grace pulled her hand away. "Aidan, it's

clear that you and I can't resolve this standing here. Please come home with me and let's work this out between us."

"I love you with all my heart, Grace. But I can't leave Emma, not right now."

She turned her face to his, the look of longing in her eyes cutting straight to his heart. "Is that it? You're going to stay here with Emma rather than coming home with me?"

Aware that things were going terribly wrong, he fought to make her understand. "Grace, it's not that simple."

"It is. Either you love me enough to put my feelings first, or you don't."

"That's not fair! I do love you."

She stepped away from him. "But not enough. Not enough to make you change your mind. I came here to convince you that we needed to sort things out, for our sakes as well as for Emma's. It's pretty clear to me that I've wasted my time," she said, her voice catching.

"You haven't wasted your time. I do want to talk, but I can't leave Emma here by herself."

"She's not by herself. She's with the one person in her life she loves best. You said yourself she is shy around you, doesn't trust you. If you gave her a little time, it would be better for both of you. While she's adjusting to her life without her mother, you and I could be working out a plan that provides for Emma's needs."

"Providing for her needs? Are you suggesting we aren't what Emma needs?"

"I'm not suggesting anything, only that we sit down, just the two of us, and work this out between us," she said, her voice so soft he could barely hear her.

"Why did you come here if you weren't willing to help me bring Emma home?" he asked, barely hiding his annoyance. "Was all that talk about having a child just talk?"

"How dare you say that? You really don't want to change anything at all. I came here to talk this out and you're being totally selfish and unreasonable," she said, turning to go, her shoulders rigid.

When she got to the door, she turned to face him. "So I guess that's it. There is nothing left to talk about. I'm going home, Aidan."

CHAPTER NINE

HOURS LATER, WITH Grace's words still ringing in his ears, Aidan pulled into the parking lot at Larry Knowles's office. He hadn't known what to do or where to turn after Grace left. He felt hollow, cut off from everything he'd known and loved, adrift trying to make sense of it. He'd been thankful for the meeting with the lawyer, anything to distract him from what had occurred between Grace and him.

Hearing Deidre's will might help him better understand why she chose to do what she did, and maybe a hint as to why she'd not told him about Emma.

After he entered the building he was shown directly into the lawyer's office.

"So good to see you again," the lawyer said, coming around his desk to shake hands. "We'll get right to the will. I've made a copy for you and will go through the major provisions set out in it."

The men sat, and Aidan picked up the

document, reminded of how easily life can be summed up in a few pages of instructions for the beneficiary. "I wish I'd known Deidre better," he said, scanning the pages.

"How's that? You and she had a relationship, didn't you?"

"I don't know what she told you. My company did work with Deidre's. Our intimate relationship amounted to one weekend. A weekend that never should have happened." He looked across the desk at the lawyer. "I don't know why I'm telling you that, other than I feel guilty that I didn't know about Emma before Deidre passed away. I didn't know Deidre was pregnant. I never heard from her again after that weekend five years ago. I guess that's part of why I was so shocked when you called to tell me I was named as guardian of Emma."

Larry leaned back in his chair. "That's interesting. Deidre didn't go into the details of her connection to you, although your reaction to my initial phone call made me suspect you'd had limited contact with her."

He rubbed his chin in thought. "Before I go through the various provisions, I'd like to tell you a couple things about Deidre that you may not have known. She always had to be in control, set the agenda. She was tough, hardworking and always very careful about whom she allowed close to her. As her friend, no one was more surprised than I was when she came to see me about her will. I'm probably overstepping my bounds, but I don't think she ever intended to have you find out about Emma. I think, like most people, she never believed she'd die young."

"Why would she do such a thing?" Aidan asked.

"Deidre wanted Emma to herself. I'm guessing here, but I believe it had to do with being an only child herself. She had told me she wanted a child, and when Deidre wanted something, she usually got it. I don't think she had many relationships. I was one of only a handful of friends. She was one of those people who made her decisions based on her needs at the time, including the people she did or did not need."

Aidan remembered that weekend, the way Deidre came on to him, seducing him with determination and eagerness. He'd been totally surprised by her attitude and her clear intention to have sex, even though he didn't have any condoms with him. He had never slept around on Grace, so had no need for such protection. Still, Deidre had assured him she was on birth control and had provided the condoms. Was it possible she'd misled him? Had Deidre intentionally gotten pregnant? Why hadn't he insisted on buying his own condoms?

As he stared at the document, not reading a word of it, his mind scrambled over his memories of that weekend—the wild sex, the total freedom and excitement.

A sickening feeling flooded him, forcing him to face the ugliness of it all. Not only had he cheated on his wife, destroying the trust between them and breaking his vow to the only woman he'd ever loved, but he'd done it without thinking of the other possible repercussions of having sex.

He had shown little or no responsibility for taking precautions during sex with a woman he didn't know well at all. He'd been careless and thoughtless.

Because of his actions, a little girl had been born without the advantage of having a father in her life. And now, because of Deidre's decision to name him as guardian for her daughter, his marriage might not survive and Emma might still end up without a mother. What a hell of a mess he'd made of things.

He sighed inwardly as he met Larry's inquiring gaze. "Obviously Deidre liked being in charge, so what else has she dictated?"

"What does your wife think of all this?"

Aidan grimaced. "She didn't know about the affair. It's really been very difficult for her, and quite frankly, my marriage is in trouble."

Larry Knowles shook his head slowly. "I'm sorry for you and your wife, but my concern is for Emma. She deserves a stable environment. She has Lisa, of course, but no family to speak of." The lawyer stared straight at him. "If you agree to the terms of the will, you have a huge responsibility."

"And if I don't take Emma, my daughter will become a ward of the state and put up for adoption," he said, returning the lawyer's demanding gaze.

"She will."

"I messed up and hurt two people who were completely innocent. Now I have to make things right for them. I love both of them very much. I never knew what it felt like to be a father, and now I have a child who needs me in her life. I plan to take good care of her and to prove to my wife how much I love her."

The lawyer's expression softened. "Then let's get to the will. Deidre left an estate of a little over five million, most of which is invested with a professional investment group here in the city. I have all that information when you're ready to deal with it. I have all the documents ready for you to sign as the guardian. Deidre wanted you to move into her house."

"But Deidre knew I have a wife, that I live outside of Charleston. Why would she think I would move here?"

"Again, Deidre looked at things from her perspective and what she wanted for Emma. Knowing her as I did, she probably thought that the combination of money and her home would entice you to move here. But I'm only guessing." He shifted in his chair. "Why don't I go through the will? If you have questions, we can address them. Would that work?"

Aidan listened to the lawyer as he read out the conditions. Sadness and regret washed over his mind. He'd hurt everyone he loved with his behavior, and now it was time to make amends. In his heart, he knew that Grace and Emma belonged together. He'd done a lousy job trying to bring that situation about. But from now on, he'd listen to his wife and do his best to allay her fears.

He was done making decisions that ended up hurting the people he loved.

An hour later, after he'd signed all the paperwork at the brokerage firm and made arrangements to set up new bank accounts, he headed to Deidre's house, relieved that all of that was finished for a while. There would be further decisions to make later, but the urgent details and paperwork had been settled.

Now was the time for him to prove to Grace and to Emma that he loved them and would care for them. It was his job to prevent any further damage to Emma. And to Grace.

Watching Emma this morning before she left the house had cemented his determination to be a good father. With her bright red curls and blue eyes, her instant smile and the adorable way she talked and played with Lisa, he couldn't take his eyes off her.

It was true that, so far, she'd avoided any direct contact with him, but he believed with all his heart that, given time, he could change that. He looked forward to the day he could hold her and play with her the way Lisa did. Until then, he would take it slow, be there for her and make certain that her life was as close to normal as possible. That meant staying here for a few days to get everything organized. It might even take a couple of weeks. He should have explained that to Grace, to make it clear he wanted to resolve the issues they faced, but from here. Not at their home, where he couldn't establish a relationship with Emma. But between Grace's anger and his inability to cope with her anger, he had, once again, mishandled their conversation and gotten it all wrong.

He heard the back door open and moved off the kitchen stool he'd been sitting on. Emma came in, tugging on Lisa's hand, a ready smile on her face. When she saw him, she slowed, stopped and stared at him. Without saying a word, he smiled at her. She gave him a tiny smile back, and his heart soared. He was making progress.

Lisa put the knapsack on the counter, then went to the fridge. "What would you like for a snack?" she asked Emma. "What about pita and hummus?"

Aidan had never eaten hummus in his life, but he was certainly willing to try. If eating hummus would give him a starting point with his daughter, he'd eat a gallon of it.

He waited to see what Emma would do.

She rushed across the room to the fridge and took the food from Lisa's hands. "I'm hungry," she said, placing the food on the counter and climbing up on a stool next to him.

"Let me help you with that," he said, reaching toward her.

She looked anxiously at him out of the corner of her eye, her lower lip jutting out. Was she going to cry? He hoped not. He'd seen enough tears for one day. "Can I have some of that?" he asked.

Emma blinked. A slight smile slowly turned up the corners of her mouth. "Mommy says we should all eat healthy," she said, popping her thumb into her mouth as her eyes moved to Lisa, who was putting the food on a plate.

"Your mom is right. We should all eat healthy," he said.

"Can I have juice, please?" she asked.

"Certainly," Lisa answered, going to the cupboard and returning with what seemed to Aidan to be a lot of similar small boxes with colorful cartoon characters on them.

Emma reached for the plate and slid it across to him. "We can share."

His heart beat hard in his chest at the kind gesture. Obviously, Deidre and Lisa had been teaching Emma to be polite and kind. "Thank you. I'd really like that."

They settled in to enjoy the snack while Lisa started to prepare dinner. Watching Emma eat and chat with Lisa, Aidan spent the most enjoyable time he'd had since coming here. He had to believe that everything would work out. He'd make sure it did. And the hummus wasn't half-bad, either.

He was laughing at Emma's antics with a piece of pita when Lisa spoke. "Aidan, we need to talk."

"Sure. Now?"

"Emma, sweetie, how would you like to finish your snack while you watch *SpongeBob SquarePants*?" Lisa asked as she gathered the remainder of the food and took it to the family room. Emma gave him a quick smile as she slid off the stool. "Do you like SpongeBob?" she asked him.

"Ah. I don't think I've ever seen it," he said, realizing that he was going to have to learn all about Emma's likes and dislikes, and clearly her favorite TV programs.

She stared at him. "Everyone watches *SpongeBob SquarePants*. It's funny." She giggled as she followed Lisa into the family room.

When Lisa returned, she had a concerned

look on her face. "I had a call from my family while I was waiting for Emma. My mother has been taken to the hospital, and I have to go."

"I'm sorry to hear that. What can I do?"

She looked at him a little strangely. "Nothing. You'll have your hands full with Emma. Having lost her mother and without me here, Emma will need all the love and support you can give her."

He had to care for Emma? On his own? The knowledge slammed into him with the force of a sledgehammer.

"I—I'm afraid I'll screw up. I mean, I'm just learning this whole parenting thing. Emma is still very uncomfortable around me. It's not a good idea to leave her alone with just me, is it?" he asked, his heart pounding hard against his ribs.

Lisa gave him a quick glance. "There really isn't anyone else I can call on, and I have to go. If you need help, I'm sure Deidre's friend Valerie Henson could step in, but she works full-time and has kids of her own," she said as she continued to peel carrots at the sink. "I'm afraid it's up to you."

"I…" What was he going to do?

"Your wife is here. She could help you."

"No. Grace went back home. She's…having difficulty coping with all the change going on in our life."

Lisa turned to him, a concerned look on her face. "I'm sorry to hear that, but I have to go. I'll leave you with a detailed list of instructions. And any contacts you might need are posted on the fridge." She pointed to what looked like sheets of information. "I'm sure you'll be fine."

She finished preparing dinner before going to pack a suitcase. Still trying to process Lisa's news, Aidan watched in horror as Lisa knelt next to Emma in the family room. "I have to go away for a couple days to see my family, but I'll be back as soon as possible."

"Don't go!" Emma sobbed, throwing herself into Lisa's arms. Lisa picked her up and carried her to the kitchen where Aidan stood transfixed by the enormity of this situation. He hadn't imagined that he might have to care for Emma alone. He'd been counting on Lisa and Grace to be around and do the things little girls needed done.

How was he to manage the care of a child he knew so little about? He had no experience with children. He had no siblings, no cousins his age and had never been around young kids.

Emma clung to Lisa. The longer her misery continued, the more Aidan wished fervently that Lisa might change her mind or at least take Emma with her. "Are you sure this is a good idea, I mean, leaving me in charge?"

"We don't have a choice," Lisa said, her voice low as if to prevent Emma from hearing what she said. She glanced at her watch. "And I have to get going." She gave him a worried look.

"I'll figure it out," he conceded as he moved closer to Emma, smiling as if his life depended on it.

For what seemed like a lifetime, Emma eyed him from under her teary eyelashes. Eventually, she pulled her thumb from her mouth, hiccuping and sniffling before putting her arms out to him.

Tentatively, he reached for her, still waiting for her to reconsider and bury her face in Lisa's chest. When she didn't, he took her in his arms, patting her narrow shoulders. What should he do now? He'd heard from someone—he couldn't remember who— that it was soothing to a child to carry them around the house looking at whatever caught the child's attention. He began moving from room to room. "Look outside," he said, pointing at the American flag fluttering on the flagpole near the garage. "What is that?"

"Flag," she said before popping her thumb back into her mouth, resting her tiny head on his shoulder and snuggling close. Love for his daughter, like a living thing, filled his chest, expanding to fill his body, shaking him to his core.

He was walking around the kitchen, pointing things out for Emma to name when Lisa appeared with her purse and a small suitcase. He really was going to be one hundred percent responsible for this little girl. "You're leaving now," he said, hearing the raw anxiety in his voice.

"I am." Lisa looked at Emma, who promptly pulled away from Aidan and reached for Lisa.

"I go with you," Emma said as Lisa wrapped her arms around his little girl.

"You have to stay here with your dad. I'll be back as soon as I can, and in the meantime, you be good, okay?" Lisa said, kissing her cheek.

Emma pulled her thumb from her mouth. "No! You stay!" she demanded, tears spilling down her cheeks.

"I have to go, honey," Lisa murmured, her eyes filling with tears as she held the little girl. She looked over at Aidan. "Can you take her for me?"

Tentatively, he reached for Emma, who immediately began to cry harder. Aidan waited, not knowing what to do, fearing that Emma would not stop crying when Lisa left the house.

"I have to go, Emma," Lisa said again, and this time she passed Emma to him. The child struggled in his arms and managed to slide to the floor, following Lisa to the door. Aidan went after her, trying to remain calm while worrying that Emma might follow Lisa to her car.

"Please stay here with me," he said to Emma as he managed to pick her up again, evoking loud wails.

Lisa turned, a desperate look on her face. "Find one of her favorite toys to soothe her," she said as she turned quickly, opened the door and walked out, to another yelp of protest from Emma.

"I don't know which toys are her favorite," he said to the closed door.

Emma scrambled out of his arms, fleeing to the window in the living room that looked out on the driveway. "Weeza!" she screamed, climbing the back of the sofa.

He went to her, unsure if he should try to pick her up and comfort her. Hoping to calm his little girl, he glanced around the room looking for a toy that might soothe her. In a corner, he spotted the black teddy bear perched precariously on the edge of a tapestry-covered bench. He grabbed the furry toy and offered it to Emma.

At first, she ignored him, sucking her thumb and hiccuping. When she did glance his way, she stared at him suspiciously. He waited, his throat constricted with worry at the possibility that Emma might simply continue to cry, and he wouldn't be able to comfort her.

Seconds later her tiny hand grabbed the bear before turning away from him and nestling into the sofa while she patted the bear's back.

What should he do now? He glanced around, trying to figure out if he could get her back to the TV in the family room. Not ideal parenting, but the TV might distract her and give him time to make a plan.

"Emma, would you let me watch *SpongeBob SquarePants* with you?" he asked, mentally crossing his fingers that the program was still on.

She peered up at him, sighed and offered her bear to him. "Blackie and I will show you."

He took the bear, grateful for the change in his daughter, and followed her to the TV. Cartoon characters he'd never seen before who seemed to live under the water flashed on the screen. How weird was that? He edged down beside her on the sofa. "So, tell me about this show. Who is SpongeBob?"

Relief whirled around him as he listened to her animated description of what seemed to be a bunch of characters making Krabby Patties while hurling insults at each other and throwing things. But he really didn't care about the storyline as long as Emma seemed content and was not crying. For now, he was happy to sit with her, watch her as she pointed and laughed at the antics of the characters.

It would seem that the program ran four episodes back-to-back each day after school, according to the onscreen guide.

Carefully he eased back on the sofa, hoping that Emma might snuggle next to him for a few minutes. Before long, she glanced at him, her gaze shifting to his lap. He took that to mean she wanted him to hold her. When he opened his arms, she climbed onto his lap, and not too long after, she fell asleep on his shoulder.

What should he do now? Would she sleep until her bedtime, then stay awake half the night crying for Lisa, or worse, her mother? He didn't have any idea and it frightened him. All he could be sure of was that, for now, things were quiet.

A little later, she awoke suddenly, rubbed her eyes. "I'm hungry," she said, sitting up straight and staring at him.

"What would you like to eat?" he asked.

"Tomato soup and crackers," she said, sliding off his lap and heading to the kitchen, dragging Blackie the bear behind her.

"Can I have some, too?" he asked, following her to the kitchen.

She raised her arms up to him. "Yes. But only four crackers," she said, holding up four fingers as he lifted her into his arms.

"Do you help Lisa make dinner?"

"Yes. I sit there." She pointed to the stool closest to the kitchen sink.

"Want to sit there now?" he asked.

"Yes."

He was pleased to make her dinner and

watch as she slurped the soup. He didn't realize that little kids liked soup, but his daughter certainly did. Upstairs, he ran a bath and helped Emma into it. He sat on the floor beside the tub and watched as she splashed and played with plastic fish and other assorted creatures.

Wanting to get her to bed so he could relax for a while, he held out a towel to Emma. "I think it's time to get out of the tub, don't you?"

For a minute, her lips formed a pout and he held his breath.

Please don't cry. Please.

"Yes!" Emma's face lit up with a smile. He scooped her up and started down the hall to her bedroom.

"We'll get you into your pajamas, and then I'll read you a story," he said.

She pointed to her mother's room as they reached the door. Oh. No. "You want to go in there?" he asked, preparing himself for the onslaught of tears he was certain would erupt if they went into Deidre's room. "Are you sure you don't want to get your pajamas on now? We could look in your mother's room later."

Emma gave her head a vigorous shake sending damp curls cascading over her face.

"Okay." He carried her into the room, the evening sky spreading shades of pink and gold across the cream-colored duvet.

Emma pointed to the mantel over the fireplace.

"Mommy's photo. You want to look at that," he said, dreading what would happen next.

Emma reached toward the mantel, picking up the photo of him next to the one of Deidre. "Daddy," she said, hugging it close, her thumb making its way into her mouth, but not before she smiled into his face.

His heart slowed to a steady thump as he held her tight in his arms. His life seemed to stand still as he met his daughter's gaze. An emotion he couldn't name swamped him, and he knew only that he'd never felt it before. "Yes. Daddy," he said, as tears of joy ran unfettered down his face.

"Don't cry," she said, her expression anxious.

"I'm crying because I'm happy," he whispered taking the photo from her tiny hands and gingerly putting it on the mantel.

"No!" Emma reached for the photo, taking it in her pudgy hands. "Mine!"

"You want to keep that?" he asked, marveling at how easy she was to hold.

"My room," she said, leaning back in his arms and peeking up at him from under her dark lashes.

In her room, she put on her pajamas and climbed into bed, still clutching his photo in her hands. Watching her, he knew he would remember every detail of this moment for the rest of his life.

Abruptly, his thoughts turned to Grace. He wanted to share this moment with her. She, better than anyone he knew, would appreciate how he was feeling. But first, he had to be sure that Emma was settled. "Do you want me to read to you?" he asked, following Lisa's instructions about the bedtime routine.

"No. Mommy reads to me," she said, her eyes dark pools of worry. "I want Mommy."

Aidan felt so sorry for his little girl, and so helpless. Nothing would change the sad truth that her mother would never be with her again, would never hold her or read to her.

He knelt beside the bed. "Well, maybe you could show me your favorite book, and maybe I could read to you sometime. Maybe even tomorrow night?" he asked, fearing that she would simply continue to cry. If she did, what would he do? There was no one to turn to. He could call Grace, but what could she do over the phone?

Slowly a small smile started on Emma's face, pushing her cheeks up into tiny pink globes. Was she going to be okay? "Can I take the photo?" he asked, hoping to smooth the tiny frown between her perfectly blue eyes.

Emma snuggled under the pink duvet, handing him the photo. "I'll put it on the bookcase, will I?" he asked, unbelievably relieved that she seemed to be settling for the night.

She nodded, her thumb slipping into her mouth. He kissed her forehead, reveling in the softness of her skin and the fresh-scrubbed scent of her. Unfamiliar feelings he could not explain filled him. He'd never felt this way in his life. She gave him a sleepy smile as she snuggled beneath the sheets. He would do anything, make any sacrifice, for the little girl lying there looking up at him. Anything.

"See you in the morning," he whispered.

"Leave the door open," she murmured, her voice filled with sleep.

"Sure. I'll check on you a little later. Sweet dreams, princess."

He tiptoed out of the room, but not before

he saw her eyelids slide closed. He took a deep breath, the first since he'd gotten her out of the tub. Overall, the evening had gone pretty well. Or, at least, he thought so. He'd be sure to check on her several times during the night, just in case. If she were afraid and lonely, would she get up and come into his room? Or would she go to her mother's room?

Back in his room, he reread the list of instructions that Lisa had left for him—all sorts of information about Emma's daily life, things he hadn't imagined he'd need to learn so soon.

He called Grace, eager to tell her what had happened and talk about everything he was feeling. The past couple of hours had been a roller coaster, from his early fear that he couldn't cope to his conviction that he could do this. He could.

"Hi, Aidan," Grace said, her voice sounding strained.

"Are you okay?" he asked.

"I'm fine. How are you?"

"I'm doing okay, mostly. I wanted to tell you about Lisa and what's been going on," he said as he started to list off the events since she'd left earlier in the day.

Grace listened to Aidan talk about his

daughter in excited, upbeat tones. Even the news that the nanny had to be off for a few days didn't seem to faze him. She was frankly amazed that Aidan hadn't called her the minute he knew Lisa had to leave.

"And you managed to get her into the tub?" she asked.

"She got in on her own. She knew which bubble bath her mom used. She got her own towel out of the linen closet, and she chose her own snack, which, by the way, she ate in the tub," he said, chuckling. "I had no idea what Ritz crackers looked like floating around in bubbles. And she is so sweet and funny. I just sat by the tub and watched her. Grace, you can't imagine what it felt like to have my daughter with me, to see her play in the bathwater and so many other things. I...I... Grace, I love her so much," he said, his voice low and filled with wonder.

He'd never been totally responsible for any child, let alone a four-year-old who had just learned that her nanny was leaving on top of everything else. "You're amazing. How did you do this on your own?"

"I nearly called you to help me, but I didn't dare leave Emma."

"I would have helped you if I could," she

said, feeling hurt that he hadn't immediately called her. Knowing that he'd managed to look after a little girl on his own made her feel as if he didn't need her.

Could she have done what he did? She wasn't sure. She'd done a little babysitting and read books on child-rearing…

Why hadn't he called her for advice and support? Maybe he didn't feel she'd be interested in what he was going through. Yet she was interested. Her misgivings over how he'd behaved earlier didn't change the fact that she wanted to know about Emma. "Aidan, despite our differences I would have helped you with Emma," she repeated, feeling the pain of not being included.

"You say that, but you wouldn't stay today long enough to meet her," he said, his voice radiating sadness.

His words filled her with remorse and a tinge of resentment. She wished she'd been there with him, to see his little girl, but she would not have found it easy to witness his love for a child she felt so ambiguous about.

"I'm really pleased for you, Aidan," she said, struggling to sound upbeat, but all she could think about was that another woman had made her husband happier than she'd ever known him to be. Another woman had given him the child he wanted. "You sound very happy," she said, as she faced the fact that her husband's happiness had nothing to do with her or with their marriage.

He hadn't said a word about them or their relationship or the way things had been left between them a few short hours ago. Once she was home, she'd prayed that he would call, that they would talk a little. As evening approached, she'd grown anxious. They'd never let the sun go down on their anger. They'd always made up before going to sleep.

How could he not have wanted to talk to her before this? How many husbands have their wives walk out after an argument and not ask how they are doing?

"Grace, are you still there?" he asked.

She wanted to ask him about where they went from here. She needed him to say what was going on with him, his feelings for her. But all he wanted to talk about was his daughter.

She realized that she sounded petulant and selfish, but she needed to talk to her husband. Needed them to agree to meet and work things out. "I'm here. I'm glad you're enjoying your daughter," she said, forcing the words around the painful lump in her throat.

"She's our daughter, Grace. And when Lisa returns, I'm going to work out a plan for us to all be together. I miss you, and I want to be with you. I messed things up when you left here, but I plan to fix all that. You'll see. I should have taken the time to call you earlier this evening. It won't happen again."

Relief appeared at his words. Despite their troubles, she wanted to believe him, to believe he was aware that she was hurting. "Oh, Aidan, I want us together, too, to work on our marriage. I want to get to know Emma. I'm sure if we talk this all out sensibly, we can find a solution that works for all of us."

"Grace, I was really down earlier today. After you left and I was finished with the lawyer, I realized that I was as much to blame, if not more so, than Deidre for what happened. I should never have had sex with her. It was stupid and irresponsible. But I can't regret Emma. I don't know why Deidre didn't tell me about her, let me be involved, but that's over. I want us to move on, the three of us. Did I tell you that Emma held my photo and called me *Dad*?"

"She did?" Grace said, her throat twisting

into a hard knot. Aidan had had the moment she'd dreamed of all her life—that moment when her child called her *Mom*. "That's lovely for you."

"I… Whatever we decide, I don't want to ever be separated from Emma again."

"Not even for a few days while we sort things out between us?" she asked, feeling a sense of foreboding. By that one statement, he had made it clear that what Emma needed and what he needed came first, ahead of their relationship. Did he have any idea how cruel and hurtful his words were?

"We can talk when she's in kindergarten any day you can get here."

"I didn't say I was coming back to Spartanburg. I'm still completely confused as to where I stand in all this and how we put things back together in our lives."

There was a long pause before Aidan spoke. "Grace, I love you. This whole experience has affected me in ways I couldn't have imagined a few weeks ago. But I realize that I'm too quick to talk about what I want and how I see things. My actions have hurt you and I'm sorry. What can I do to fix this?"

Had he not heard a word of what she'd said?

"Do you think this can be fixed by making a list of things to be done?"

"Well, not exactly a list. My weekend with Deidre was almost five years ago, Grace. I've hurt you, made it difficult for you to trust me. I realize that. But I love you. We have a beautiful life together, and now we have a child."

"Aidan, you're asking me to accept your daughter by another woman without you helping me work through how I feel, what I want to see happen. I need you to listen to me, to my feelings."

"I am listening right now, Grace."

"I don't know if I can accept Emma into our lives. Every time I look at her, I will see a part of you and be reminded that you were unfaithful to me. When I see you in her, I will remember what you did to us, and to our marriage. I will remember that when I thought we were focused on creating a child, a family together, you had sex with someone else."

"Do you suppose you could get over those feelings and start thinking differently if you met Emma, formed your own bond with her? Deidre isn't competition. She never was."

"I know you believe that, but in my heart I'm afraid that I can't handle living with Emma every day without remembering where she came from and how I feel about that." She made a frustrated sound. "And in contradiction to those feelings, when you didn't want my advice on Emma, I felt left out."

"You're not left out. I've just been a stupid person to let you feel that way."

Did she dare hope that they were making progress? Was he really willing to take her into his plan as an equal and not as simply someone he needed? "I want what you want for Emma. But I feel we're moving too fast without consideration as to how this will work in the long term."

"Grace, a few weeks ago those words would have been my words. I'm the one who likes to sit back and deliberate on what to do and how to do it. But Grace, there's no problem here that I can see. What I'd like is get you and Emma together. Believe me, all your worries will disappear. Would you consider that?"

Grace felt they still weren't communicating well, but for now, she didn't want to go any further. Aidan did seem to be trying to see her point of view, which was a start. "I guess the best thing for me to do is to wait and see whether or not you want to discuss bringing Emma home with you."

"Grace, I can't come home without her. The lawyer says she needs a stable environment. We can give her that."

"No, we can't, until we resolve some of our own issues."

"Grace, please give my plan a try. Emma needs to feel part of a family."

Pain and hopelessness spurred her to hang up the phone without saying anything more. She wasn't angry; she was completely discouraged by their conversation. No one mattered more to him than his daughter.

She thought back to that time five years ago when Aidan had gone to Spartanburg. His company had been finally hitting the big time, had been sought after by a lot of high-powered companies, and he'd been working day and night and sometimes weekends.

When he'd called to say he wouldn't be home for a couple more days, she worried about him being overtired. She remembered that weekend he'd spent with Deidre because they had planned to go with friends to a community theater production of *Wicked* and she'd been looking forward to it. Not wanting to go alone, she'd given her tickets to another couple and had stayed home to work on a quilt.

If she'd had any idea Aidan was with another woman that weekend... And yet, what had changed? Five years later, she was once again waiting for Aidan, hoping that he would consider her feelings in the decision he was making.

And she was left out of it.

Despite being fed up with him, she waited, hoping that he'd call back, looking for an explanation for her quick hang-up.

In their entire married life, she had never hung up on him. Reason enough for him to call her back. The fact he didn't showed her how completely and utterly preoccupied he was with fatherhood and what it meant to him.

With a sinking heart, she decided to go for a walk, anything to not feel so completely abandoned by the one person she'd loved all her adult life.

CHAPTER TEN

IN THE DAYS that followed their phone call, Aidan had few moments when he wasn't thinking about Grace and how she'd behaved. He should have called her back, but he'd been too hurt by her attitude to find the words that might help them, and he feared that if he did call, they would fight. What they needed was some time together where they could face each other and work things out.

To fill the void of Grace, he'd thrown himself into Emma's life while he waited for Lisa to return. He'd managed to get Emma off to kindergarten without a huge flood of tears, and he was navigating the whole which-book-to-read-at-night thing. It had seemed complicated in the beginning, but really came down to allowing Emma to deliberate in front of her bookshelves about which book he could read.

A neighbor had dropped by offering to help him if needed, and the postman had dropped off a parcel. Not knowing what to do with parcels addressed to Deidre, he opened the package to find half a dozen new outfits for Emma from an online store specializing in clothing for young girls. It was clear from the invoice that Deidre had spent an exorbitant amount of money. He looked them over, realizing that he had no idea what size Emma wore or where to buy clothes for her. For future reference, he made a note of the company and its address.

There had been moments in the past two days when he'd wanted to call Grace to find out why she'd hung up on him. He wanted to, but she'd been acting so weird lately he was frustrated. She only seemed to be able to see all this from her perspective and what she wanted, and he didn't have the ability to cope with all of her concerns when his days were filled with learning to manage his daughter's life.

Besides, he was pretty certain that Grace would come around. She loved children and they now had a daughter. Once she could accept that and look forward to what their life now was, everything would work out.

He realized that he needed to include Grace in whatever way he could until she had the chance to meet Emma.

Ultimately, what he needed to do was convince Lisa to move home with him, and that way Grace would see how wonderful everything could be. He didn't want to simply bring Emma into their lives and expect Grace to take over. It would be nice if he could, but that couldn't happen as long as Grace felt the way she did. Until she changed, Lisa would be a good buffer. And she would give Emma some continuity while she got used to living with them.

The timing was becoming problematic. He needed to get back to work soon. Lucas had called with questions and decisions they needed to make, and he'd spent hours on the phone last evening after he put Emma to bed while they worked on the more urgent problems. It wasn't right for him to be away from work too long, especially when their marketing efforts to grow the business were paying off in substantial sales increases.

He checked his watch again. Lisa had called and said she'd be here by noon. He couldn't imagine what she'd say to his idea of moving in with him and Emma, but he had to give it a try.

When she walked through the door, she didn't waste any time. "Where's Emma?"

"She's at kindergarten," he said, surprised at the question.

"Seriously? I thought she'd want to stay home when she realized I wouldn't be here to take her. I always take her to school." Lisa looked around. "How did you make out otherwise? Did she cry a lot?"

"A little the first evening after you left. She really missed you."

Lisa's smile brightened. "I missed her, too. She's like my own daughter, and now with her mom gone…"

"How's your mom doing?"

"She had to have a stent put in, but she's doing okay."

"I'm glad to hear that." Lisa's presence would allow him to focus more on work, on the moving plan…and on Grace. "I wanted to talk to you about Emma and her future, if you have time."

Lisa perched on a stool in front of the kitchen island. "I have all the time in the world, or until Emma needs to be picked up."

"I'm thinking about taking Emma home with me. I've been working with the lawyer and a lot of Deidre's will has been settled. I really need to get back to my wife and my business. Of course, I want to take Emma with me."

Tears glistened in Lisa's eyes. "What about this house? What about Emma and her kindergarten?"

"I won't put the house on the market just yet. First, I want to have Emma's life in order, get her settled in my home. If she's really upset by the change, it might mean that we come back here, so I'll keep the house for now."

He glanced at her for approval, but saw none. "The thing is, I'd like you to come along. Emma would be happier with you in her life, and you could be a tremendous help in helping us adjust and adapt to her needs. Would you be interested in being part of the plan?"

Lisa squared her shoulders. "Yes. Of course, I'll come with you. It's important that some part of Emma's life remain constant." She sniffed. "But you have to know that I have had other job offers, and if your wife will be staying home with Emma, you won't need me very long. I would like to be free to take another nanny position as soon as Emma is settled with you and your wife."

"I understand, and I appreciate you being frank with me."

"When do you plan to move?"

"I thought this weekend. I haven't had a chance to look for a kindergarten near our home, but I'm sure Grace and I can find one."

"I don't mean to interfere, but your wife and I didn't hit it off when she was here. If my going with you should cause a problem, I won't stay more than a couple days. As much as I love Emma, she is not my child. She's yours. You have the final decision on everything related to her. And, to be honest, I don't want to live in a hostile environment."

He was once again surprised by Lisa's matter-of-fact tone. She obviously loved Emma, but she didn't seem to be happy about the move. "Emma is my first priority, and will be Grace's, as well. This has been very difficult for my wife, as she didn't know about my relationship with Deidre."

Lisa's eyebrows shot up. "What? You mean she only found out when Deidre died?"

He didn't want to tell this woman more than was necessary, but he did want to clear up any misconceptions. "Yes. I hadn't said anything because it was a long time ago, and that was the only time I broke my marriage vows. Finding out what I'd done was very hard on my wife."

"I had no idea…" Lisa said, a frown forming on her face.

"We are working out our problems."

She gave him an odd look but said nothing. "I'll drive in my own car," she said. "That might be better…for everyone."

"Sounds like a plan. I'll call Grace and tell her the good news."

GRACE HAD JUST returned from the grocery store. She struggled to find something she wanted to eat, as her appetite had abandoned her after that last conversation with Aidan. She didn't know what to do about him, about their marriage, in the light of his obsession with Emma.

She'd tried to talk to her brother about it, but he'd had several work emergencies and had gone out of town on business. She wondered if Lucas had spoken with Aidan about the backlog of work that wasn't getting done. If he had, she doubted that Aidan was listening. He was probably too preoccupied with his daughter to even notice the stress Lucas was under.

Aidan certainly hadn't noticed anything

about her during his last call. All he'd talked about was himself and his daughter.

She had just placed the last of the vegetables in the fridge when the phone rang.

Aidan. Taking a deep breath, she picked up. "Aidan, I apologize for hanging up on you, but I was upset. I hope you're calling so we can talk."

"I want that, too, sweetheart. And I think I have the answer. I can't be away from you any longer, and I am so anxious for you to get to know Emma. I've decided to come home and bring Emma with me."

"You what?" she yelled in disbelief. "How can you take that child away from everything and everyone she knows so soon after her mother's death, with no plan on how to look after her? Aidan, you're not thinking straight. This isn't fair to Emma or to me or anyone else in your life. Lucas needs you at work. I need you. You need to get back here and get your life straightened out—our lives straightened out—before you move Emma here."

"Grace, I talked to Lisa and she's willing to move in with us and help with Emma, getting her settled and into a routine. Emma will be just fine with Lisa along."

"And how long can Lisa stay with us?" she

asked, anger rising. Totally ignoring her had become Aidan's modus operandi and she was sick of it.

To think he could bring a child into their home without discussing the arrangements with her was so hurtful she could hardly breathe. What had happened to Aidan? Why was he so determined to bring this child into their lives without considering her?

"She hopes to stay about a month. If that's all right?"

"Why didn't you talk this over with me first?"

She heard a long sigh and knew that Aidan still didn't get it. He was determined to act without her input. He was so sure he knew the outcome, knew how to make the situation bend to his will. But she didn't care what he did anymore. He had tramped all over her feelings and her concerns and now he was moving strangers into their home—*his* child and her nanny.

"I thought you'd understand. We've been over all this. We have a little girl. We're a family. Let's concentrate on that for now." He lowered his voice to a soft, intimate tone. "Honey, once we are all under the same roof together, loving and caring for each other and

Emma, we will be happier than we've ever been in our lives. Please trust me on this. I want you to be happy and to have a family. Emma is only the beginning."

So, now that he'd had a taste of being a father, he believed that they would proceed to have more children. She fully expected him to bring up the subject of adoption in his excitement about being a parent.

"Is this how it's going to be, Aidan? You make all the decisions where our marriage is concerned, where my life is concerned?" Her hands trembled so much she could hardly hold the phone.

"Grace, honey, please don't be upset. We'll be there in a few hours. You and I will sit down together and talk about all of this."

Tears began their steady movement over her cheeks, down into the corners of her mouth, tasting salty on her lips. "We'll talk, will we? Like the last time?"

"No. We will really talk. I promise."

Funny thing how easily her world had shifted. She had wanted to talk things over since the beginning, but only now, when he was on his way back here with his daughter—putting her in the unbearable position of having his child in her home—did he think about her and her feelings. "Aidan, you can do whatever you like. I won't be here."

His abrupt intake of breath reached across the connection. "You don't mean that. You wouldn't leave me. I love you with my whole heart. Look, whatever it takes, I'll do it. I—"

"I've heard you say those words repeatedly since that first hideous phone call, but nothing has changed. I've seen so little effort from you and you continue to make decisions to suit you, without consulting me. So I'm not sure we can, Aidan. I've waited my entire married life to have you show as much enthusiasm for having a child with me as you have over your child with another woman. I can't listen to your excitement and your plans anymore just because suddenly you see what it means to be a parent. But you have a baby that is yours…not ours."

CHAPTER ELEVEN

THE SOUND OF the dead connection stabbed Aidan like a knife. This couldn't be happening. What was he going to do without Grace? Glancing around at the messy counter and the load of laundry sitting by the door of the laundry room, he felt adrift and lost. He'd never faced anything like this. Even the loss of his parents hadn't been this painful.

Why had he rushed this? He could have stayed here for a while and given Grace time to adjust. Maybe he could have even gone home for a few days, talked to Grace and gotten caught up at work. After all, she'd been here twice, which proved she cared. But Grace had made it clear from the start she didn't want him to bring Emma to their home.

He should have given her time to adjust to his plan. What was going on with him? In hindsight, choosing to take Emma home so soon was a little erratic, but he seemed to be doing a lot of things lately that were not like him.

The real truth was that he wanted his little girl in his life so badly that he couldn't think of anything but her and what he wanted to do for her. Everything else paled in the face of those feelings.

"Are you all right?" Lisa asked, coming into the kitchen with another load of laundry.

He eyed the load. "Sorry I didn't get all the laundry done."

"Do you know how to do laundry?" she asked skeptically.

"Yes…" He didn't have a clue. Other than the years in college, his mother and then Grace had always done the laundry. "No. You're right. I haven't done laundry in a very long time."

"I suspect you haven't had to do much around the house," she said, eyeing the counter.

"Yeah. My wife stayed home. We wanted a family and I wanted her to be free to care for our children, not having to divide her time between work and family."

"Better for you, as well," she said. "Aidan, are you sure your wife wants me there with you and Emma?"

What was he going to tell her? He couldn't admit to himself that Grace had left him, let alone explain it to someone he hardly knew. But he had no choice if he wanted to leave for home tomorrow. "It's been a big adjustment for Grace. All of this."

"I should say. You didn't tell her about the affair. Did you talk to her about what you should do about Emma?"

"I tried to, but I didn't get it right."

"So she was okay with you coming home with Emma and me?"

"No. To be honest, she wasn't."

"Then why would you decide to do it without getting her support for the move?"

"I thought she'd go along with it." He scrubbed his face as realization dawned. "I've always assumed that Grace would go along because she always has. Even now... What am I going to do?"

Lisa placed her hands firmly on the island that separated them. "I don't know if it's such a good idea to take Emma to your home until you settle your differences with your wife. I can stay here with her, and keep her life as quiet and normal as possible while you and your wife figure out what you're going to do."

His stomach burned at the thought of leaving Emma. He had to have her with him. Needed it. "I—I need you to understand how important this is. I have to get back to my work. We're really busy and I have to be there. I can't leave Emma. I know you'll take good care of her wherever she is, but I need to get home. I can't lose Grace." He willed her to understand.

She stared at him, her eyes dark. "You have gotten yourself into a terrible mess, haven't you?"

"I have. And it's my fault…all my fault."

"It is." Lisa squinted as if in thought. "I will go with you on the condition that you talk to your wife and work this out. I will not stay if you don't make a real effort to settle things with her."

His shoulders slumped in resignation. "I thought I had. That's how badly I've messed up. I thought she wanted what I wanted."

"It's my guess that, in your eagerness to take over Emma's life, you haven't been listening to Grace. If you'd been listening, you would not have allowed her to leave here without talking everything through. Why do you think I disappeared that first day? I could tell you two weren't on the same page over any of this. And anybody with half a brain would have seen how upset your wife was. If you ask me, you need to start over with her." She gave him a wry smile. "There. I'm done. But it had to be said. And one more piece of advice. Don't move Emma for a few more days. It's been only a few weeks since her mother passed away. Give her a little more time."

Lisa's words hit him hard. He was so self-centered. And he'd taken Grace for granted. "I don't want to do anything to upset Emma, but the truth is I need to get back to work. My business is suffering with me being away from the office."

"You can use Deidre's home office. It's completely equipped, including two desktop computers. You already have access to the Wi-Fi."

"I hadn't thought of that, but you're right, I could."

She walked ahead of him to Deidre's office, across the hall from the living room. The office looked much as it had five years ago, although the equipment had clearly been updated. With a network connection, he'd be able to access the company system. He wouldn't be able to do all of his work, but he'd make some inroads.

He could call Grace and arrange a Skype call with her. That way he could try again with her. It wasn't ideal, but it was the only thing he could think of at the moment. The only thing he knew for certain was that he couldn't make another mistake where Grace was concerned.

GRACE WAS SO relieved when Lucas pulled into the parking lot of his condo. She had called him in tears after the conversation with Aidan. When Lucas heard how upset she was, he'd told her to meet him there. He was at a meeting in Greenville, but he'd said he would be home as soon as possible.

She jumped out of her car and raced over to him.

"Gracie, I'm sorry you're so upset. What's Aidan up to now?" he asked, pulling her close.

"I'm so relieved to see you."

"I'll always be here for you, sis," he said, hugging her tight. "It's kind of nice to have my baby sister need me."

"I always need you, silly," she murmured into his shirt.

"Not in recent times. Even with all your baby-making efforts, you kept your biggest worries to yourself," he said, clicking the locks on his truck key fob before starting up the walkway toward the condo entrance. "Let's go in so we can talk."

Once inside, he led her over to the sofa. "Now, spill the beans. You and Aidan are fighting about how he's behaving over Emma and Deidre, right?"

"Yes. It's as if he's taken complete control of our lives."

"Have you told him how you feel?"

"Yes."

"What did he say?"

"That he was willing to talk, but that was after he'd left me feeling as if I didn't matter in his life."

Lucas looked at her, his affection for her clear in his expression. "I'm here to encourage you to not let go of what you and Aidan have. I realize that's not easy, given what a mess he's managed to make of things, but you can't give up."

"What am I supposed to do? Every time we speak, it's all about his daughter, his concerns. I feel so angry at him—"

"That you clam up, right? You get angry and you walk away."

"That's not—"

"Let me ask you something, and be honest with yourself."

"Go ahead," she said, feeling very uncomfortable with the conversation.

"Do you think there will ever come a day when you can forgive Aidan for what he did?"

"I—I don't know. There is so much between us that is good, but the past few weeks have left me unable to trust him. I don't believe in him anymore. I'd really like to have our old life back, but I realize that's not possible under the circumstances. We will always have a child he had with another woman in our lives. I'm not sure I can get past that."

"Oh, sis, I wish I could kick Aidan's ass to Mars and back for what he did. Believe me, Aidan seriously regrets what he did. Hell. He's called me every day since your first trip to Spartanburg, full of remorse, begging me to help him convince you that he didn't mean to hurt you."

"So what am I supposed to do?"

"I have no idea. It's certainly been a wake-up call for me where Maria is concerned. She and I have talked every night about being willing to share everything, no matter how difficult it may be. And, oddly enough, our relationship has gotten stronger. To think it took your marriage problems for me to make changes in my relationship with Maria."

"I'm glad someone is getting something positive out of this mess," Grace said ruefully.

Lucas gave her a sad smile. "I am certain that Aidan will try to win you back. And you know how convincing he can be when he wants something. All I can say for sure is that you have to be prepared to forgive him. Otherwise, your marriage is over. If you can't forgive him, you can't move on. The intimacy will be gone. The shadow of what he did will hang over you and Aidan for good. If he can't convince you that he's sincere, and you can't let go of your suspicions, there's little hope."

There was a solid ache around her heart. Her throat felt parched. "How will I ever be able to forgive what he did? How do I get past feeling so betrayed by him? And there are times when I wonder if there were other women. I worry I'm a bigger fool than I thought."

He frowned in surprise. "Gracie, if only you could see Aidan when we go on the road together. It's a traveler's nightmare. I've shared a room with him, heard stories from other engineers who've traveled with him. He's either going full-out, talking up a storm or fast asleep. We've nicknamed him the Whirling Dervish. Take my advice. Do not go on a business trip with him."

He gave her a sappy look that had her throwing her head back and laughing for the first time in weeks. It felt wonderful. "You are so good for me. I have this image of you trying to go to dinner in some city and Aidan insisting on working the entire dinner."

"I swear. Some nights I would insist on pizza delivered to the room, just to get a break while he went out to dinner with colleagues or clients. But he would always return so fast I wondered if he'd simply inhaled his food and left the others at the table."

His expression turned more serious. "Grace, you have to decide where you stand on what Aidan did and how much of it you can forgive. I'm hoping you can forgive him, as I don't want to face down another brother-in-law. And I read somewhere that women usually pick the same kind of man. And with my luck, there's another Aidan out there somewhere." He grinned at her. "Just kidding, but you get my point, don't you?"

"I do." She leaned into his shoulder feeling a little better. "I'm so happy you found Maria. I really like her."

"Whoops." He glanced at his watch, pulling his cell phone off his belt. "I was supposed to call her as soon as I learned what your problem was. I hope you don't mind, but I'm not staying the night here. There's a beautiful woman who is more than able to say what she needs. And she needs me. As for you, there's only so much a brother can do, if you get my drift."

"If you had said you planned to stay here with me without Maria, I was going to boot your butt. Go and have a good evening. I'm fine."

"What are you going to do?" he asked before leaving a message for Maria to call him back.

"I'm going to have a long soak in the tub and think about what you said. Maybe I can't forgive him." she said, her throat tightening.

"Don't say that, please," Lucas said. "You will work this out. The entire office is rooting for you."

"Stop it. You're not taking me seriously," she grouched.

He took her shoulders in his powerful hands and looked straight into her eyes. "You are going to find a way to talk to Aidan or Maria and I will hold an intervention. I'm serious. You have to work this out, one way or the other."

An hour later, she was about to settle into the tub when her cell phone rang. Aidan. At first, she wanted to let it go to voice mail, but the old need to hear his voice won out.

"How are you?" he asked when she answered.

"I'm okay, I guess."

"Grace, I realize you're angry at me and with good reason. But I was listening to you when you said we needed to work at making a plan for Emma and how she fits into our lives. I'm going to try and work from here for a week or so while Emma gets really comfortable with me, rather than coming home right away. In the meantime, I wondered if you and I could talk on Skype."

She thought about it. Despite her anger and disappointment over his behavior, she couldn't resist a chance to see him while they talked. "I would like that."

"Would you like to do it now?" he asked, his excitement clear in his voice.

"I'd need to get over to the house to go on the computer. I'm at Lucas's condo."

"I can wait," he said softly, his voice soft and intimate in her ears.

"Okay. I was about to take a bath, but it can wait."

"No. I don't want to rush you about this, and I know how much you love soaking in the tub. Why don't you call me when you're at the house and on your computer?"

"I will. See you in about an hour," she said, a smile edging along her lips.

Excited and upbeat, Grace drove over to her house, took a shower, blew her hair dry and put on makeup. Touching up her lipstick, she felt as if she were going out on a date with Aidan, rather than simply talking on Skype.

Settling in front of the computer in the den, she dialed Aidan's Skype number, startled by how quickly his face appeared on the screen. "You look great," he said.

He seemed anxious, his eyes searching her face. "You, too." She smiled at his compliment.

"So, what do you want to talk about?" she asked as she searched his face, waiting to see if anything had changed.

"Ah... I... You're right. We do need to work a few things out around when I bring Emma home. I've thought about what you said. I'm not putting our personal problems on the back burner while I stay here. I thought it might be better for both of us if we worked on Emma's needs while I'm with her. I can only really make amends for what I did to you by being with you and working through our problems." He cleared his throat nervously. "I… What do you think?"

She didn't like his plans to stay longer in Spartanburg rather than coming home. Yet he was willing to communicate with her where Emma was concerned, which made Grace feel hopeful for the first time in days. She would have preferred that they talk in person, but given the circumstances, she was willing to compromise. "I agree. We need to put together a plan for Emma. How is she doing?"

"She seems okay, but I'm not sure. I have no idea how to recognize the symptoms of emotional distress, and I don't want to do something that would cause her any permanent damage." His concern was evident on his face. "I wonder if we should hire a child psychologist for her. At least to do an assessment. What do you think?"

Realizing that he was asking for her advice, she impulsively touched the screen. "I think that might be a good idea. Neither of us knows enough about grief in children. We need all the help we can get. What does Lisa say?"

"I haven't really asked her that question, as I feel it's our decision to make." He smiled at her, lifting her heart. "Do you have any other ideas on what we need to do to help Emma?"

"You could ask her kindergarten teacher how she's doing. Other than Lisa, that's someone who would know if there has been a change in her behavior."

"That's a great idea. Why didn't I think of that? Or Lisa, for that matter. I will arrange to meet with the teacher and see what she says… I miss you."

"I miss you, too," Grace said, a yearning for him and their life together sweeping through her.

After a few minutes of staring at each other through the screen, Aidan asked, "What are you planning to do until I get back? I mean, are you planning to stay at Lucas's?"

She wanted to stay in her home, and maybe she should. With Aidan willing to make concessions for her sake, it meant they might have a chance to work out their problems. "I'll see—"

"Sorry to bother you," a voice broke in.

Aidan turned away from the camera. "What is it, Lisa?"

"A parcel arrived for you from your office," she said, passing a large brown envelope to Aidan.

"Where are you, Aidan?" Grace asked.

He faced the screen, a small frown on his face. "I'm in Deidre's home office. It's a great workspace. See?" Aidan panned the room for her.

Grace studied the background, the framed photos of Deidre and Emma, searching for any pictures of Aidan as her pulse pounded in her throat. "You're working out of Deidre's office? You didn't rent space for the weeks you're planning to be there? Why did you do that?"

He shrugged. "It just made sense to stay here to be near Emma. There's almost everything I need here." He turned the envelope over in his hands. "And this looks like the documents I need for the Perlman Project."

"You don't get it, do you?" she said as disappointment flooded her.

There was a long moment of silence during which Aidan stared at her, his expression slowly changing into one of disbelief. "I— Grace, I didn't think about how this would feel for you. I just saw the opportunity to be near Emma while I worked... Sorry."

Pain and loss rose in Grace. Her husband was working in the same office he'd worked in with Deidre that weekend. She remembered clearly that he'd said they'd been working from her home. She imagined her husband in that room with Deidre, alone, with their attraction to each other building. She imagined the touches, the stolen kisses, the foreplay... Had the first time been in that room? She felt sick.

"Aidan, I have to go," she managed to say before rushing to the bathroom across the hall. Sinking to her knees over the commode, all the anger and hurt, betrayal and fear flowed out of her. She was sick of it all—the fear, the hopelessness, the loss. Finally, when the convulsions eased, she leaned against the vanity.

She could hear Aidan calling out to her over the Skype connection but couldn't bring herself to answer him. There was no way he could help her. Only she knew the raw emotion of betrayal and abandonment. She wiped her mouth, got off the floor, found her purse and headed out the door of her home. Once in the car, she clutched the wheel to steady herself.

She's been so upbeat, so hopeful when he'd asked to Skype with her. And he seemed so conscious of doing the right thing, including for her...while he sat in the office of his former lover. A part of her couldn't believe how hard this had hit her. But she hadn't expected to find him in Deidre's office, nor had she expected him to be so nonchalant about it. She had a long way to go before she could ever trust Aidan with her feelings. He had no idea how much his past had hurt her and continued to hurt her.

CHAPTER TWELVE

As THE NEXT few weeks dragged on, Grace fell into a funk, feeling aimless and at odds with everything around her. She'd cleaned her brother's condo from top to bottom, gone online and read articles on quilting, gone to the local magazine shop and bought every magazine they had on quilting and hooking rugs, all to no avail. The days still continued to drag by.

She couldn't face talking to Aidan again because she didn't know what to say to him. He'd left several messages apologizing and wanting to know that she was okay. She'd sent him an email explaining why she'd gotten off the phone, but she couldn't talk to him. He offered another apology but it didn't help how she felt. Once she'd settled down a bit, she realized that seeing Aidan in Deidre's office had reinforced the fact she'd been lied to and cheated on.

Aidan believed the past was over—his affair was done and Deidre was dead—so they should move on.

Grace knew it wasn't over and it wasn't done. Not for her. She couldn't simply move on.

In a way, it was a relief to have him out of town so she didn't have to worry about seeing him unexpectedly or having friends ask why they weren't together. Thankfully, Lucas had told her that Aidan was coming back later today, so she'd had the chance to prepare herself.

She supposed she should go to clean up the house since Emma and Lisa were accompanying Aidan, but Grace couldn't bring herself to do it. Every time she thought of him, she remembered seeing him in Deidre's office.

Seeing him there, so comfortable in that space, brought back all the times she'd put his needs first, thought of nice things to do to make his life easier. She had loved and cared for him, waited on him and wanted to bear his children. But none of her caring mattered. It hadn't mattered when he decided to have sex with another woman. And it didn't matter now, when he was in another city, leading a life that made her feel jealous and left out.

There was something she should do at the

house before Aidan got home. Her flower garden had been overlooked in her lethargy. Despite Aidan's suggestion that they hire a landscaper and have the backyard done professionally, she had been adamant that she do it herself. She loved every minute she spent in the garden and had taken a horticultural course to learn about plants and their preferred places and relationships.

To her complete surprise, she'd discovered a rabbit had taken up residence, a delightfully shy creature that she first found nibbling on baby lettuce in one of her raised beds.

She was anxious to see if the rabbit was still around and how her hibiscus shrubs were doing, not to mention the black-eyed Susan plants she had acquired last spring. According to Lucas, Aidan wasn't expected until early evening. She had time to at least assess what needed to be done.

She was on the way out the door, thinking that she needed to pick up a few groceries on the way over to the house, when it hit her.

You're not living there anymore. Your marriage is in trouble, and you still think you should be putting groceries in the fridge?

Getting her purse and keys, and avoiding the street that went past the grocery store, she headed down the wide boulevard that led into the subdivision. A pang of longing shot through her at the sight of her window boxes showing off the bright red geraniums she'd planted. And the peonies at the corner of the house nodded their large pink blossoms.

Only weeks ago she'd been very reasonably happy in this house. Despite not being able to have children, she had concentrated on her crafts and her love of wool and fabrics, her gardens. Now, as she pulled into the driveway, she yearned for those moments before all this happened when she believed she could convince Aidan to adopt a child.

Determined not to think about any of it, she made her way around the house to the garden in the back. The sweet scent of lavender wafting up from the herb bed greeted her, filling her with a sense of calm. At least here she had control of what went on. It was, after all, her design and her effort that had converted this into a flowered space that her neighbors and friends praised. She enjoyed their compliments and freely shared gardening tips with anyone who asked.

She recalled the day Aidan had hurt his shoulder moving the lumber into place for her raised beds, the day he nearly stumbled carrying an armload of sod to fix the ground around the koi pond in the center of the garden. She remembered rubbing his sore muscles with an anti-inflammatory cream to ease the pain. She also remembered the love-making after they'd showered together that day.

How had they come to this place where they had trouble talking to each other and no longer shared even the simplest things?

She longed for those innocent years when everything seemed to go their way, when trying to get pregnant was fun, not reduced to an anxious endeavor, fraught with insecurity.

She glanced around her garden, taking it all in, remembering each shrub and plant she'd lovingly planted. She must not dwell on the past weeks, but instead let her garden and its serenity soothe her.

What she needed was to get her hands dirty, feel the soil on her fingers and enjoy the results of her hard work. She walked the stone pathway leading to the rear of the garden, then opened the wooden shed and went in to the dark, moist space in search of her gloves, a spade and a rake.

The first area in serious need of her attention was the herb garden. The rosemary had developed long scraggly branches and the cilantro was suffering from lack of water. Getting into a rhythm of digging and weeding, the smell of the earth and the wind sighing in the maple tree over her head, relaxed her.

She'd been working diligently, feeling the sense of accomplishment she always felt as she cleaned up and weeded a garden area, when she glanced at her watch.

Two hours? Aidan would be here soon with Emma and Lisa. She didn't want to be around when they arrived. It would be too difficult to face him when she was still so uncertain about everything. And this was not the time to see him with his child. A small surge of anger struck when she realized he probably expected her to be here, to have filled the fridge with fresh fruit and vegetables.

Scooping up her tools, she headed to the shed. Just then, she spotted the rabbit hopping in front of the trumpet creeper, a climbing shrub that clearly needed to be trimmed— but not today. Today she had to get back to her brother's condo.

Thankfully, she left without encountering Aidan. She was relieved, even though a small part of her wished they could meet. She missed their conversations about their everyday activities, the little things that happened that contributed to the story of their lives. She missed coming home to him after being out somewhere. She missed hearing him singing off-key in the shower, the way he towel-dried his curly hair.

Getting out of her gardening clothes, she took a quick shower and washed her hair, then settled in to read. Finally, she tossed aside the latest quilting magazine, wishing she'd stopped long enough at the house to grab her sewing machine so she could put together the quilting pieces she'd meticulously cut out last month. Surveying the space, the austere maleness of her brother's condo, she faced the truth. She was bored and lonely and wanted to see Aidan.

MEANWHILE, IN SPARTANBURG, Aidan and Lisa loaded his rental car, then placed Emma's car seat in the back. "Thanks for all your help," he said, trying to wedge the trunk of the SUV closed. "I had no idea how much gear a child needed. And that car seat was complicated to install."

"Get used to it," Lisa said, laughing as she turned toward the house. "I'll put Emma in the seat for you."

"Thanks," he said as he checked for the keys and linked his cell phone to the online security system. He had to call Lucas as soon as he could. Working in Deidre's office was okay, but not the same as being where he had everything—files and paperwork—at his fingertips. Thanks to Lucas and one of the other engineers, he'd managed to put out a few fires, but a lot of work was still pending.

He'd make some phone calls on the drive while Emma slept. At least, he assumed she would sleep. Who wouldn't sleep after waking up at four in the morning? He wished he could sleep, but there wasn't a chance until he got home.

Emma and Lisa came out of the house, Emma hugging her black bear. He opened the back door. "In here, sweetie," he said, feeling upbeat and ready to take his daughter home where she belonged.

Grace hadn't taken any of his calls since the day he'd Skyped with her. He'd been so sure that they were working things out, but he'd seen how upset she was about his being in Deidre's office. Still, he couldn't do anything about that if she didn't take his calls.

He knew she was living at Lucas's condo. He also knew there was no way Grace would be happy living there for very long. She loved her gardens, her sewing room and all the other nice touches they'd built into their home specially to please her.

He would see Grace once he got home. When he got Emma and Lisa settled, he'd convince Grace to meet him somewhere, maybe for coffee or dinner. And this time he'd work on how to alleviate her fears about their relationship. Whatever it took to bring her home with him and Emma…

Emma stomped down the driveway to the back door of the SUV, her bear crushed against her chest. She stopped. "No! I want to go with Lisa."

"Emma, I explained that you and I are going with your daddy today. We'll be living in his house."

"No!" Emma screamed, racing toward the house and crying at the top of her lungs. "I want Mommy! Mommy!"

He started toward her, but Lisa touched his arm to hold him back.

"I'll get her. You stay here," she ordered before walking up the driveway.

He watched in agony. Emma's tears hurt like a physical blow. He waited while Lisa knelt in front of Emma and talked soothingly to her. In a few minutes, Lisa returned holding Emma's hand.

"What do we do now?" he asked Lisa, trying to remain calm. "I suppose we could always put the seat in your car."

"Not a good idea. Your car is bigger and safer. Besides, it will take even more effort to change the seat. I think it's best if we simply go," Lisa said.

Emma stood next to Lisa, her tiny shoulders shaking, her face buried in her bear's neck. "I want Mommy," she sobbed over and over.

Aidan could barely breathe over the anxiety knotting his chest. His heart hurt for his little girl but he didn't know what else to do to help her.

"Emma, you and I are moving to your new home with your daddy. I need you to get in his car. I'll be driving my car right behind you. Whenever you want, you can get your daddy to call me on his cell phone and you can talk to me. How's that?"

Emma looked up at him, her tearstained face wrenching his heart. He saw an opportunity to convince her that she had to go with him, all the while fearful that he'd made a horrible mistake in insisting on moving home.

"Emma, if you'll go with me, I promise you that we will stop at a McDonald's and a park on the way so you can have fun on the trip. It isn't just about going to my place. It's about having fun along the way, isn't it? And Blackie would like to go on a set of swings and eat in a restaurant, wouldn't he?" Aidan asked, feeling an overwhelming sense of relief when his daughter smiled up at him.

"McDonald's has toys," Emma said, hugging her bear close, the beginning of a smile forming on her face.

"Well done," Lisa whispered as she helped him get Emma into her car seat. "You're catching on fast."

The drive proved he hadn't caught on all that fast. Emma talked, hummed or cried all the way. The only break Aidan got to make calls was at the rest stops and standing outside in the rain at a McDonald's. Completely exhausted when he got home, he was pathetically grateful when Lisa offered to unpack the car and settle Emma in her new room. There was nothing to eat in the fridge, bringing home to him in no uncertain terms how big a role Grace had played in keeping his life operating smoothly. He'd never seen the fridge as empty as it was today.

"I guess I'll have to go to the grocery store before dinner," he said as Lisa entered the kitchen.

"I guess you will," she said, placing the booster seat on a chair at the table. "Emma is up in her new room putting her books on the shelf. That room is ready for a baby. You'll have to take the crib down and put up her bed. I assume you have a single bed some-where...or I could put her in one of the other bedrooms for tonight if needed."

He let the fridge door close. Memories rushed him. The hours his wife had spent painting the room, the bookshelves they'd scoured antiques shops looking for, the hours spent huddled over wallpaper samples. All of it for a baby they'd never had. He choked back his sorrow, seeking to answer as normally as possible. "I'll put the twin beds back and take the crib out."

Lisa gave him a sad smile. "You can tell me to mind my business, but in a way, this is my business because of Emma. You need to make amends with Grace. You can't go on living like this. And neither can Grace."

"But if she wanted to be here, she would be. I pleaded with her to stay. She chose to go."

"So now we're going to do the I-can't-do-anything-because-she-walked-out-on-me dance?" Lisa asked, a disgusted look on her face.

He looked at her and realized that no one had ever talked to him the way she did. She could have stayed out of it, and in fact, he'd started out wishing she would. But she was helping him see what a mess he'd made of things, and she was right. "Thanks, Lisa. I'm going to call her right now and see if she will meet me somewhere, anywhere we can talk."

He picked up the phone and dialed Grace's cell phone. When it continued to ring, he started to worry. She knew he was coming back. Had she decided not to take calls from him? How could he make amends if she didn't talk to him?

As his call went to voice mail, he felt so isolated, the feeling of the distance growing between them becoming more acute. What if she wasn't willing to sort things out because she had gone to a divorce lawyer?

An empty sensation settled in his stomach at the thought. What a fool he'd been. Grace had been very upset about the office thing, and he'd done little or nothing to assuage her feelings. If he didn't hear from her soon, he would call Lucas and invite himself over to the condo. He'd stay right there until Grace was willing to talk to him. In the meantime, he'd keep trying to reach her.

To EASE HER BOREDOM, Grace decided to watch an old movie. She'd poured a glass of wine and was about to settle in front of the TV when her cell phone rang again. Aidan.

Undecided as to whether she wanted to talk to him, she let it ring. Then, feeling a need to hear how he was doing, she picked it up.

"Grace, I just arrived, and wanted to see you. I miss you. I need to talk to you. Going on Skype with you in Deidre's office was wrong—I was an insensitive idiot."

"Aidan, will you slow down?"

"Sorry. I was afraid you might hang up before I said what I needed to."

"Aidan, I think that what you need to do right now is look after Emma."

"But I thought you wanted to talk, to work on things. You told me that I was making decisions without you, but I'm not. I want to hear you say that you're willing to work with me to fix our life," he said desperately. "I can't live without you—"

She heard screaming in the background

and realized that Emma was upset. "Sounds like you have your hands full."

He sighed. "Yeah, we got in about an hour ago. I need to get a few groceries so Lisa can make dinner. Emma is exhausted from the drive, and to be honest, so am I. She cried, sang or talked the entire way. My ears are hurting. Seriously."

"Welcome to the world of children," Grace said, enjoying his anguish while knowing how unsympathetically she was behaving. "Lots more to come. Have you looked into kindergarten for her?"

"Haven't even started that. I should have made a few calls last week, but it's been hectic."

"I can imagine," she said, absolutely reveling in the idea that Aidan was experiencing the results of doing little or no planning before bringing Emma here. It was probably mean of her, but she couldn't help how she felt. If he'd listened to her in the first place, none of this would have happened.

Besides, nothing had changed between them. Their relationship was in jeopardy, and until he faced up to that fact, she didn't want to be anywhere near him. It wasn't that she didn't love him, although there had been times over the past few weeks…

"Aidan, I need to stop by to pick up some of my quilting materials."

"That would be great. I would love to see you. This house isn't the same without you. When would you like to come? What about this evening?" he said eagerly, and for a moment, she felt the old closeness.

And despite everything that had happened and all her negative feelings toward him, hearing the sweetness in his voice she gave in. She missed him "Why don't I drop over this evening after Emma is in bed?"

"Come over anytime. Really. Lisa is great with Emma, and I'm sure we could find a quiet place to talk," he said, over another loud scream.

"I'll see you then," she said, aware that she was in danger of doing whatever he wanted of her. She hung up quickly before she fell for the intimate tone, the enthusiastic response. Aidan had always been so enthusiastic about everything going on in their lives, his boyish spirit and drive being two of the main reasons she'd fallen in love with him.

In the quiet of Lucas's condo, she faced her thoughts. She loved Aidan. She needed him. But she couldn't continue feeling left out, of little importance except to do as he wanted and fulfill his needs. She wished she could believe in him again. But the man she'd married was rapidly disappearing behind his plans, his dreams, his obsession. Not hers. And not theirs.

Aidan had to change if they were to have any chance to save their marriage.

An hour later, she pulled into the driveway. Seeing a car she didn't recognize parked on the street, she hesitated. Who would be visiting Aidan so soon after he got home? Lucas had said the office staff had been waiting for Aidan. What if one of them was a woman who cared more than she should for Aidan? Aidan was vulnerable right now, and might have accepted an offer of help from one of his staff.

How had she so easily jumped to that conclusion? As the question formed in her mind, she recognized that she continued to worry that Deidre hadn't been Aidan's only affair. How would they ever resume their marriage with her feeling this way?

Biting back her suspicions, she went to the front door, feeling really strange that this was her home and yet she didn't feel comfortable enough to walk in.

Anxiously she rang the bell, and Aidan opened it immediately. "I've been waiting for you," he said, his words punctuated by Emma's yelling about not wanting to go to bed.

After an earsplitting shriek, he said, "She wouldn't eat her supper, and we don't know what to do with her," he said apologetically.

Grace glanced at him, saw the strained look on his face and the bags under his eyes. Aidan was not having an easy time of it. "You're still getting unpacked, I assume," she said, wanting to touch his cheek, to massage the worried frown on his handsome face, to feel the smoothness of his skin.

"Trying to," he said just as Emma came running down the hall toward the door.

She stopped. Her red curls bounced around her head. "Who are you?" she asked as she put her thumb in her mouth and stared at Grace, smudges of tears evident on her cheeks.

"I'm Grace. I'm here to pick up a few things," she said, unable to keep the smile off her face. With her bright blue eyes, Emma was a charming little girl.

"Do you live here?" Emma said.

"I...have, yes." Grace couldn't help but

smile at the way Emma pursed her lips and scowled.

"What things do you want?" Emma asked, speaking around the thumb in her mouth.

"I make quilts and I need some fabric and stuff from upstairs. Would you like to go up with me and help me find what I'm looking for?"

Stepping away from Aidan, Emma held her hand out and looked into Grace's eyes. The sudden sense of connection charged through Grace like an electric current.

"Yes." Emma tugged on Grace's hand. "Let's go."

Aidan let out a long sigh. "This is great. Please let Emma help you get your materials while I try to get the ringing in my ears to stop," he said, a wry smile on his face as he led the way to the stairs.

Grace exchanged a quick look with Aidan. "That bad?" she asked.

Aidan rubbed his jaw. "Emma isn't happy with me or Lisa right now. She hasn't eaten anything since we got home."

"Emma, I haven't eaten, either. Maybe once you help me get my fabrics you and I could have a peanut butter sandwich together. What do you think?"

Emma smiled as she headed up the stairs, her pudgy hands gripping the handrail as she took the steps one at a time with Grace following.

"We need to go in here," Grace said when they reached the top.

A big smile spread over Emma's face. "Next to my room," she said excitedly as she hopped up and down. "Want to see my room?"

Grace hesitated. It had been the room that held all her hopes and dreams for a child of her own. And now another child—her husband's child—occupied the space Grace had imagined spending time in, rocking her baby, watching her child fall asleep after reading her or him a story.

Could she go in there and not break down in tears? Aidan and Lisa would not appreciate another round of crying from anyone at this point. But she had a little girl waiting for her answer... "Show me your room."

Emma grabbed Grace's hand and pulled her to the door, her fingers warm against Grace's skin. "See. These are all my teddy bears. I love bears. Do you?"

Grace's eyes moved around the room she'd so lovingly decorated as she waited for the news that she was pregnant. The one thing she had prayed for had been denied her.

Her heart sank at the changes in the room. The crib was gone and in its place a single bed stood between two dressers. The bed had been hastily made up. The mobile that had hung over her baby's crib was dangling off the end of the bookshelf. The wallpaper looked decidedly infantile as a backdrop for the toddler and little-girl objects. Her throat ached with loss and regret.

"Are you crying?" Emma asked, her voice gentle and oddly quiet as she tugged on Grace's hand. "Mommy says that tears are needed sometimes." She slipped her thumb into her mouth, then pressed her face into Grace's leg. "I want Mommy," she said, her voice breaking.

Grace scooped Emma into her arms and sat on the edge of her bed, rocking her back and forth to ease the little girl's distress. "Your mommy was right. Tears are very needed sometimes, aren't they?" she asked, still holding the child, feeling the warmth of her little body.

She held Emma as emotions long kept in check flooded over her. The powerful connection created by soothing and caring for such a precious little girl left her suspended in a place where only she and the child existed. This was what she'd waited for all her life—the touch of a child. Her child.

She stroked Emma's head soothingly, letting her snuggle. In this moment, she and Emma had a bond. They'd both lost a part of their lives they'd wanted. Emma had lost her mother. Grace would never give birth to a child. Smoothing Emma's brow, Grace whispered into her curls, "Emma, this room was decorated for a little girl just like you."

Emma leaned back in her arms. "Like me?" she asked, a quizzical expression on her face.

"Yes. Your dad and I wanted a baby just like you."

"Did you have one?" Emma whispered, her eyes wide ovals of deep blue.

"No. We didn't. But now you are here," Grace said, looking directly into the toddler's eyes, feeling a sudden sense of finding something for the very first time.

"I'm staying here," Emma said.

"You are. For sure."

"Will you be here?"

She didn't know how to answer Emma, but in her heart, she knew that more than anything she wanted to be here with this wonderful little person. "Would you like that?"

Emma's eyes darkened. "Lisa is here, but she's not staying very long," she said.

How does she know that? Has she overheard a conversation between Aidan and Lisa?

"Emma, there will always be people who love you even when they can't be with you," Grace said, her heart pounding in dread. Emma had to be tired. And tired children could get upset very easily. She didn't want Emma to be afraid that she might be left alone by yet another person. How could Lisa even think about not staying here with this little girl? "Your dad loves you very much. He will always be here for you."

"My mommy is gone. She's in heaven with the angels," Emma said, a forlorn look on her face.

Life was so unfair. "Yes, your mommy is with the angels and you can pray for her whenever you like. I'm certain she's looking down on you and loving you from heaven."

Emma gave a long sigh and snuggled closer.

Grace held Emma in her arms as gently and lovingly as she could, and decided that whatever it took, she would try to work out her differences with Aidan. It would take time, but it was worth the effort. Not just for Aidan or for her, but for this wonderful little girl so in need of love and reassurance. She kissed the top of Emma's head. "Why don't we go downstairs and I'll make you the best peanut butter sandwich you ever had."

"Better than Mommy's?" Emma asked, her face turned up to Grace's.

Looking into the child's eyes, she was reminded how fragile life could be. A car accident, a few seconds of distraction or misjudgment had forever altered this little girl's life. "No. Not better than your mommy's. Nobody could do it better than she did," Grace said as she took Emma's hand and led her down the stairs. She hadn't grabbed the pile of fabric she'd wanted, but it didn't really matter at the moment. All she wanted to do was to keep Emma from being sad.

"No. Mommy's sandwiches were really, really good," Emma said as she hopped down each step while still holding on to Grace's hand. It was a bumpy trip down the stairs, and when they reached the bottom, Aidan was waiting.

"Want to join us in the kitchen? I'm making

peanut butter sandwiches for Emma and me," she said to him, watching his eyes search her face, warming her heart.

"I'll make them," Emma called out as she moved ahead of Grace.

"You know how to do that?" Grace asked, her eyes still focused on Aidan.

"Of course! Mommy showed me," Emma said proudly, her tiny chin tucked into her chest.

Grace and Aidan shrugged at each other. "Well, Grace, I guess it's time for us to see what sort of culinary skills Emma has," he said with a smile as they followed Emma down the hall toward the kitchen.

"She has cried ever since we got here, until you arrived. How did you do that?" he asked, his fingers brushing hers.

Grace looked into Aidan's eyes and recognized pain and uncertainty, eagerness and caring, all in a glance. She wanted to touch him, to tell him everything would be okay for Emma and for them.

But she knew it wasn't that simple. If they were to make any of this work, they needed to take it slow, not say things that might end up being worthless a few days or weeks from now. "She cried a little while we were in her room, and I let her. She needed to cry. She's missing her mom."

"And I can't figure out how to help her," he said, as they walked into the kitchen. His hand brushed hers, sending an exciting thrill up her arm.

"Emma, your daddy is going to be your assistant and help you make the sandwiches. Is that okay?" Grace asked, at once pleased and lonely to be entering her kitchen. But she didn't live here anymore, and might not ever live here again.

"What's an assistant?" Emma asked.

"It's the person who helps the person making a meal," Aidan said, smiling his thanks to Grace as he went to the cupboard to get out a loaf of bread.

"I do it," Emma said, taking the bread and pulling the fridge open. Reaching into the shelf on the door, she took out the peanut butter.

"Let me help you," Grace offered.

"Okay." Emma put her arms up to be lifted onto a bar stool at the kitchen island.

Grace got a knife out of a drawer. "Why don't you lay out the bread slices, Daddy, while I get the jam? Then you can help Emma put the peanut butter and jam on the slices."

"Sounds great," he said, helping Emma to spread the slices with a thick layer of peanut butter and jam.

At the sight of her husband being so caring to his daughter, she had to turn away to hide her tears. When she turned after composing herself, Aidan was watching her.

"Okay. Done." Emma patted a sandwich until peanut butter oozed out of it.

"I'll put the sandwiches on plates and take them to the table," Aidan said, his eyes still on Grace, making the heat rise in her cheeks. He took dishes from the shelf, his arm brushing against her as he moved around the kitchen.

"What does everyone want to drink?" he said. "If we were not being observed by the princess, I would kiss you right about now," he whispered, leaning closer as he opened the fridge.

"I want milk," Emma called from the table.

"I'll have water," Lisa added.

"What about you, Mrs. Fellowes?" Aidan said, continuing to whisper.

"Water is fine," Grace said, feeling the heat of his body, smelling the scent of his skin. She wished they were alone.

"Daddy!" Emma called. "I want milk."

"Coming right up," he said, pouring a glass.

"This is the best," Emma said excitedly as she munched on her sandwich.

"You bet it is," Grace said, glancing around the kitchen, feeling connected and happy.

Yet, as it stood right now, she didn't belong here. Although Aidan had been very kind and expressed his appreciation of her efforts, at no point did he say anything about their situation.

When they finished eating, she put the dishes in the dishwasher, a simple act, but one that filled her with longing for all she'd lost. This wasn't her home. It had been her choice to leave, and yet what had driven her out hadn't changed.

Feeling out of place, she slipped quietly upstairs to retrieve the materials she wanted. Returning to the kitchen she said goodbye to everyone. "I can see myself out," she said, not wanting to interrupt the happy scene.

"No. Wait." Aidan came around the table. "I'll walk you to the door."

"Do you know when Lucas will be back?" she asked, feeling awkward when they reached the door. Would he try to kiss her? If he did, what would she do?

"He should be here tomorrow," Aidan said, his eyes searching her face. "Grace, I would like a chance to talk to you. Can we meet somewhere tomorrow? Maybe for coffee?"

"That would be nice," she said, resisting the urge to move into his arms.

"Grace, you were fantastic with Emma. Thank you."

"You're welcome." She fidgeted with the bag of fabric, and pushed the strap of her purse up her shoulder.

Aidan shifted from one foot to the other, jamming his hands in his pockets as he did so. "I just want to say that I'm so sorry we never had a baby together. You are a fantastic parent. All this time you waited to do something that comes so easily and naturally to you. I can only imagine how painful it has been, and I'm so sorry I wasn't more caring and didn't support you the way I should have."

The expression on his face, the way his eyes searched hers made her see that he was sincere. She wanted to reach out to him, to touch him, to show her appreciation for his saying that, but she couldn't. If she did, she'd cry, and she'd cried enough these past few weeks, endless days of wishing things had been different in their lives and in their marriage.

More than anything, she wanted to talk about how difficult it had been for her, but that would have to wait until she was emotionally able to share everything with him and have him listen with his heart not his mind. She knew he was waiting for more, but she didn't have anything she could offer him. "I'd better go."

"Can I call you tomorrow?" he asked as she opened the front door.

"Yeah. That would be good." She didn't look back as she went down the walkway. She couldn't. If she did, she would surely run to him, to his arms, to the life she'd lived for the past ten years as his wife.

But that would mean she'd have to give up on her belief that he had to change, that he had to be willing to really listen to her. Being the one to relent, give in over an argument, had always been her style. She'd always taken the first step after any disagreement they'd ever had. She couldn't this time. There was too much at stake, too much of who she was, who she believed herself to be, to be the one who offered to reconcile their differences.

She opened the car door, placed her material on the passenger seat, climbed in and drove off into the lonely night.

CHAPTER THIRTEEN

AIDAN CALLED THE next morning just moments after Grace had gotten out of bed. "It was great to see you yesterday. And I wondered if you might be available for coffee or tea this morning. I could bring coffee over if you'd like that."

Stifling a yawn, she said, "Don't you think it's a little early? I just got up."

"You never sleep in. Are you all right?" he asked, concern evident in his tone.

She wasn't about to tell him that she'd lain awake for hours last night, missing him lying beside her, reaching for him knowing he wasn't there. Waking up to an empty condo with no one to talk to, to share things with, had been heart wrenching. It all felt so final somehow, so awful. She didn't want to live like this, but she needed Aidan to change his attitude where she was concerned. She needed him to really see her and not simply

the things she could do for him to make his
life better.

"I'm fine. I slept in a little bit, that's all. I
used to do that when you were away on business, or don't you remember?"

"Yeah, now that you mention it I do remember calling you when I was away on
business and waking you up." He gave a low
chuckle. "So, what do you say? Will we go
out for coffee or will I bring it over to the
condo?"

She needed somewhere quiet to talk to him.
"Why don't you come over here?"

"Great. I'll bring coffee and your favorite
banana muffin and be there in a few minutes. Can't wait to see you, Grace," he said,
his voice thick.

"Me, too," she said before hanging up the
phone.

She rushed through a shower and was
about to apply a little blush and eye shadow
when the doorbell rang. "I'm coming," she
called out as she strode toward the door.
When she opened it, Aidan stood there holding a bouquet of her favorite yellow roses and
a cardboard carrier with two coffees and a
bag of muffins.

"Grace Fellowes, I want this to be our first

date of our new life together," he said, passing her the roses.

She took the flowers as her eyes met his. "It's been a while since we had a first date."

"Eighteen years, four months and thirteen days, to be exact," he said, following her to the kitchen.

"You have a better memory than I do," she said, putting the roses in a vase and adding water, all the while delighted that he'd remembered with such accuracy.

"I wanted to impress you, so I did the math and counted up the time. We met when we were sixteen. We've been together for over half our lives."

"Leave it to the engineer to figure that out," she said, seeing the ardent expression on his face.

"Grace, I've missed you. I can't live like this anymore. You have to come home. Please."

She wanted him to cross the kitchen floor and kiss her senseless, but she knew if he did, she would give in and move home with nothing being resolved. As much as she wanted her husband, she couldn't go back to the way it was.

"First we have to talk, really talk, about

what has gone on in the past few weeks." She took the coffee and muffins to the table.

"Anything." He sat across from her, took the lid off her coffee and slid it across to her before opening the bag and passing her a muffin with a napkin. "First, I'd just like to say how much I appreciated you coming over last night. Lisa and I were at our wits' end. And the peanut-butter thing was pure genius. Emma asked where you were when she was having her bath and went to bed without a tear."

He took a sip of his coffee. "Emma got up this morning and was her old sweet self. Of course, yesterday was a difficult day for her. I should have realized that it was too much, but I really felt that getting here was the best solution."

"To what?" she asked, hoping to get him to talk about them, about what was going on in their lives. She was eager for him to express his concern for her and how she was coping with all of this, if only to have him recognize how much of her time had been devoted to him, and would be, if only he'd include her in his plans.

"To this. Us living apart. Everyone is talking at the office about what is going on. They know about Emma and naturally are asking about you and how you're doing."

"And what do you think is the answer?"

Telling him flat out how she felt, how much he'd hurt her hadn't worked. And leaving him to cope hadn't worked. But maybe he'd figured it out himself.

"Look, Grace, I really messed up when I didn't talk to you about what we should do. As I said before, I was so focused on helping Emma that I lost sight of what was really going on between us. Then, when I tried, I did it while sitting in the absolute wrong place."

Was he finally going to talk about all of that? She felt her body relax in relief. "You left me out completely. Even though you were aware that all of this was a shock to me, that my belief in us as a couple was shaken to the core, you didn't get the fact that I felt abandoned while you and your daughter came first."

"I get that now. But how do I fix it?"

"You can start with telling me why you had an affair with Deidre."

"It wasn't an affair. I spent two nights with her five years ago. I told you it was a mistake and I'm sorry that it ever happened."

"Tell me why you had the affair," she repeated, clasping her hands tightly in her lap, her coffee cooling in front of her, her stomach threatening to reject the bite of muffin she had swallowed.

Aidan sighed, looked up at the ceiling, then back at her. "I doubt you realized what was really going on when we started trying for a baby. Our every moment together was taken over with having sex at the right time, whether or not you were pregnant, whether or not there was a physical reason why we couldn't have a baby. I felt as if I was a cog in a wheel, a person whose only function was to produce enough sperm at the allotted time to get you pregnant. It was awful."

"Why didn't you say anything?"

"I tried to a couple of times, but you always seemed so preoccupied, I felt as if you weren't listening. There never seemed to be a time when we could stop and look at what we were doing to each other. The three years we were married before we started getting involved in fertility testing, when we thought we could have a child easily were good, but then when we realized that we had to seek help everything seemed to change. We didn't go anywhere together except for some appointment or other. Instead of holding you in my arms and talking about you and me, and how much we loved each other, we talked about when you'd probably ovulate again. I knew the inside of the fertility clinic waiting room in more detail than I did our living room."

"I've never heard you talk like this before. I had no idea that you felt so…pressured by all of it."

"Didn't you feel that way?" he asked.

"At times, yes. But I believed, in the end, we'd have a child."

"Well, that's where you and I saw it differently. The longer it went on, the less I believed that we'd succeed. I'm not blaming anyone or anything. I just didn't feel the whole thing was going to work, and I didn't know how to say that without upsetting you."

"So you went away on business, saw an opportunity—"

"Grace, don't say it like that. It wasn't that I saw an opportunity. I was…confused… lonely. The days I spent with Deidre were wrong and I felt terrible about it, but she listened to me. We actually talked about what was going on in the world. About politics. We…just…talked." He looked across the table at her, his eyes dark, his face pale. "And as stupid as that sounds, I needed someone to hear me."

Grace searched his face. He was telling her the truth. A truth she didn't want to hear. Had she been that unaware of him and what he needed? "I thought you were as involved as I was in getting pregnant. You never told me you weren't."

"How could I let you down like that? When all the testing started, I believed it would work out, and we'd have a baby. But as time went on, and I realized it probably wouldn't work, I didn't know how to tell you what I was feeling without adding to your concerns. You wanted a baby so badly, honey, I felt I had no choice but to continue no matter how I was feeling about it."

"All those months you went along with trying for a child because you felt you couldn't disappoint me?"

"I did. You were so much more committed than I was. I began to think that I didn't want it as much as you did. You talked about it all the time. I wanted to have the old Grace back. The one who liked to spend a morning reading the papers in bed, having sex simply for the fun of it, going for a walk without checking the clock or talking about the latest test results."

"I had no idea you were so unhappy."

"It wasn't that I was unhappy. I felt guilty that we hadn't had a child. I wanted you to have everything. I'm your husband. I wanted you to be happy, and I knew how much a baby meant to you. I felt inadequate seeing you so anxious. The week that Deidre and I spent so much time on a computer problem in her business, I felt part of what was going on, enthusiastic that we would succeed.

"Deidre had a successful start-up of her new computer system thanks, in large part, to my company. I was completely engaged in what I was doing. When we ended the week by crossing that business line, I felt lousy. Really lousy. I never told you about it because I was ashamed. You're my wife. I love you with all my heart. And I did something I should never have done."

He reached across the table, his fingers touching hers. "I don't want to dwell on the past. We have a bright future ahead of us. I want to resolve things so that we can be a family—you, me and Emma. What can I do to make that happen?" he asked, his smile wrapping around her in a wave of love that left her breathless and her heart thudding against her throat.

They were all wonderful feelings that couldn't mask the hurt roaring through her at his admission. "Did you ever consider how hard trying to get pregnant was for me? Yes, I did want a baby more than you did. So you can imagine how painful it was for me to learn that, after a couple of nights with a virtual stranger, you were able to have a child with her, a woman you claim not to care about.

"And even worse, when you find out you had a daughter by this woman, you act as if the only people who matter are you and Emma. You make your plans without talking them over with me. And I'm expected, as usual, to simply go along with what you want."

"And that was a mistake on my part. I want to change how I do things. From here on, we will talk through things, and you will see that I'm serious about taking your feelings into account."

"Okay, so you're back and suddenly what I want and think is important to you." She didn't try to hide the skepticism she was feeling.

"Grace, I don't know what to say or how to say it. Only that if we continue to go over all the mistakes I've made, we will never be able to move on. As much as it hurts you, there is no way to change the past."

"How would you suggest I move on? How do I get over your mistakes, your lack of respect for me?" she asked, trying to ease the anger building up in her.

"I never meant to hurt you. You don't believe that right now, but it's true. I didn't mean to leave you out, but there was a little girl, and I was responsible for her."

"And you had a wife who had just gotten the shock of her life when she learned that her husband had had a child by a woman he hardly knew. You never once asked me what I needed, how badly I was feeling or what I thought we should do. You were bringing your child into our marriage without ever consulting me on how we should do it," she said, her voice rising.

Aidan looked startled, the smile on his face disappearing, replaced by a tiny frown. "Grace, I admit I made a mistake in not talking everything over with you. I'm here now to fix that. But since we're talking about the past, I did everything you wanted when we were trying to get pregnant without having much say in the plan. I trusted we were doing the right thing for you and me. I was happy to go along because I trusted that what the doctors were saying and your belief in what we were doing would give us what we wanted. I never once balked at anything, or questioned what was going on. I was simply trying to make you happy."

"Making me happy. Is that what all that effort and loss meant to you? You went along with getting pregnant to make me happy?" she asked, searching for a way to stay calm. If Aidan thought that all of this was only about making her happy…

"I had no say in it either. I went along with the plan as you did. I had things done to my body, things I never would have imagined, all to have our baby."

"And I love you for that. You were the one facing all the changes in your body, and I was powerless to do anything about it. Even though we both found it hard, we were together on trying to have a baby. I want us to do that now, talk to the adoption lawyer, make plans to have the family we've always dreamed of."

"Then why are you willing to do it now

when you weren't before Emma came into your life?"

"Because…" He rubbed his hands through his curly auburn hair. "Grace, those first couple days in Spartanburg, I was so anxious to see that Emma was taken care of."

"But she had a nanny who was perfectly capable of caring for her, better than you and I, right?"

"Well, me for sure." He gave her a wry smile, the same one that emphasized the dimples in his cheeks.

"Aidan, taking on a child is something we've never done. There is no best way, no predetermined plan that is known to work. It was supposed to be you and me facing the arrival of a child in our lives. And you left me out of every part of it, until now."

Aidan met his wife's anxious gaze. That this conversation was painful for her was evident in the hurt and uncertainty he saw in her eyes. His heart thudded in his chest. He felt as if he'd betrayed her all over again and it broke his heart.

Fighting to remain cool and in charge, he thought of all those times they'd sat across from each other in the college library, studying, laughing together, sharing the same jokes and loving the same things. It was as if they'd been born for each other. He'd never felt that way about anyone in his life. Never, in all his wildest dreams, had he imagined anything but the blissful happiness they'd experienced from the first time they'd locked eyes on each other.

He and Grace not getting along was out of the question. Everyone who met them couldn't miss how much in love they were. He had been such a dumb ass in so many ways, but right now, all he wanted was to have his wife back in his life. "Grace, I would do anything to make this better. Believe me. All I want is for you and Emma to be loved and cared for. If you're willing to help me, I swear, I'll make it up to you."

"If I believe you, and I want to..." She played with the edge of her coffee cup, her eyes focused intently on him. "How do we do this? How do we start over? Where do we go from here?"

"I'm not sure. All I am sure of is that I don't want to make any more plans without you involved." Their old connection, the intimacy they'd always shared, rolled over him. There would never be anyone for him but her, and it was time he put it all on the line. "Grace, would you like to go on a date with me?"

"What?" she asked, her dark brown eyes wide with surprise.

"We can't figure out how to move forward, or at least, I can't. I'm beginning to see that I've not only hurt you over everything I did, but I haven't been treating you like my wife. I have taken you for granted. Sure, I can come up with reasons, but they'd probably only sound like excuses to you. The fact is, you've always been there for me, and I've always assumed you would be."

Her hands stilled on the cup. "What did you have in mind for a date?"

Where would be the best place to go to dinner? Some place she loved. "I'll make reservations for Dominique's and pick you up. We'll have a wonderful evening together. Just the two of us. We won't talk about anything going on in our lives. We'll simply enjoy each other's company. I'd like to start new, date... the way we used to do. Then, once we're both feeling more at ease with each other, we can move on to planning our future together. What do you think?"

Thrilled by his words, Grace wanted to lean across the table, run her fingers through her husband's curly auburn hair and kiss his lips. Yet she knew only too well how easily succumbing to his charm would distract her, make her forget her very real concerns. He was right when he said they weren't connected in the same way anymore. If she were to be totally honest about it, she'd gotten comfortable with her crafts and her craft group. She had gotten her life into a quiet routine broken only by her efforts to have a child, a dream she still clung to, despite the disappointing results. Perhaps she had taken him for granted, too.

She'd let him come here because she believed the only way forward was to insist on marriage counseling. She needed help to find it in her heart to forgive him for the way he'd behaved all those years ago.

Yet his words of explanation touched her deeply. That he'd shared his feelings over the fertility testing, his shame over what he'd done, made it possible for her to see his actions and choices a little differently.

Maybe there was a new way to approach this. It might not be a perfect way to resolve their issues, but if they went back to where they had started—their attraction to each other, their caring—they might have a chance to rebuild the trust between them. "I accept your invitation to dinner, but I'll drive."

His wide smile filled her heart with desire. There had never been a time in their marriage when she didn't want him to make love to her, making what he'd done even more painful. But she would work on moving ahead, starting over.

"Why do you want to drive?"

If she drove, she could control what happened after the dinner. As much as she cared about him, the date could not be about making love. She was well aware what would happen if she allowed it. He'd kiss her, hold her and the rest would be inevitable.

She was not going to let that happen because she needed to believe he was truly changing and not just doing this to get her to agree to whatever he wanted to do about Emma.

She needed to be convinced that he was genuinely interested in her as a woman, a partner. Her confidence had taken a beating after the revelation of his affair and Emma's existence. Grace needed to be assured that he respected her as well as loved her. Nothing less would do.

"Aidan, if we're going to do this, it has to

be on my terms. We're in this mess because of your behavior." She clasped her hands in her lap to keep from reaching for him.

The anticipation of starting fresh, of getting to know each other all over again thrilled her. "We've lived for all these years thinking we knew each other. Maybe we don't. It's time we found out," she said.

"I'm all for that. What time are you picking me up?" he asked, a smile spreading across his handsome face.

CHAPTER FOURTEEN

GRACE APPLIED LIPSTICK, her hand shaking so much she was afraid of smudging it. She'd spent the entire day getting ready for their date, including buying a new dress in shades of green and gold with a wide skirt and a narrow waist. She'd never owned a dress like this one, and she loved the way it swayed around her legs as she walked.

She could still feel Aidan's eyes on her as she'd made the peanut butter sandwiches with Emma, the rush of exhilaration when he'd walked her to the door.

After applying a bit of blush to her pale cheeks and putting gloss on over her lipstick before checking her face one more time in the mirror, she put her makeup away. Turning around in a circle in front of the full-length mirror, she smiled at her reflection. She felt so good, pleasure bubbled through her. She hadn't been this excited in years. This was like a whole new beginning.

"Maria and I are here waiting in the living room to see you off on your date," Lucas said, coming down the hall toward the bathroom. "Ready or not, we want to see how you look."

She opened the door and stepped out into the hall. Lucas gave a long, slow whistle. "Sis, you look spectacular," he said, pulling her close. "Aidan won't know what hit him." He led her to the living room. "Maria, what do you think? Is my sister not the most beautiful sister in the world?" His voice was filled with pride.

Maria strode across the room to hug Grace. "That dress is perfect on you. It brings out your eyes."

Maria's job as fashion coordinator for the local department store meant that she always dressed well, another trait Grace admired about her. She had been so kind since Grace had moved into the condo. "If you like it, then I'm good to go," Grace said.

"The only thing I'd add is a smoky tone to your eye makeup," Maria said, heading toward the bathroom. Quickly and with complete confidence, she applied the shadow to Grace's lids. "Aidan is one lucky man. That's all I can say."

Maria's gaze met Grace's in the mirror. "I think Aidan needs his butt kicked for the way he's behaved. I mean, he had everything and he tossed it for a hookup. Men. Sometimes I wonder…"

"You're not wondering about Lucas are you?" Grace asked.

"No! But before Lucas I was involved with someone who didn't tell me that he'd had an affair on the side. I was so hurt and angry. I had invested my total self in the relationship only to find out that he'd been with someone else."

Grace touched Maria's arm. "I'm so sorry."

"Thanks. It was really messy at the time, but when I realized that he was the one who made the mistake, not me, that I was the excuse he used to justify what he did, I got angry. And getting angry saved me from slipping back into those patterns of thought." She gave her forehead a gentle smack. "Sometimes I wonder what we women use for brains when it comes to men."

Grace experienced an odd sense of comfort. What had happened to her had happened to someone strong and amazing like Maria. "You're right. This isn't my fault at all. I wasn't the one who broke our marriage vows."

"That's the attitude, girl. You just remember that you deserve a man who knows how to treat a woman. Someone like your brother," she said, winking. "And if Aidan doesn't come to his senses and behave like a loving husband, he'll have my man to deal with." She teased Grace's bangs a little. "You look like a sexy woman on a mission."

"How serious are you and Lucas?" Grace asked.

Maria nodded her head slowly, a smile filling her face. "Very serious."

"Oh! That's great!" Grace hugged Maria.

"Isn't it? I'm excited. He's asked me to go looking for a diamond with him, but I'm a little more traditional. I'd like him to pick something he likes. As for me, it's not about the diamond. It's about our future together."

"I couldn't agree with you more. It's not about the ring. It's about the love and the future together. I can't wait to have you as my sister-in-law."

"I'm so lucky. We're both taking it slow, getting used to being with each other, to sharing our lives, our interests." Maria glanced at her watch. "You'd better get a move on. You're going to be late picking Aidan up. By the way, I think it's totally cool that you're driving—shows him you're in control."

"I hope so." Grace hugged Maria a second time, went to find her evening bag, kissed her brother's cheek, then headed for the door. "Love you. See you both later."

"I guess I can't ruffle your hair the way I did when we were kids," Lucas said.

"Not a chance. After all the work Maria and I have put into my appearance, you cannot touch my hair."

"I'll be waiting up for you, to hear all about your date," Maria said.

The traffic on the parkway was light and Grace got to the house earlier than she expected. She thought about slipping in the back door, but decided to come to the front instead. Like a real date. A scream of delight greeted Grace as Lisa answered the door. Emma peeked out around Lisa's leg, her thumb slipping into her mouth, a smile of welcome on her tiny, upturned face. Unable to resist the little girl with the mischievous grin, Grace knelt down. "Hello there, Emma. What's up?"

Emma pulled her thumb out of her mouth. "I'm playing with my Barbie doll. Do you want to play with me?" she asked, stretching out her hand toward Grace.

"I would like that very much."

"Aidan's been on the phone for the past hour," Lisa said. "He just now headed upstairs to get dressed."

Emma tugged at Grace's hand. "Come on. I've got lots of dolls," she said. The soft touch of the little girl's skin filled Grace with happiness. As they entered the kitchen, she stopped. Everywhere she looked, there were toys. The TV was turned to a *Thomas the Tank Engine* program. The late-afternoon sun streamed over the counter where a little pink sweater dangled from the corner.

This was exactly how she'd imagined her kitchen would look when she and Aidan had a child of their own. She'd imagined making breakfast while her toddler played, Aidan coming downstairs, scooping up their child and squeezing in between her and the island to kiss the nape of her neck. She'd imagined so many wonderful moments. Moments that had never come true. Struggling to maintain her composure, she swallowed over the lump in her throat.

"I didn't realize that four-year-olds played with Barbie dolls," Grace said.

"Her mother bought a lot of toys, from dump trucks to Barbie dolls, and let Emma make the choice of which to play with."

"Wanna see my dump trucks?" Emma asked still holding Grace's hand. "Or we can sit at my table and have tea." Emma pulled Grace to the child-size wooden table and chairs near the window. "Please, Lisa, can we have tea? Just the three of us. And Daddy, too." She popped her thumb back into her mouth as her gaze moved to the door leading to the hall. Emma had clearly begun to feel at ease around him. The idea warmed Grace.

She was suddenly overwhelmed with caring and concern for this little girl who had been through so much and still faced the loss of her nanny when Lisa went back to Spartanburg. How would Emma cope with her dad at work and Lisa gone? Grace couldn't imagine what it would be like to be so young and face so many changes in her life.

"I would love tea," Grace said, kneeling next to Emma's table, patting her narrow shoulders as Emma moved the dishes around in a businesslike fashion.

"We have to get tea for Sam and Pedro, Barbie, Ken and Tammy," Emma said, going to the dolls propped up on miniature furniture by the fridge.

"Is everyone having tea?" Grace asked, loving this moment of make-believe with Emma.

"Oh," Emma said, her lips rounded and her eyes bright with anticipation. "Do you want to make a peanut butter sandwich? Like we did the last time? All my dolls like peanut butter."

"That sounds like fun." The way Emma's eyes widened when she was excited about something was cute.

Lisa wiped her hands on a towel, folding it neatly. "Emma, honey, you've already had your dinner. We need to get you ready for bed. Besides, Grace is here to pick up your daddy."

Emma's lower lip trembled. "Are you taking my daddy away?"

How difficult it must be for Emma to understand what is happening in her life. To think that she would fear someone taking her daddy away broke Grace's heart. She hugged Emma, smoothing the curls from her face and looking into her anxious eyes. "No. Never. No one is going to take your daddy from you. I'm going out to dinner with him so we can talk."

"About me?" Emma asked, leaning closer

to Grace as she played with the gold necklace she was wearing.

"Probably some," she answered honestly. She saw the downcast look in Emma's eyes, and wanted to hold on to her forever. "Do you mind?"

Emma snuggled closer to Grace. "Has my mommy really gone to be with the angels?"

"Yes. Your mommy is in heaven with the angels."

"How do you know?" Emma asked, her dark eyes wide in question.

"I just know. Someone who loved you so much would definitely be in heaven," Grace said. What if she'd said the wrong thing? What if Lisa or Aidan had given Emma a different explanation? She glanced hurriedly at Lisa, to see her nodding slowly.

Grace clung to the little girl, feeling connected to her, imagining what it would have been like to hold her own baby. What would it have been like to give birth to a wonderful little girl just like Emma?

No! She couldn't think those thoughts anymore. She would never have a baby of her own, and she had to stop wishing she could. With Aidan able to have a child, and despite the gynecologist saying they could find no reason she couldn't conceive, the fault for not having children had to be hers.

She sensed someone standing behind her. Glancing up she saw Aidan, an expression of wonder on his face.

"Emma needed a little comforting," she offered, the air seeming to be suspended between them. She searched for words to express her feelings, the changes this child had wrought. Changes that went so deep they rocked Grace's belief in herself.

He knelt beside her. "You are so good with Emma," he said, his eyes dark with awareness as his hand touched her shoulder.

For the longest minute, she wanted him to take her in his arms and kiss her breathless, show her how much he cared by making love to her. It took all her willpower not to act on her feelings. But if everything went well in the next few weeks, she might not have to resist her feelings.

"I think it's time we got to the restaurant," she said, holding back the loving, bittersweet emotions his touch sparked.

"Whatever you say," he offered, taking Emma in his arms and brushing the curls off her face. "Emma, Daddy is going out with Grace, but I'll be back." He kissed her round cheeks, making her laugh, a beautiful sound that tugged hard on Grace's heart. She needed to leave before she lost her determination to stay removed from this scene.

Still in her father's arms, Emma reached for Grace. "Hug. I want a hug."

Stepping closer to Aidan, Grace kissed Emma's cheek and, in doing so, breathed in the cologne she'd given Aidan for Christmas. She felt light-headed at the nearness of him, the possibilities of the evening ahead. "Good night, Emma."

"Good night," Emma said, giving Grace a big, noisy kiss and a smile as she waved.

It took every bit of energy to move away out of Aidan's reach. Grace wanted to touch him, to feel his skin, soak in his scent, but it was too dangerous. She had to keep her head clear, focus on working out the issues between them.

Tonight was the beginning of the changes needed to make her feel included, be part of Emma's life and to find a way to resolve her feelings of betrayal. If they were to have a life together, it had to be on equal terms. Even the thought of what would happen if it all went wrong again made her frightened, her courage deserting her.

Lisa's voice was gentle as she said, "Emma, it's time for bed. Say good-night to your daddy."

"Night, princess," Aidan said, kissing Emma before handing her to Lisa. "I'll be back real soon."

"And in the meantime, Emma will have her bath and I'll read her a story," Lisa said.

What would it be like to put Emma to bed, read to her, then kiss her good-night before seeking Aidan to enjoy the rest of the evening? Feelings of remorse flowed through her at the memory of the words they'd said to each other, their inability to find a way to be a family.

She wanted to be part of Aidan's life and Emma's. Everything she'd ever wanted and everything she stood to lose was in this house. Quietly, she went to the door. He must not see her tears. He would want an explanation and she couldn't give him one without admitting how much she loved him.

When they got to the restaurant Grace was feeling a little more in control. Aidan, true to his word, had kept the conversation light and fun as she drove. They listened as the maître d' told them a humorous story about his eight-year-old son learning to play the violin, then ordered their favorite food.

When the meal arrived, they talked and ate as if nothing was wrong between them. "Do you remember the first time we went to the movies together?" Aidan asked.

"Ah… *Miss Congeniality.* Benjamin Bratt and Sandra Bullock. We laughed all the way through it."

"And how many times have you watched since?"

"Probably three or four times," she said, savoring the taste of Alfredo sauce.

"I've never known anyone who enjoys watching reruns of movies like you do." He picked up his wineglass. The old connection, so strong between them even after all these years, came alive. It was as if they'd never been apart, as if none of the events of the past weeks had happened.

Nervously, she smoothed her hair, her fingers touching the necklace at her throat. "How is work going?" she asked to keep the conversation on a safe topic.

"Busy." Aidan sighed, putting his wineglass down. "In fact, we are going to exceed our profit projections for this year based on the first six months."

He continued to talk, giving Grace a glimpse into the business that excited him. She'd always loved his passion for his work, even though she didn't understand most of what he did. Yet his enthusiasm triggered a sense of loss. A few weeks ago sharing their day over dinner had been normal—something they'd taken for granted and maybe not appreciated. But because of the past weeks, it had completely and utterly changed.

The man sitting across from her had kept a part of his life a secret from her, had let her believe that he'd been faithful to her. And all the while, his infidelity, his thoughtlessness had threatened everything.

A chill settled in the pit of her stomach. Their life would never be the same again, no matter how much either of them tried to put it back together. They could never go back to how their life had been, to that time of innocence and total trust. Deidre MacPherson—a woman Grace had no real knowledge of and one her husband claimed to not really know or care about—would always overshadow their lives.

But the worst of all was that Aidan could have had a casual relationship with a woman he claimed no real connection to. That he could be so cavalier about something she considered sacred. And now there was a child who would forever represent that fundamental difference in their values. How could he be so careless about sharing his body with another person? What sort of person could have sex with no emotional involvement with someone he'd had no contact with after?

"Sorry. I tend to talk too much about business." He leaned back in his chair, glancing around for a waiter. "What would you like for dessert?"

"Not tonight," she said.

He waited while the waiter took their plates. He looked into her eyes, stirring her affection despite her train of thought. There had never been anyone else for her but Aidan.

"Are you sure? What about lemon gelato? It's your favorite."

He can remember my favorite dessert but not understand how I feel about his infidelity.

Did he have any idea how much he'd hurt her? He was sorry, and repentant, but was that all? Would he have felt as she did if the situation had been reversed, if she'd been unfaithful?

There was an awkward moment after he convinced her to order dessert. Even though there was a lot going on inside her, she couldn't seem to think of anything to say. At least, anything that wouldn't lead to what was really uppermost in her mind.

They were supposed to be on a date, but it didn't feel that way. It felt more like being suspended in a bad dream, unable to wake up. Every time she tried to rein in her thoughts, her mind circled the pain of the past few weeks.

Aidan watched her, a pleading look in his eyes. "Grace, I would give everything I have if you would come home with me this evening. I love you, and I miss you in a way I've never missed anyone in my life." He smoothed his hand over his hair, a sign he was nervous. "I'm well aware that we have issues to work out, but it's lonely without you. I miss our early morning talks. It's hard to get up and head out to work without saying one word to you." He blinked rapidly. "Do you suppose we could go for a walk, somewhere more private so we can talk?"

She wanted that more than anything. "It's impossible the way it is," she said.

"What do you mean?"

"We can't ignore or gloss over what's going on between us."

"Let's drive out to Foley Beach and watch the waves. We always loved doing that," he said.

His suggestion called to mind the days when they had no money and went to the ice cream shop near the pier. More bittersweet memories. Still, a walk on the beach would be pleasant and distracting. "Why not?"

"Will you let me drive?" he asked.

"Why would you want to drive my car? Aren't you the one who claims that it drives like a grocery cart?" she asked, slipping easily into their teasing banter.

"I'm doing my good deed for the day by saving all the oncoming traffic from my wife, the centerline hugger."

"While Mario Andretti, here, thinks that the speed limit is for turtles," she said, laughing for the first time this evening. It freed her.

He shifted in his chair, his smile warm, his gaze intense. "You look gorgeous," he said. "I love the sound of your laughter...the way your nose crinkles when you grin."

I love you was on her lips, but she held back. Her laughter was one of the first things he'd complimented her on when they'd started dating, and something he never failed to remark on. Funny, how he'd always been able to make her laugh. And she'd always said she loved him when he did; a habit honed from years of loving the same man.

They arranged to take their desserts and coffee with them, then headed out onto the highway to the beach, the windows down, the air ripe with scents of tidal water and muddy inlets. The street leading to the beach was lined with shops selling trinkets, and restaurants with patrons spilling onto the sidewalk.

"I love this town," Aidan said as he pulled into the parking lot next to the pier, searching for a space.

"It's certainly busy tonight," Grace said as she watched him maneuver her car into a narrow parking place.

"Do you want to take our desserts out to the boardwalk or eat here?" he asked, turning off the engine.

"The gelato is probably melted, so maybe staying here would be better," she said, opening the bag and passing him his coffee and chocolate cake. Placing her coffee in the cup holder, she opened the tiny container and peeked in. "Yeah, I'd say it's minutes from being totally melted."

"Why don't you simply drink it?"

"What?"

"Just drink it. Never mind using a spoon." He grinned. "Be adventuresome."

Grace sipped the delicious liquid. That worked—tart and creamy, and delicious.

"Grace, you are so beautiful," Aidan said, his voice low and husky.

Sitting inside the darkened car, listening to the radio, made everything feel so perfect, so normal. She licked her lips, tasting the lemony sugar, feeling his gaze on her. She knew that look. "Aidan, we can't. There is so much that isn't right between us."

She saw the disappointment on his face, but makeup sex wasn't going to solve their problems.

"I'm aware of that," he said. Focusing on his dessert, Aidan finished, then dropped the container in the bag. "Let's go for a walk along the beach."

He came around and opened her door, then led her to a path that reached the shoreline. "Grace, you may be angry at me for saying this, but we're so good together and always have been. I can't let that slip away without doing everything in my power to prevent it." His hand held hers in a firm but gentle grip as they moved across the sand, the setting sun sending long, gold cones of light around them.

Despite all that had happened between them, she knew he was speaking from his heart. "Aidan, I'd like that, too."

He slipped his arm around her shoulders as they moved closer to each other. "I've known that since the day I met you—"

She put her fingers on his lips to silence him. "Just listen to me. Being a mother means everything to me, but I never imagined it would happen like this. That you would have a child with someone else. All I ever wanted was to have our baby, to be part of bringing our child into the world, our lives, our home. I wanted the excitement of being pregnant, of giving birth to our baby. That's not going to happen for me.

"Instead, I am faced with another woman's child who has come into my life uninvited and unintended. It's not that I don't adore her. She's sweet and bright and a beautiful child. But she's not mine. I don't know how to explain this any better than that."

He pulled her into his arms, his warmth, his embrace a shield from the world. "Grace, if I could turn back time, I'd go back to Spartanburg, the first time, and do it all over with you. I would. I'd include you in everything I said and did back there. But that's not possible." He paused, then said slowly, "If it would change how you feel about me, I'm willing to move Emma and Lisa back to Spartanburg while we sort things out between us."

She wished with all her heart that was possible. "You can't do that to Emma. She's been through enough, from losing her mother to losing her home. But don't you see what's happening here? You're looking to make things right without thinking it through or considering the consequences. You're looking for a quick fix and there isn't one."

His expression was bleak as he held her closer, his forehead pressed to hers. "But I can't live without you. Maybe we can all move to Spartanburg for a few months."

"You can't believe that such a move would work. Your business is here. Our lives are here. You wouldn't be happy living in Spartanburg. Emma is here now, and she has to stay here. You and Lisa are all she has, and together you'll work through it," she said, tilting her face to his.

"But what about us?"

"Isn't that what we're working on now?"

"Then what do we do?" he asked, touching

her cheek, sending waves of desire spiraling through her.

She fought off the urge to succumb, to kiss him, to hold him… "I wish I knew. For me, it feels as if my life has been broken in ways I can't fix. I feel as if you've turned your back on me."

He held her shoulders in his powerful grip, his face a mask of shock. "No! I haven't, Grace. Yes, I made a mistake, more than one. But I am not intentionally turning my back on you."

"But I can't get past the idea that when you were faced with the opportunity to claim your daughter, you put your needs ahead of mine. You shut me out."

"Grace, I'm not shutting you out now," he said, easing her head against his chest. The sound of his heart reverberated through her, tampering with her will.

Aidan stroked her cheek. "Grace, you mean everything to me," he whispered, touching her cheek, eliciting a sigh of need.

As his dark eyes searched hers, he kissed each finger slowly and deliberately. "I want to make love to you all night. I want your skin on mine, our bodies together." He nibbled on her lip, his mouth hot against her.

She sank into his embrace, her head spinning, her body angling closer to his. He smoothed her face, his breath warm, his eyes on her lips. "Grace, please," he breathed as he pressed his body into hers. "Please."

She fought for air, her heart tumbling in her chest. She wanted him, his skin, his body, his words, everything. As his gaze, simmering with passion, met hers, she faltered. There had never been a time when they didn't enjoy each other's bodies.

But she couldn't help wondering if he'd held Deidre the way he was holding her now. Had he spoken similar words of endearment to Deidre before he made love to her?

"Aidan, we can't do this," Grace said, seeking to put a little space between them. She wanted him, needed him, but she couldn't do this…not here…not now.

His face was lit by the setting sun, spotlighting his desire. "Grace, we need to find our way back to each other. We could always shut out the world and love each other. We need that now more than any other time," he said, his deep baritone voice playing over her, toying with her resolve.

"Aidan, what we need is to work things out. To talk, to act differently. I can't make love to you, not yet. When you're close to me, I can't stop myself from imagining you holding another woman."

"That was five years ago, Grace," he said, disappointment seeping through his words.

"Not for me," she said. "I found out only a few weeks ago, so for me it feels as if it happened yesterday."

Sighing, he pressed his lips into her forehead. "You're right. This is not a good idea at all. I don't want you to feel pressured," he said. "I meant for us to simply spend the evening with each other. No expectations."

Glancing down the beach, he said, "Let's go into the hotel and have a drink. Maybe reminisce a little." He took her hand and tucked it against his body.

She matched his stride as they walked. "I can't remember the last time I was inside that hotel," she said, allowing the evening to chase away her disturbing thoughts.

"The last time I was in this hotel was when we came here for dinner to celebrate our new office space. Do you remember that?" he asked, sounding completely in control, as if the past few minutes hadn't happened.

"I do," she said, matching his carefree tone, even though she wasn't feeling very carefree.

She felt as if she'd let him down, somehow. But maybe that was her guilt talking. She'd always done whatever he wanted, whenever he wanted it.

At least going into the hotel bar might distract them enough that they'd keep the conversation light and upbeat.

"One of our first dates was at this beach, having hot dogs at the little takeout on the pier. That was one of the most memorable dates we had. I was so sure I'd blow it and you'd go off with Peter Woods and I'd be left holding the beach bag."

"You're kidding. Me and Peter Woods? Never," she said playfully. "He wasn't after me. He was after Sue Beck. Remember her?"

"Yeah. How I remember her…all that black hair," he said, glancing at her out of the corner of his eye, a smile teetering on his lips.

"You told me you didn't like her—you're teasing me."

"Of course I am. Wonder what we'll find when we get to the bar. Probably a bunch of people staring at their cell phones."

"And, of course, you've never stared at your phone," she said, giving him a gentle poke in the ribs.

He laughed, pulled her close and kissed

her. "Guilty…" His gaze caught hers, held her…and then he slowly looked away. "You can't imagine the fantasy playing in my mind at the moment. You. Me. Our big four-poster bed…"

Struggling to recover from the force of his kiss, she said way too quickly, "I wonder if they've redecorated since we were here last."

He took her hand and pulled her along with him. "I hope so. It wasn't the most elegant bar I've ever been in."

They entered the lobby of the hotel and went into the wide-open space of the bar. Taking a table by the window, they sat in deep, comfortable chairs across from each other, their hands touching casually.

She glanced around. The color scheme had changed from taupe and grays to mostly black and turquoise with splashes of white and cream. The room was filled with small tables along the windowed area, while the bar with high stools and tables occupied the rest of the space.

She liked the way they'd opened the bar up to be part of the lobby area. Young couples and singles milled about. "New color scheme."

"Different crowd. They seem a lot younger than I remember," Aidan said.

"And you might be showing your age," she teased. "I remember when we were in our twenties, when everything seemed possible… our ambition limitless."

They ordered wine and continued to people watch. "This must be a popular bar by the size of the crowd."

"We were here to a wedding reception once and there was a dance floor over there." She pointed to the back of the room near the entrance. "I wonder if they ever have dances here."

"No. This is probably a bar for hookups. People coming on vacation looking for a quick fling. I hear my staff talking about how dating works today. Were you aware that there are apps you can get for your phone that allows you to find someone to hook up with on a moment's notice?"

Is that what you did? Did you and Deidre hook up in a bar like this one?

He said that they'd been working, but what if they went to a bar for a drink after work? She couldn't stop the sudden rush of images. Her husband touching another woman, kissing her in public…laughing…sharing a joke.

Deidre flirting with him, making it clear she wanted him. No strings attached. Just sex…

She felt the blood drain from her face. "How do you know that?" she asked, her voice sounding distant, not part of her body.

Surprise dawned on Aidan's face. "I—I know because of some of the people I work with."

"Is this how you and Deidre got together? Did you go to a bar?"

"No! We worked long hours together…" He rubbed his face with his hands, his eyes bleak as he met her desolate gaze. "Look, I never hang around bars when I am out of town. They don't have any appeal for me. I eat in the dining room of the hotel, then head upstairs to work. I've always done that."

"Except when you hooked up with Deidre," she said, aware of how angry and judgmental she sounded, but she didn't care. Seeing these people behaving in such a casual way, enjoying themselves—some of them probably cheating on their partners—made her want to throw up.

"Grace, talk to me," Aidan said, taking her hand in his. "I've never been in a bar like this without you. I swear."

"But you did have a casual relationship. How could you?"

Aidan put his hands in his lap, his face impassive, his tone quiet and controlled. "I've told you how it happened."

"How do I know that what you're saying is the truth? Look around. Whether innocent or not, these people are here for something besides a drink."

"I swear to you. It only happened that one time, Grace," he said, his gaze searching the room as he took a deep breath. "I'm sorry I brought you here if it reminds you of what happened. I'm truly sorry," he said, defeat in his voice. "I think we should leave."

Numbly, she followed him out to the car, her heart breaking. But she couldn't help lashing out. And even worse, she was still so angry at him, at what he'd done and how it had destroyed her happiness. When they reached the car she slid into the seat, despair filling her.

Aidan climbed into the driver's seat and started the car. "Grace, we have to resolve this somehow." He gripped the wheel and stared straight ahead. "You are my life. I want you to be with me and with Emma. I want you to be part of everything we do. But if you and I can't get past your fears…pain…what then?" he asked, his voice haggard.

"I just can't believe that someone as caring as you are would have casual sex, Aidan. It's not like you. That's the part I can't accept."

"You're right—it's not like me at all. That's my whole point. It was a onetime thing."

"You say that, but I find it so hard to accept that you could be so indifferent about something so intimate. It makes me feel inadequate, as if I wasn't enough for you."

She swallowed against the futility of it all. This shouldn't be happening. She longed for the days when they were excited and hopeful about having a baby, rather than this. This awful, hurtful experience that had destroyed her self-confidence and her trust in her husband. "Regardless of how you felt about everything going on with us and your work, why did you do something so demeaning to me, to our marriage?"

Aidan sighed. "I don't know, Grace. I was lonely and working long, hard hours with her, eating in her office. We were together and suddenly… I… Things were all mixed-up in my head. It was a long time ago," he murmured, pain and hurt flowing through his words.

She stared across the small space separating them and felt as if she were looking at a stranger. She didn't know this man nearly as well as she thought she did, and it broke her heart. "I don't know, either."

His gaze met hers, his face drained of any emotion. "I'm out of ideas, Grace. Please help me figure out what to do."

Grace felt sick. The marriage she'd dreamed of was about to disappear. "I have no idea." Sadness wrapped around her heart, crushing her spirit. "I really have no idea how we're going to work this out."

"You know what frightens me the most?"

"What?" The desperation in his eyes made her fear his answer would make things worse.

How she wished she'd never said what she had said. It only made more trouble for them to deal with, adding to their problems, and maybe for no reason if he was telling the truth. And if he wasn't, there was nothing she could do to alter the past and the hurt they'd both experienced, widening the gulf between them.

"I'm scared that we can't fix this. That you will never forgive me for what I did. That Emma and I will live our lives without you. I wish things were good between us, the way they were. We were happy together, regardless of what happened these past few weeks. You have to admit that." Turning, he pulled out of the parking lot. "I'll take you to Lucas's place, and bring your car back in the morning."

CHAPTER FIFTEEN

THE DRIVE TO the house was easily one of the worst of Aidan's life. He drove slowly, frustrating the drivers behind him, but he didn't care. Her withdrawal from him was a physical, tangible thing. Every minute that passed took Grace farther out of his reach, away from their life together.

He struggled to think of something to say that would give him an opening, an opportunity to make one last try. She was still upset, and he didn't blame her for that, but if they were to ever to get together again she had to help him find a way he could make it up to her.

He'd been glancing her way every couple of minutes, but she didn't look at him. He wanted to pull over to try to reason with her, but hadn't dared to do that, fearing that he'd only make things worse.

All he could do now was encourage her to

call him tomorrow. He didn't feel he could call her, under the circumstances.

When Aidan pulled into the entrance to Lucas's condo building, Lucas was walking toward the door. He retraced his steps when he spotted Grace's car. "Hey, sis. You're back early," he said, a quizzical frown on his face.

"I'll explain later," she said, not looking Aidan's way. She picked up her purse and got out. "I'm really tired," she said, hugging her brother.

"Talk to you tomorrow?" Aidan asked, aware that his brother-in-law would have a long talk with Grace tonight or tomorrow, then Lucas would call, demanding to talk to him.

Grace didn't turn back, didn't make eye contact or smile. "I'm sorry for tonight," he said, hoping she'd at least say good-night.

Instead, she walked toward the condo building without turning back.

Lucas got into the passenger seat Grace had just vacated. "Okay, buddy, what did you do to my sister?"

"It didn't go well," Aidan said, feeling defeated.

"If you don't make this right, you need your head read," Lucas said, giving Aidan's shoulder a light punch. "The last thing I expected was to have her show up looking like she'd been hit by something."

Aidan stared in surprise. "I would never—"

"Relax. I know you wouldn't. But you are messing up badly. What is going on?"

"I don't know. She won't listen to me. She says I ruined everything, and she has no idea about how I can make it better. And I don't, either. I'm going to lose her, Lucas. And I can't seem to turn this around. I need your help."

"You got it. But first, I want to check on Gracie, see if I can help her. Maybe I can get a handle on what's happening with her. I might be able to sit down with you tomorrow if I can get out of going to Nashville again."

Aidan's heart sank at the stiff expression on Lucas's face. Did he think that there had been other women besides Deidre? "Lucas, I didn't have any other relationships. Deidre was the only one. I swear to you. Man-to-man. I never, ever, intended to do what I did. You have to believe me. I wouldn't intentionally hurt Grace."

"I'm not sure of anything where you're concerned. You had everything a man could want, and you tossed it over for a fling with a stranger." Lucas got out. "I think you should face facts. If you don't put your wife first, you're going to lose her."

GRACE LEANED ON Lucas for support as they went into the building, wretchedness dragging her every step. She could still hear Aidan's words of entreaty, proving he didn't get it. She was hurting so badly, was so desperate to understand what had driven him to another woman. And yet when they needed each other, needed to share their feelings, to talk it all out, he was ready to give up on them rather than work to solve their problems.

When did feelings need a time frame? Why couldn't he accept that nothing this serious was over and done with on a schedule? Her stomach ached at the memory of his words.

"You'll be all right, Gracie, really," Lucas said as he pressed the elevator button and the door closed behind them. "I'm getting you upstairs, then we're going to have a talk about what's going on with you and Aidan."

"Please. No lectures. Not tonight. I'm too tired, and besides, there's really no point." She leaned against the wall as the stress of the evening washed over her. She could still feel

Aidan's body pressed to hers, his mouth on hers, desire for his touch flooding her senses.

"I'm not going to lecture you, but we need to sort this out. I'd like to kick his butt, but it wouldn't do much good. Aidan can be a brickhead when it comes to personal connections. But this isn't news to you, right?"

"Yeah," she said, her whole body feeling lethargic, her mind in complete turmoil.

Lucas touched her shoulder. "Don't mean to be hard on you, sis, but there has to be a way to get this settled. I've never known two people who loved each other the way you two do."

"Maybe it was all just a sham," she said.

"You don't believe that. Not for a minute."

"No. Aidan and I had everything but a baby. I want to believe that if we'd been able to have a child, this wouldn't have happened. But I'll never know, always be left wondering if all that wanting to have a baby ruined my marriage."

"Do not believe that. Do not," he said emphatically.

"I may not have a choice if he doesn't want to work things out. Actually, that's not it. He wants to work things out but he can't accept that it's not an easy fix."

"You can't change the past, and don't go blaming yourself here. Aidan was the one who made the mistake."

She walked ahead of him from the elevator, heading down the hall toward his condo. "What do you mean?"

"Let's go inside first."

"Is Maria here?"

"No, she's doing inventory at work this evening."

"I really like her, Lucas. Are you going to propose to her?"

He tilted his head at her. "We are not discussing my love life. We're discussing yours. I'll make us a hot chocolate like Mom used to make. Remember how good that tasted? The ultimate comfort food."

Whenever they'd needed a little cheering up, their mom would get out the saucepan to make real hot chocolate—none of those just-add-water packages.

"Yeah. I miss her so much, and even more now with my life in such a mess. She taught me everything about quilting and knitting. Sometimes when I'm knitting, it's as if she's there with me."

"You've been knitting while you've been

here, but I haven't seen you working on a quilt."

"I finished what I brought with me. I'm waiting for new fabric. I ordered online and it should be delivered to the house this week."

"Will you go pick it up?"

"Probably when I get the call from Lisa or Aidan that it's arrived."

"How will you feel about that?"

"I'm not sure. It makes me so lonely to go over there. I was happy in that house with Aidan. But now...it's just hard to make conversation, to see that little girl...feel the loss all over again."

Lucas busied himself mixing the ingredients together, the scrape of the spoon on the pan the only sound. He turned the burner on under the saucepan. "Sis, honestly, I don't have a clue how I'd feel in your shoes. Wanting a baby, then finding out that Aidan had a child by another woman."

"Lucas, can we not go there tonight?" She pushed her hair off her face, irrationally feeling Aidan's skin against hers when he'd kissed her forehead on the beach this evening.

"Sorry. I didn't mean to start there, but we have to start somewhere. You need to decide what you want to do about it."

"Like what?" she asked.

"Well, if you and Aidan aren't going to settle your differences, then you'll need to look for somewhere to live. It would make sense for you to stay at the house, but he'll have to move his daughter somewhere—another move for the little girl. Not the best choice. Or you could find a condo or an apartment while you get to work on your divorce."

"Divorce! I don't want to divorce Aidan."

Slowly Lucas turned with the saucepan in his hands, filling two mugs with the steaming brown liquid. "If you don't want to divorce him, what do you want?"

"I—I want Aidan to understand that he's hurt me, and I need time to get over it."

"Then maybe you should simply get an apartment while you decide if you're ready to forgive him or not."

"You make it sound like I'm punishing him."

"Aren't you?" Lucas cocked one eyebrow at her.

"No! I'm the one being punished. I'm the one who has to find a way to live around my husband's infidelity."

"Gracie, that was five years ago. Five years during which you've been happy, right?"

"Yes…except for not having a baby."

"But you are working on that, right? I mean, you've been in touch with an adoption lawyer."

"I have. But Aidan wasn't keen about it. When the whole mess with Deidre happened, it got left behind. Besides how can he pretend to want to adopt when our marriage is in danger?"

"Gracie, that's not fair. Did Aidan say he didn't want to adopt?"

"No. He just didn't act very excited when I told him I'd found a lawyer."

"Okay. So you were in the middle of considering adoption when all this happened, and now you're convinced that Aidan wouldn't be interested in adopting a child." He took a sip of his hot chocolate, a concerned frown on his face.

"What? Why are you looking at me like that?" she asked, annoyed that her brother was taking Aidan's side.

Lucas put his cup down. "Gracie, if you want your marriage, I suggest that you get over there and talk to your husband about Emma, about what you want out of life, about the child you'd like to adopt. Get the ball rolling."

"It's not that simple," she said, feeling defensive, something she rarely experienced around her brother.

"It is simple, if you love him. If you don't love him, then get out of his life. He's my brother-in-law and I'm mad at him for what he did to you. But he's also my friend and my partner. In all the years I've known Aidan, he has been an honorable man who loves you. I've envied him that happiness. As I've gotten closer to Maria, I've learned something that is key to loving someone. You have to talk to each other, no matter how painful the subject is, no matter how difficult or even embarrassing it is to share how you're feeling. If you love someone, you talk, you listen."

"We've been talking," she said, wishing this conversation could be over.

"Have you been listening? Seriously listening?"

"I have. I'm very aware of how Aidan feels about all that has happened," she said remembering how emphatic Aidan was about his responsibility to Emma.

"Then you heard how unhappy he is. How he's willing to do whatever you want if you'll come back."

She couldn't deny that. "Yes."

"And despite knowing that your husband is ready to do whatever it takes to win you back, you're still willing to throw all of that away because you can't forgive him for doing what he did."

Lucas took Grace by the hand and led her to the sofa, where they sat. "You've been married a long time. Your husband, the man you love, made a mistake in judgment five years ago. If you can't listen to him, understand his side of things, and find a way to accept his mistake, you need to move on and let him go."

She hadn't let her thoughts go there, to the step of officially ending her marriage to Aidan. She stared at her brother as his words hit home. "You think Aidan and I are headed for divorce?"

"I have no idea. All I know is that you need to face the reality that if you can't find common ground, a way to settle your differences, you may end up facing the very real possibility your marriage is over. Aidan loves you and he loves his daughter. If you cannot accept that and become part of it, you could end up living without him."

Lucas tucked her hand in his. "Gracie, you've always wanted to be a mom. I realize that this wasn't the way you'd imagined

you'd become one. And although it is a little
unorthodox, you have a little girl in your life
who needs a mother."

An ache started under her rib cage, slowly
moved toward her heart. "What if it's too late
for that? I mean, Aidan and I don't seem to
be able to figure this out. Nothing is going
right between us. What if he feels forced to
choose between me and Emma?"

"Don't let that happen. I'm the one person
who has been around since the beginning of
your relationship back in high school. You
two were meant to be together."

CHAPTER SIXTEEN

IT HAD BEEN a rough few days for Aidan. He'd driven to the house in her car, and the next morning he had Lisa follow him while he dropped Grace's car off, leaving the keys at the desk in the condo building. She hadn't called since.

He couldn't stop thinking about what Lucas had said. Lucas hadn't been able to get out of his Nashville commitments, so their talk had been postponed. Aidan understood better than anyone why Lucas had to go, that he couldn't ask someone else to head up the meeting on a project that would see them break into the Nashville market.

Yet Aidan had nearly called Lucas to ask him to come home. The last thing he wanted was to lose Grace, but he felt powerless to reach her, to get her to see how sorry he was for everything.

He had called work this morning to let them know he wouldn't be in. He had several large files, pricing reports and some new project proposals he needed to review, and his home office was the quietest place he knew.

But he was home for another reason. He needed time to think. He had left messages for Grace, including one that a parcel had arrived for her. And there had been no response. He had driven by yesterday, looking for her car, but it hadn't been in the parking lot.

She was making it clear she didn't want to talk to him, and he had nowhere left to turn... unless Lucas could help. But Lucas wasn't very happy with him and certainly had made it clear his loyalty was to Grace.

Aidan had to admit he'd seen subtle changes in Lucas this past week whenever they talked on the phone. Usually their conversation was open and easy. But in the past few days, Lucas had seemed distracted, distant in a way Aidan hadn't noticed before.

The first time, he hadn't let it bother him, but now he worried that what was going on between himself and Grace had spilled over into his relationship with Lucas. He had to admit that he wasn't surprised. But their personal relationship was key to the success of their company.

He couldn't lose his wife, and he didn't want to lose his best friend and partner.

The dilemma had cycled through his mind, until the previous night when he'd woken with an idea. It was a poor one, at best, but it was all he could come up with.

If he took Grace away to Hilton Head for a few days without any outside interference, he might get a conversation going again, show her that he wanted to include her in Emma's life and his.

If he could get today's pile of work finished, he would be able to devote his time to his wife, and hopefully give them an opportunity to talk things out without his work cell ringing.

He still had to find a good kindergarten for Emma. He had two recommendations from staff at the office, and he had an appointment with each of them before the weekend. But he could send Lisa in his place if he managed to get Grace to consider a trip to Hilton Head.

He was about to open his computer and start his workday when Lisa came downstairs into the kitchen. "Aidan, while Emma is playing in her room, I have to talk to you."

Aidan's heart jumped into his throat. "Is it

about Emma? Is she all right? She's not sick, is she?"

"No. Emma's doing really well. I'm truly amazed at how easily she's settled in here. It's me I need to talk to you about. I've been offered a job in Spartanburg. It's full-time, looking after twin boys. It will mean I'll be near my mother and able to care for her when needed. The pay and accommodations are good. The only problem is they want me on the job by the end of the month."

That was a little over two weeks away. He'd planned on Lisa being here for another month, at least, so he had made no effort to replace her. "That sounds like the perfect job for you."

She glanced at the pile of paperwork, then at him. "I hate to leave you so soon, and Emma is still missing her mom so much. But I feel that I need to take this position. Losing Deidre and watching Emma grieve has been very hard on me. I had always believed that I would be with them until Emma went to high school. They were as much a part of my family as my brothers and sisters, but that's all changed now.

"I realize that you have plans for Emma, and I truly believe you will work things out with your wife. She's a lovely person and Emma adores her. For me, an offer like this won't come my way again, and I do need to be near my mother. Her health isn't good and I'm the only daughter living here in the United States."

Struggling to understand the effect this would have on Emma, Aidan tried to focus on what he needed to do next.

"It's not going to be easy to replace you, Lisa. I wouldn't have been able to manage without you these past few weeks. But of course, I understand. I'll start looking for someone right away."

"Thanks, Mr. Fellowes. I hope that you get your issues resolved with your wife. She is a natural when it comes to children. Emma is always asking when she's coming to the house."

"Thanks for saying that. There is nothing I'd like better than to have my wife back here with me, and with Emma…"

Lisa touched his arm consolingly. "You'll figure it out. Over the next week I'll stock up on supplies of food and things that Emma will need, regardless of who is caring for her. And I will look at those kindergartens, then give you my evaluation. I know what to look for where Emma is concerned. I helped Deidre pick the one in Spartanburg."

"Thanks, Lisa," Aidan said with regret. "We'll have to tell Emma together."

"I dread that the most. She will be upset, and so will I. How do you think we should do this? How do I tell my little girl I'm leaving her?" Lisa asked, biting her lip and turning away.

With a loud clatter, Emma arrived at the bottom of the stairs. "Oops! My dump truck fell. Just fell. Like that." She flipped her hands open and shrugged her tiny shoulders in a show of disbelief.

"Emma, you're going to put your dump truck in the toy box, aren't you?" Lisa asked, a forced smile forming on her lips. She glanced anxiously at Aidan, who gave a barely perceptible shake of his head.

"Yep. When are we going to the grocery store?" Emma asked. "We need more peanut butter. And I want more cheese but no yogurt. Yogurt is yucky," she said as she wandered into the kitchen, chatting all the way.

"When will we tell her?" Lisa murmured.

"I'm not sure," Aidan said.

"I will miss her so much," Lisa said with a catch in her voice.

"And she'll miss you."

Lisa nodded as she smoothed her cheeks, removing the remnants of tears.

They followed Emma to the kitchen. She crouched in the middle of the room, focused on arranging several of her trucks and her tractor. "I'm building a house today. That's why I got to dig a giant hole in the ground." She looked over her shoulder at them, then walked to Lisa. "Why are you crying?"

"I'm not."

Emma planted her hands on her hips. "You are, too."

Lisa ruffled the red curls forming a halo around Emma's head. "We have to get ready to go shopping."

"What are we buying?" Emma asked, smiling up at Lisa. "I love to shop."

"Spoken like a woman," Aidan said to lighten the moment. How was he going to tell Emma that Lisa would be leaving them? And who could come to help him on such short notice?

Grace sprang immediately to mind, but he shied away from the idea. She would likely feel he was using her, further reinforcing her feelings of being left out of the decisions being made.

Lisa gathered the grocery list and her car keys. "Let's get your jacket and we'll head out. Where did you leave it, Emma?" she asked.

Emma swung around. Her lips pursed in thought, she turned all the way around one more time and pointed to the back of a chair in the dining room. "There it is."

"Then get it on. I need to speak to your dad for a minute, so you wait in the hall for me, okay?"

"Sure." Emma ran for her jacket. Pulling it on, she rushed for the door leading to the garage. "We'll play dump trucks when I get back," she said, dropping the one she held in the toy box behind her.

With Emma out of the room, Aidan turned to Lisa. "We have to tell Emma as soon as possible. We need to give her time to adjust to your leaving."

Lisa's eyes swam with tears. "Maybe I could wait and take another job. That way it would be easier on everyone. My biggest concern back in Spartanburg is my mother. She doesn't seem to be doing as well as the doctors suggested she would. It's all such a worry," she said, glancing furtively toward where Emma was playing.

Aidan wanted Lisa to change her plans and stay longer. He wanted that more than anything, and for a few minutes, he considered calling her new employer to negotiate a different start date for Lisa.

With less pressure, he would have a better chance of finding someone with Lisa's skills. All sorts of scenarios went thought his mind at once. Lisa had the right to take a new job. So he had to find a solution as soon as possible. Otherwise, Emma would be even more unhappy and he'd find himself working from home indefinitely.

Abruptly he stopped and looked around. He was doing it again, making decisions for everyone. He'd done it to Grace without a thought. Slowly he reconsidered what he'd been about to do. He didn't need to take charge of Lisa's problems. He wasn't responsible for her. He needed to provide for his daughter.

"Lisa, in all of this, I've not considered what it must be like for you—losing your friend and now having to give up a child you love as if she were your own."

"I am going to be so lonesome for her, but she belongs here with you. That's what Deidre wanted. I have to confess that I was pretty concerned when you wanted to bring her here so soon after her mom's passing, but she is settling in well."

Awkwardly, he patted her shoulder in an attempt to stem the flood of tears. "You do whatever is best for you. We will manage. But maybe you could come back to see us."

"I'd like that," she said, taking a tissue from her pocket. "I'd like that a lot."

"Talking to Emma isn't going to be easy. Should we try for this evening?"

Lisa frowned. "I don't think so. She's usually so tired at the end of her day, which makes her really fussy. It might be better to talk tomorrow morning. She's going to be upset enough. No point in adding to it by timing it badly." Lisa sniffed and looked at him apologetically.

"Okay. Let's plan on after breakfast tomorrow. I'll call and let them know I won't be in the office tomorrow. I feel pretty sure that she'll need reassurance from both of us."

Lisa met his gaze. "Aidan, you're a good dad and a good person." She picked up her purse. "If there's anything I can do to make things right between you and your wife, I'd be willing to do it. It was pretty clear that first day I met her that she was hurt and shocked by what she'd learned. I feel guilty about the way I brought up the photo of you because it hurt her, something I didn't mean to do."

"You were pretty upset yourself, Lisa. We all made mistakes in those first few days."

With a sad heart, he watched Lisa and Emma go down the driveway. He felt empty and alone. He had so much to consider. First, he had to talk to Emma about Lisa leaving. Then he had to find someone to take over the house and care for Emma while he was at work.

Whomever he found would have to be able to start as soon as possible, but it wouldn't be the same as having Lisa, who clearly loved his little girl. He began to realize how much he had counted on Lisa to be here with Emma while he convinced Grace to move back home.

He waited until Lisa's car had turned onto the next street before he turned to the job at hand. He called his office, asking his assistant to see if she could help in the search for a new nanny, then put a call in to the two kindergartens to move the appointments up so that he and Lisa could go together.

He was concerned about how tomorrow would go, how upset Emma would be to learn

Lisa was leaving. The chaos underscored his need to have Grace here. Especially while he talked to Emma.

Grace would know what to say, how to handle this. Emma liked Grace. She was so strong. So capable of seeing what was possible, what would work best for Emma.

He'd been sitting staring at his computer screen, trying to deal with the paperwork spread out around him. All he wanted to do was see Grace, a futile wish, given that she hadn't returned any of his calls. If there was a bright spot to his day, it was that the parcel meant he had an excuse to call her again.

He was still thinking of Grace when the phone rang. With trepidation, he answered, "Hi. What's up, Lucas?"

"You are, you silly bastard," Lucas said. "Like I promised a week ago, I'm coming over to your house. Put the coffee on," he ordered.

Whoa. Lucas's tone said he was angry, which said that Grace was, as well. But if he could reach Grace by having it out with Lucas, he'd do it. "Okay. See you in a few minutes."

"You got it," Lucas said before hanging up.

When Lucas arrived, a scowl dominated

his features like a cloud before a downpour. "Coffee's on," Aidan said, taking two mugs from the cupboard. "Two creams?"

"Yep." Lucas took the cup, had a quick sip, then leveled a look at Aidan he'd never seen before. "When are you going to fix things with my sister?"

"I've tried. She is still very angry about everything."

"And that's your excuse? Hell, Aidan, you can do better than that."

"Lucas. She won't talk to me. Ever since we stopped in at the hotel bar at Foley Beach the other night. She acted really strange and I could tell she was upset with being in the bar, being around singles... Or I assume that's what it was." Aidan put his cup down. "And I made a really dumb remark that didn't help things."

"Acting dumb is going around like a flu bug, it seems."

"Why do you say that?"

"I talked to Grace."

"What did she say?"

Lucas sipped his coffee, a glum expression on his face. "Not much."

"Grace is still convinced that my relationship with Deidre went on a lot longer than it did."

"Did it?" Lucas asked, his gaze fixed on Aidan.

"No!"

"Then get your act together. Grace is hurt over your infidelity. That's influencing everything for her."

Aidan nodded slowly as Lucas's words cut into him. "What a complete fool I've been." Aidan scrubbed his face, felt the stubble along his chin. "My second mistake was to think that Grace would go along with what I thought was the best plan."

Lucas nodded slowly. "Well, I can tell you that Grace is miserable, She just sits in my condo and knits. She doesn't seem willing to talk to us, but something has to change. I just can't watch my sister being so unhappy and not do something about it."

"Lucas, I had an idea last night, but can't do much about it if Grace won't talk to me."

"What's your idea?" Lucas asked, a quick look of interest on his face.

"I thought I'd see if Grace would go away with me for a couple days. If we could find time alone, just the two of us, without any interruptions, maybe she could be persuaded to come home and try again with me."

The emptiness of the house seemed magnified by his thoughts of Grace. "I miss her so much. I can't imagine my life without her."

"Okay, here's what I'm going to do. I'll talk to Maria and get her advice on how to convince Grace to see you. You let Grace know about the quilting fabric, didn't you?"

"Yes. I did, but she didn't answer my message."

"My sister loves her quilting fabrics. That might be the easiest way to convince her to come over here. The rest will be up to you. Unless you have another idea…"

Rubbing his jaw in thought, Aidan said, "Emma's nanny, Lisa, is leaving at the end of the month. She and I are going to talk to Emma tomorrow morning. What would you think if I asked Grace to be there? Am I being a total idiot to think she might be interested in being part of that?"

Lucas stared at him for a few minutes. "I honestly don't know how she'd react. I'm pretty sure she likes Emma. In fact, my sister loves all children and wouldn't want to see any child hurt. I guess you could call her and see what she says."

"If you can get her to return my calls."

"Maybe the best answer is for you to go to my place and talk to her. Just give me fair warning you're coming so I can be out before you get there."

"I could give that a try. Would you be willing to give her a message?"

Lucas scanned the ceiling before answering. "I'll put in a good word for you, but you need to make the effort. I'm headed to the office and then out of town on the McLellan project. It's all up to you, buddy. Good luck."

Relief flowed through Aidan like a warm summer breeze. "I'll try anything."

"By the way, if Grace is willing to go away with you, be sure to turn off your work cell. Nothing kills a romantic moment faster than a call from work." He tapped his chest. "I found out the hard way a couple weeks ago. I've never seen Maria more upset."

"And if I disappear for a couple of days, that will mean more work for you," Aidan said.

"All for a good cause. I need you to focus more on work, and Grace needs you back. Not to mention what Emma needs in all this."

Lucas put his cup in the sink and slapped Aidan on the back before heading to the door. "Try not to blow it, Aidan."

CHAPTER SEVENTEEN

GRACE SAT ALONE in her brother's condo, trying to sort out her feelings. She'd hardly slept since her talk with Lucas. His words, his serious tone, had filled her with dread.

More than anything that had happened so far, Lucas had made her aware of how fragile her marriage was, how little it would take to end it. She'd never truly considered that she and Aidan might not be able to resolve their differences. Yes, she'd had moments of frustration when they seemed miles apart. But underlying that frustration had been the deeper confidence that they would fix their relationship. They'd always been able to talk over any problems in their marriage, but this time was different. What had happened five years ago was tearing them apart.

Deep down she knew she'd been hiding out at her brother's place, taking solace in knitting and watching TV. But she needed to do something to move on with her life, to figure out what she should do with her marriage.

She wanted to deny that she'd been unable to accept what had happened to her and Aidan in the past few weeks. Lucas couldn't possibly understand how painful it was to face up to the fact that Aidan had a child with another woman. And how could Lucas possibly believe that what Aidan had done to her was acceptable in a marriage based on love and trust? She'd come up with all kinds of reasons Lucas had to be wrong, but none of them made sense in the darkness of her room each night.

Was she simply unwilling to accept what Aidan said? That he'd made a mistake a long time ago, and it had nothing to do with his love for her?

And what about Emma? She couldn't help but love the little girl. Yet if she wasn't an equal partner in raising Emma and making decisions involving her, the rest of their relationship would suffer the consequences.

Still and all, she missed Aidan so much, found herself thinking about him all the time. What was he doing? What was he feeling? Was he eating, looking after himself? Between his new family responsibilities and his work, he had to be under even more pressure.

She'd been at the table with Lucas and Maria several times over the past days and heard how busy Lucas was, which meant that Aidan had even more work responsibilities than she'd been aware of. She wanted to call Aidan, to let him know she was here if he needed her. But she wasn't going to do that. Not without some resolution about her role in Emma's life.

She glanced at the phone, uncertain what she should do. If she called Aidan, what would she say? How could she begin a conversation about them when she wasn't certain where to start? And the way she was feeling right now, she was afraid that what she did say would come out as an accusation. And what was the point in that?

Of course, her fabric had arrived. Having waited weeks for the expensive tapestry material, she wanted to see it. She'd chosen the fabrics online and intended to use them to make a wall hanging for her church.

Could she simply return his call about the fabric? That would be a neutral topic, possibly a place to start. She touched the phone, her fingers tapping along its smooth surface. "Do it!" she said to the empty room.

She reached for the phone just as it rang. Caller ID showed Aidan's number. Suddenly nervous, she picked up. "Aidan?"

"It's me, Grace." She heard him sigh and wanted to reach through the phone and touch his cheek. "I—did you get my message about the fabric?"

"I did. I was thinking that I might come over today sometime if you're going to be around. Or this evening, maybe," she offered, aware of how much she needed to hear his voice.

"I'm working from home today. Come over anytime you want," he said, his words tender in her ear.

Her body warmed at the memory of other times when he'd spoken to her like that. There had always been such warmth between them, such a powerful connection, and yet...

Her heart pounding in her throat, she clutched the phone tighter to her ear, willing him to talk to her about how he loved her, needed her and wanted her in his life. He'd said it the other night, but in her anxiousness, she needed to hear it once more.

In that moment, she faced what had been

uppermost in her heart. She would give anything to see him. But she needed to move quickly before her courage deserted her. "What about now? Or maybe in an hour?"

"No. Please. Come over now. I'm right here. I'll close up my computer and turn my cell phone off so we can talk," he said, his words coming fast.

"Okay. I'll be over in a few minutes," she said, her heart pounding in that old familiar way it did whenever she talked to her husband.

Grace drove carefully through the streets toward the house she loved and the man she'd married and had loved with all her heart. Did she still love him after all this, or was she simply wishing for her past life? Would he ever understand how much he'd hurt her? Despite how she felt about him, what he'd done five years ago would always be between them, influencing how they felt about each other, if they couldn't find a way to overcome it.

Would they be able to connect, to put the past behind them? If she were willing to try again, how long would it take before she could trust him with her feelings? And if they were to start over, to put their marriage first in their lives, how long would that take? What if they discovered, after months of trying again, that their love hadn't survived what they'd been through?

What if she got to the house only to learn that nothing had changed, that Aidan insisted on convincing her that she needed to see things his way? If he did, what would she do? She suddenly realized that she'd been placing all her hope in a meeting like this, one where they could share their concerns as a starting point. And if it didn't go that way...

As she pulled into the driveway, she noted that Lisa's car wasn't there. She had felt uncomfortable around the woman from the first moment she met her, mostly because Lisa seemed to know things about her husband she shouldn't have known if Aidan had only been at the house once.

No matter how hard Grace tried, she couldn't shake the feeling that Deidre and Aidan had been in touch after their short affair. Underneath everything that had gone on, Grace was afraid that Aidan hadn't told her the whole truth. And no matter what they said to each other, how hard Aidan tried to convince her otherwise, the fear she felt at his behavior was the direct result of his infidelity. A betrayal she might not be able to move beyond. If she were unable to put the past behind her, there was little hope for their marriage.

Pushing her worried thoughts to the back of her mind, she got out of her car and went up the front walkway. The door opened and Aidan was standing there with a huge smile on his face, making her heart tumble in her chest.

He moved toward her...then stopped. "You're here." He sighed out the words. "Come on in. Do you want coffee?"

She glanced around at the smattering of toys lying about the front hall and the pink hoodie hanging on the newel post at the bottom of the stairs. "Is Emma here?" she asked, not wanting to have the little girl overhear their conversation.

"No. She's with Lisa, running errands." He smiled again, a smile so warm and inviting she wanted to walk into his arms.

"I was pleased to hear my fabric had arrived," she said, glancing around the living room, seeing the dollhouse at the end of the sofa and the Lego blocks on the coffee table.

"I've put the parcel right here." He pointed to the long flat box propped near the door.

"Thanks. I'll get it on my way out," she said, going down the hall to the kitchen.

The kitchen area was in disarray with the piles of files and the laptop on the counter, toys scattered everywhere. The sun caught the edge of the table where coloring books were spread out. Everything looked so lived in, so much the home of a child who was loved and cared for. "Emma must keep you busy."

"She does. She's basically taken over most of the house with all her stuff. And today I have a bunch of files that are in the way." He glanced at her anxiously. "Let's go to the living room. It's probably the least cluttered part of the house," he said, placing his hand in the small of her back, the heat of his fingers, the ease of his touch so familiar.

They faced each other, their eyes locked, the air between them charged with unanswered questions and emotions that neither could express.

Finally, Aidan said, "Grace, I'm so glad you're here. I wanted to tell you how sorry I am that I messed up our date. I never considered that being in a bar would be so difficult for you and my thoughtless remark..." He glanced away. "I don't seem to get anything right with you anymore."

Seeing the anguish in his eyes, she reached for him. "You are having as much trouble with this whole thing as I am. I came here wanting to see if we can work through this somehow." She gave him a wry grin. "Lucas read me the riot act the other day."

His expression brightened and he reached for her hand. "Me, too. But he was right about everything. I need to listen to you."

"And I need to understand where you're coming from." Her breath seemed to be stuck in her throat at his touch, the encouragement shining in his eyes.

"Why don't you start? I promise to listen." He led her to the sofa.

She eased down beside him, acutely aware that he still held her hand, his touch so warm. "I am having trouble accepting what happened, but you already know that."

He sandwiched her hands in his. "The time I spent with Deidre was wrong and disrespectful. But I wasn't keeping it from you for any other reason than that I didn't see any point in hurting you over something that was done before it began. It was never anything more than a working relationship that got out of hand."

"But finding out about Deidre, then being left out of your plans for Emma, made me feel worthless, not really part of our marriage anymore. As long as we've been married, I have supported you, been there for you during all your business ups and downs. Yet, when it came to the most important part of our lives, you decided to go it alone. You made me feel as if you didn't need my support, not as your wife nor as your friend," she said, feeling the rise of resentment in her chest. "I really wanted you to allow me to be part of the decision."

"I see that now. I really do. I did try that day on Skype, but it didn't work out..." He tugged her fingers closer into the palms of his hands. "Grace, I want to explain something that might help you understand where I was coming from, what I was feeling and thinking."

The look of vulnerability in his eyes touched her. Aidan had always seemed so in charge, so capable of taking care of anything. Yet now she saw the exhaustion in his eyes, the worry lines around his mouth. She didn't say a word while she waited for him to continue. Her only movement was to gently squeeze his hand.

Aidan took a deep breath to steady his racing heart. Looking into her clear blue eyes, he was reminded of the day they met. He'd been waiting for an excuse to talk to her, and her math problems gave him an opening. He still remembered how she chewed her lip as she listened to him, the way she was doing now.

"You and I have wanted children all our married lives, and I was so certain that we would have them. Then, when it became clear that we couldn't, I was as brokenhearted as you were. The only difference was that I felt I needed to be strong for you, to protect you from the pain of knowing there wouldn't be a baby for us. I came home every day, saw the sadness in your eyes and felt helpless to do anything to ease your sorrow."

"You have no idea what it was like, because you were busy or away from home," she said, tears shining in her eyes.

He touched her cheek, wiping the damp spots with his fingers. "I left you to fend for yourself because I wasn't doing well with it, not just for me but for you. I wanted you to have a baby even more than I wanted a baby for me."

"But you didn't tell me that. You left me to believe that I was the one suffering the most, facing up to my sadness."

"That's where I went so wrong. I should have talked to you about my pain, my loss, instead of shielding you from it. I believed I was doing the right thing, but I realize now I wasn't. Grace, there hasn't been a day that I didn't wish with all my heart we had a child, our child," he said.

"We should have been more open about our feelings," she said. "When you found out that Emma was your child, I needed you to understand how I was feeling. Not just the sense of betrayal but also how left out I felt by your need to charge ahead and do what you believed was best."

"As difficult as this is for me to say, I was so happy to learn that we had a child. All I could think about was bringing our child home to be here with us. I know I handled it badly, but all I wanted was for us to be a family. I had a child who could make that happen, who we could share. The circumstances were not what I would have wished for. But in my mind, it was the next best thing. That's why I rushed into it, organizing everything, thinking that I could fix your loneliness, your need for a child simply by taking charge of Emma's life."

She nodded slowly as her eyes moved over his face.

He felt her gaze like a blessing, a loving thought exchanged between him and his wife. "I could have waited and I should have. I should have left with you that first day so we could talk this over. It was so stupid of me. And the worst of it is that I can't go back and fix any of it. I can't take back your pain at feeling left out or the loneliness my crass behavior caused you." He squeezed her hand gently, willing her to believe him. "I can only try and make it up to you now."

"Then why wouldn't you see an adoption lawyer with me?"

He wanted to tell her what she wanted to hear, but was it true? Did he want to adopt? "I'm not sure. I guess I felt that, after all our efforts to have a child, the way our life had been taken over by the desire to have a family, I needed a break from it all. I needed you to myself for a little while, needed you and I to be a couple devoted to each other."

He wanted to pull her into his arms and kiss her, show her how much he loved her. But he was afraid that if he moved too fast, she would feel he was pressuring her. He didn't want that. Never. "I don't have the words to explain my behavior. It was wrong of me to make you feel so alone. Since you've been gone, I wake up every morning facing an empty bed. I can't go on like this. The long nights of lying awake, missing you. No morning talks. No discussions about our days. We belong together. There's never been anyone for me but you. Only you."

"Oh, Aidan..." She moved closer to him.

He closed his eyes in torment. He had to get this right. He had to. "And it's because I love you that I'm willing to accept whatever it is you decide you want. I'm here for you. I've tried to make it clear how I feel, how sorry I am. I won't pressure you into a decision about us. I'm powerless to change how you feel about what I've done to you."

"Aidan, I want us to be happy again, but I don't know how to do it, how to fix what went wrong between us."

Aidan fought the urge to crush her to his chest, to plead with her to move home. But if there was one thing he'd learned through all of this, it was that he had to give Grace time to accept what had happened and how sincere he was in trying to make amends.

"I would like for us to go away together. So much has happened since Charleston. I really believe that if we spent time together, really shared our feelings about everything that has happened, we can find our way back to each other. I've already talked to Lucas and he's willing to take over for me. I promise to never touch my business cell phone from the minute we leave here until we get back."

He stopped, confused by the look on her face. Was she crying? "Oh, Grace, darling, I didn't mean to make you cry. I really wanted to do something nice for you, spend time with you, but if you don't want to—"

"I do," she said quickly. "I would love to go away with you."

He held his breath, uncertain as to what to do next. "Are you sure?"

"Yes, I am. More than anything we need to work things out between us."

His throat thick with emotion, he pulled her close and kissed her gently—and with so much bottled-up feeling he thought he would burst with happiness. When her arms moved around his neck, he took her face in his hands and kissed the last traces of tears from her cheeks. "Grace, whatever happens from here on, we're in this together."

His cell rang, startling both of them. Holding her close, he pulled the phone from his pocket. The caller ID showed the kindergarten he'd hope to enroll Emma in. "Sorry, but I need to take this call. It's about Emma's kindergarten. Do you mind?"

For a moment Grace hesitated, her teeth biting her lower lip. "No. Go ahead."

Thankful for Grace's support, he answered the phone.

"I'm sorry, Mr. Fellowes, but we won't be able to offer your daughter a place at our facility because we don't have the space for her. I can leave you on the list and if there's a cancellation, we could see about fitting her in."

He gave a sigh of disappointment. "I'm sorry to hear that. I was hoping you would be able to accommodate her. Thank you for informing me of your decision."

He ended the call and put the phone away.

"What happened?" Grace asked.

"I was trying to enroll Emma in a kindergarten recommended to me. They don't have an opening, at least, not now. Maybe later."

"How soon do you need a kindergarten? I understood that Lisa was staying on with you to give Emma lots of time to adjust to her new life here."

He grimaced as he leaned forward resting his elbows on his thighs. "Lisa's not going to be here much longer."

"Why?" Grace asked, curious as to why the nanny would be leaving before Aidan had everything in place. But maybe he had found a pediatrician and a dentist and all the other things Emma would need to be healthy and happy. Maybe the kindergarten was the last piece. Her feelings of being outside the circle saddened her. She wanted to be part of that, part of putting Emma's life together here in her home.

The urge surprised her a little. Yes, she'd wanted to be involved, but her motivation now had less to do with her role in her marriage and more to do with wanting what was best for Emma.

"Lisa has a job near where her mother lives. I hate to let her go, but feel I have no choice. It's been difficult even with her here—I have no clue how I'll manage when she's gone."

"And there is a problem over the kindergarten?"

"More like several problems. No kindergarten arranged yet. I haven't been able to spend the time to get Emma settled the way I'd planned, what with work commitments.

Worst of all, I have to tell Emma that Lisa is leaving. I don't know how to do it, and I'm afraid that she will be so unhappy without Lisa…"

He needed her support, her understanding. Forgetting her own concerns, she said, "Emma will be upset. You can't avoid that. She's a strong little girl, but to be losing the one person who has been with her, who was there from the beginning, will be very painful."

"Lisa and I are going to talk to her about all this tomorrow morning. I'm worried about her reaction. Lisa is upset over leaving Emma but feels that she has to take this job offer. I don't know what I'll do if Emma becomes inconsolable."

"That's awful," Grace said, imagining how hard it might be for Emma to get over Lisa's departure.

Aidan nodded. "I'm sure Lisa won't want to give up her new job and I can't, in clear conscience, ask her to do that simply because Emma is upset. So I guess I have to find someone to replace Lisa. But there won't be any time of adjustment. I don't see where I can have someone hired in enough time to work with Lisa before she leaves. I mean,

I can't be careless with this decision. The nanny has to be someone who is right for Emma."

"What do you believe is the best answer for Emma?" Grace asked, seeing the defeated look in her husband's eyes.

Aidan took her hand. "I wish I could answer that without making it sound as if I called you here because I am desperate and you're the only person I can trust. Although that is the truth. There is no one I can call on to help me but you." He got up, his body tense as he clenched his hands and paced the room.

She rose and stood beside him, in the middle of the hall, in their home, hearing Aidan's words while her heart melted at the pain in his eyes. She'd been so absorbed in her own problems, her own feelings of loss and anxiety, she'd failed to realize that Aidan was struggling, too. Only he had a child to care for, regardless of how he was feeling. "What is it you want from me?"

"Grace, I have no right to ask this. You have had a real hard time because of me. But I'm desperate to make Emma happy. Yet I'm worried about her ability to cope with another loss in her life."

His hand moved up her back, around her

shoulders, pulling her into the safety of his arms as they stood together at the entrance to the living room, the room where they'd started to create their home, their new life together.

The memory of those early days of love and caring, and their dream of children filling every room, made her loss even stronger. Overcome with emotion she turned to face him, and the love in his eyes stole her thoughts.

"Would you be willing to be here while we talk to Emma? Emma really likes you. She might feel less upset if you were with her. It's asking a lot, I know."

Seeing the agony etched on his face, Grace had to look away. Her knees shaking, she made it to the sofa in the living room, thankful to be able to sit. Aidan followed, easing down beside her.

"Talk to me, Grace," he said, his words coming out in a hoarse rasp. He reached for her hand.

Aidan's body was so close to hers, his heat surrounded her, his hands offering her strength and certainty. She remembered the first days after Deidre's death, her anguish at finding out her husband had had an affair, that there was a child from the relationship.

Her disbelief that he'd left her alone, uncared for, in his eagerness to meet his needs and those of his daughter. Those had been the worst days of her life.

Yet as she sat next to the man who had caused her so much agony, listening to his concern for Emma, she was at a loss as to what to do. If she refused to help him and walked out, their marriage would be over. If she stayed and helped him sort out his problems, she would once again be putting his needs ahead of hers. Rather than resolving their issues, she would be choosing to smooth things over for Emma's sake.

Looking around at all the toys, the books, all the things that made a little girl happy, she realized that she had no right to withdraw her support. Not if it meant that someone as precious as Emma could benefit from her help.

Emma did not deserve to be caught between them over issues she had no knowledge of and events that had been out of her control from the beginning. This little girl had lost her mom, the worst thing that could have happened to her. Now Emma was about to lose the second most important person in her life. Someone she loved dearly and would miss so much.

There was only one thing Grace was certain of at this moment. What was going on between her and Aidan could not be allowed to destroy Emma's happiness. "You said you were talking to her tomorrow morning?"

"Yes, but if you're here and willing to be part of it, maybe we should talk to her this afternoon when they get back."

"So, they could be here at any moment?" she asked, feeling pressured by the thought that her decision had to be quick.

"Yes. But we can wait, if you need more time." He patted her hand, ran his fingers across her palm, driving her crazy with need.

Was she ready to be involved with him? Could she put aside her concerns and help him? If she did, this might be a place for them to start. If she didn't, she might lose the one chance she had to get him back.

She'd spent all these days wanting him to come to her, to explain himself to her. She wanted him to face up to what he'd done. He hadn't come to her in the way she'd wanted or expected. But he was here now with her, pleading for her help. She might not be willing to forgive him, but she was willing to help him for Emma's sake. "I'll stay. I'll be here when they come back."

He took her in his arms, kissing her so gently and with so much slow-burning passion, she was lost in his embrace. Wrapping her arms around him, she stroked his face, returning his kisses, her body arching to his. "Grace, I want to make love to you right this minute. Is that what you want?" he asked.

"Yes," she breathed, her hands moving over his chest.

Sighing deeply, he whispered, "We would be upstairs now if I didn't know that Emma and Lisa could be home any minute. But if we weren't facing this situation at the moment..." He leaned back, pulling her into the crook of his arm, easing her head onto his shoulder. "I am so glad you're here with me."

For the first time in a long while, she felt hope flooding through her. "Emma deserves all the love and caring we can give her," she said, feeling the impact of her words, the love growing in her heart for Emma.

Aidan hugged her close as he led her to the kitchen, walking side by side as they'd done so often before. "Let's have a cup of coffee to celebrate. I'd like to have something stronger, but that can wait until we're alone."

The door to the garage opened. Emma stood there staring at them. "Daddy!"

CHAPTER EIGHTEEN

EMMA RACED IN, trailing a plastic grocery bag behind her. "We got Cheerios. Lisa says they are good for me. Do you like Cheerios?" she asked, coming to a halt in front of Aidan as she dropped the bag and put her arms out to him.

"I love Cheerios. We'll have them for breakfast, will we?" he asked, lifting her into his arms and kissing her cheek.

"We can have them now," Emma said, planting a big noisy kiss on Aidan's cheek.

He hugged her, his arms cradling her body as he swayed back and forth. "We can do whatever you want, Emma girl."

Emma spotted Grace and leaned back in her father's arms. Her eyes widened. "Do you want to make peanut butter sandwiches?" She wiggled out of her father's arms to go to Grace. "I help Lisa, but after that we could make some sandwiches," Emma said, putting her tiny hands on her hips, the way Aidan did so often.

Grace, her heart filling with love for the little girl who had made her husband so happy, glanced at Aidan. "Like father, like daughter?"

"Oh. You mean this," he said, resting his hands on his hips.

"Exactly."

Aidan's smile radiated happiness. "She is amazing, isn't she?"

"Come on." Emma took Grace's hand, leading her to the cupboard and opening the door, peering inside before pulling out a jar of peanut butter. "You get the bread."

"Are we being just a little bossy?" Lisa said as she entered the kitchen, her arms full of grocery bags.

"Let me do that," Aidan offered, taking the bags from her and placing them on the counter. "I'll get the rest of the groceries out of the car."

Turning to Aidan, she said, "Can you take Emma out with you for a few minutes?"

"Absolutely," Aidan said. "Emma, Daddy needs your help with the other groceries." He held out his hand.

"Yeah!" Emma raced past Lisa, red curls circling her head.

"Thanks," Lisa said, nodding at Grace. "It's nice to see you."

"It's nice to see you, too." Grace helped take the groceries out of the bag, feeling more relaxed than she had in weeks. Was it being back in her house again, or was it simply being with Aidan?

She stopped to consider, a bag of Oreo cookies in her hands. It wouldn't be her kitchen again until she could accept everything that had changed these past weeks, changes that both she and Aidan had to cope with if they were going to be part of each other's lives.

With Emma out of the house for a few minutes, she turned to Lisa. "Aidan tells me you're going to Spartanburg soon."

Lisa hesitated for a few seconds. "Yes. I'm worried about how Aidan will manage. I've gotten to appreciate him. He's kind and considerate, and he is a great dad. The only reason I feel I can leave is that Emma is perfectly happy here with him. At first, it didn't go so well, but now I have no doubt that everything will work out. The only other thing I wish for Emma is that she have a new mom," Lisa said, a knowing look in her eyes.

"I want that for Emma, too." Grace wanted to be involved in Emma's life, but first she needed to resolve her feelings, find a way past them if she was to be a good mother to Emma.

She hadn't wanted to face the thoughts that had played in her mind as Aidan talked about kindergarten for Emma. They were thoughts that frightened her, left her feeling alone and inadequate. For all her wishing and hoping for a baby, during which she'd planned and pushed Aidan to continue the treatments to conceive a child of their own, there had been one unexpressed thought lurking in the back of her mind.

After all the effort they'd had to put into getting pregnant, would she be a good mother to the baby she'd wished and prayed for so long? Being younger than her brother, Lucas, she'd never experienced what it felt like to care for a child. And her only babysitting jobs had been with children who were in school.

She'd read every child-rearing book she could find, haunted the library for information on childhood diseases, all in preparation for having a baby. Grace's friends had often teased her about her obsession with being the perfect mother. Little did they or anyone else know despite all her preparation she was afraid of failing at the one part of her life that meant so much to her.

According to Lisa, Aidan was a good parent, something that surprised her a little and thrilled her a lot. Now it was up to her to follow his lead if she wanted to be part of Emma's life.

"Grace, you and I don't know each very well, and we got off to a rough start. If I caused you pain over what I said, I want you to know it was never intended to hurt you."

"You were going through a difficult period, too," Grace offered.

"I was in shock after Deidre's death. She was my employer, but she was also my friend. She was a good mother and one of the best people I ever worked for. I miss her. She did everything she could to give Emma a good life, and that included providing for her should anything happen." Lisa met Grace's curious glance. "If Deidre had loved Aidan, she would have said something to me. She certainly would not have allowed him to walk out of her life."

At Lisa's words Grace recognized that her

suspicion had come from her fear that Aidan had lied to her. Now that Lisa had told her what she knew about Deidre's relationship with Aidan, she stopped to consider what it must have been like to have a baby and decide not to contact the father of the child.

While Grace had been preoccupied with conceiving a child to complete her family, Deidre had chosen to face being a parent alone.

Grace glanced at Aidan as he came into the kitchen carrying grocery bags, Emma following along behind him. Her husband had been hurt, as well. What had he felt when he realized that Deidre chose to keep him out of his daughter's life? That phone call saying that he was Emma's father had to have been very difficult in ways Grace couldn't imagine.

How must it feel to learn that you had a child you didn't know existed when you wanted one so badly? All the lost chances to be with your child, hold her, watch her take her first steps, be there when she went to day care, dream of her future.

"Grace!" Emma called from her perch on the edge of a chair at the table. "I need you."

"The queen has spoken," Aidan said, putting the last bag on the counter. "I've learned that resistance is futile," he said, smiling softly at Grace.

Grace looked into his eyes as he towered over her, his closeness framing her thoughts. She wanted to touch the auburn curls along the nape of his neck, hold him close in her arms and feel his body on hers. She loved this man. She'd loved him since that day in high school. "Can we talk a little more about going away together?" she whispered.

His face brightened. His smile widened. "You mean it?"

"Yes, I do," Grace said, leaning close to him, breathing in his scent, feeling at peace and at home in his world.

He picked her up and swung her around, holding her as they danced around the kitchen. "You have made me the happiest man on the planet. We can go anywhere you want," he said, kissing her lips, hugging her body to his.

"No! Don't take my daddy! No!" Emma screamed, racing to her father, pushing on Grace, pinching and crying. "Go away!"

It wasn't the pinch that hurt so much as the feeling of separation that rocked Grace. Emma's fierce response made Grace feel isolated and in need of reassurance. It was obvious how frightened Emma was of losing her father, and how angry she felt.

Still, Grace wondered how she and Aidan were to talk out their problems if Emma made this kind of fuss over them talking a little bit? But they weren't only talking...

Lisa glanced from Grace to Aidan and moved quickly, picking Emma up in her arms, patting her back and trying to soothe her. "There, it's okay. You shouldn't pinch anyone, Emma. That is wrong."

"I didn't mean to." Emma stuck her thumb in her mouth as Lisa picked her up. "I want Mommy," she whispered, her tearstained face looking into Lisa's.

"It's going to be all right. You'll see," Lisa said, her pleading glance reaching across the room to Grace.

What should she do? Should she offer to take Emma and soothe her? Or would that simply make things worse?

Undecided, she stood rooted to the spot.

Emma began to cry again. Squirming, she stretched out of Lisa's arms, reaching for her father. "Daddy," she pleaded as big sobs shook her body.

Aidan reached for her, pulling her into his arms, forcing him to move away from Grace in his eagerness to soothe Emma, leaving behind an empty desolate space.

Grace watched helplessly as Aidan cuddled Emma, swaying with her as she sobbed into his neck. Grace didn't belong here.

"I'm sorry. I didn't mean to upset her." Grace said, struggling to maintain calm, to not cry. Everything had been going so well, so much better than she could have hoped.

Aidan gave her an anxious smile. "This has happened before. She'll be all right in a few minutes."

Emma glanced at her suspiciously, sniffling and clutching her father's shirt. "You can't have my daddy," she said, a dark frown on her face.

Overwhelmed with worry, Aidan felt trapped between his wife and his daughter. He'd never been in this sort of situation before, where everything hinged on how he behaved and whether or not Emma could be convinced to let Grace be around him.

He could see the hurt look on Grace's face and wanted to hold her and reassure her that she was in this with him. They were a team. He had this moment of opportunity, one he wouldn't let get away from him now that he was so close to having Grace in his life once again. "Lisa, can you take Emma for me?"

Lisa put her hand on Emma's back, speaking gently to her. "You come with me, sweetie. We'll play dump trucks in the living room. You like driving them over the carpet. I think there's a bunch of new building blocks in the garage. Why don't we get those?"

Emma's sobs faded to soft hiccups. "I want to stay with Daddy." She nestled into his shoulder.

Aidan struggled to figure out what to do. He didn't want to upset Emma, but he couldn't let Grace feel left out.

He couldn't believe she'd agreed to go away with him. He'd started out today fully prepared to accept that Grace and he were finished, but now, with her willingness to be with him, everything had changed.

"Emma, Daddy really needs to talk to Grace. I need you to go with Lisa, just for a few minutes. I won't be long, okay?"

Emma snuggled closer into his chest, her suspicious glance still on Grace.

Clearly unhappy, Grace moved away from them, over toward the kitchen table. "I'm going to sit here for a little while, Emma. You and Daddy talk a bit. You love your dad, and he loves you." She sat at the table, her eyes meeting his, his heart flipping sideways at the look of consolation on her face.

She understood what was going on and had decided to remove herself from the situation. It had been clear from Grace's expression that she'd been hurt by Emma's abrupt response, but she'd recovered and had put Emma's needs first.

Looking into her eyes, seeing her sincere need to alleviate Emma's distress, he couldn't remember a moment when he loved her more than he did right now. Seeing her like this, cold reality hit him. He didn't deserve this woman who loved so deeply, who cared with her whole heart. But if he had a chance to keep her, he would love her unconditionally forever.

"Or I can go out into the garden, look at the fishpond and see if the bird feeders need filling while you talk to your dad. Would that be better?" Grace asked, smiling warmly at Emma.

Aidan could have hugged her for being so kind, for helping him manage the situation. He mouthed, "Thank you."

She nodded, a small smile starting at the

corners of her mouth. "I'll also check for bunny rabbits while I'm in the garden."

"Bunny?" Emma asked, brightening, a look of interest on her face. "Where's the bunny?"

"I'm not sure," Grace said, "but maybe if I take a carrot out to the garden, he'll come to see me. We have a small shed at the back where I keep my gardening tools. Maybe he's there. What do you think?"

Emma wiggled out of her father's arms and came to Grace. "What's his name?"

"He doesn't have a name yet. He's big and brown, and he loves lettuce. I usually buy lettuce just for him. But why don't you and I see if we can find him, and in the meantime, you can come up with a name for him. How would that be?"

Emma fidgeted for a moment, looked over her shoulder at her father before turning back to Grace. "I can find the carrots in the fridge. You want to come with me?"

Grace's smile was bright as she looked across the room into Aidan's eyes. Their eyes held. His heart swelling in his chest, he whispered, "I love you."

"I love you, too," she whispered back.

"What are you saying to Daddy?" Emma

asked, a small frown forming between her blue eyes.

"Saying? I'm telling your daddy something really special." Grace laughed, the upbeat sound filling the kitchen, a sound Aidan had feared he would never hear again.

Aidan, his love for Grace a soothing balm easing the fear that had plagued him since she'd come to the house, couldn't help but smile as he followed Grace and Emma out into the garden. Hanging back just a little, giving the two people he loved most in this world a chance to be together, he felt at peace and happier than he could remember.

GRACE LED EMMA out to the rear of the garden, hoping that the rabbit would be somewhere near the shed. That's where she'd last seen him. "Emma, what do you think would be a good name for the bunny?" she asked as she searched the area just beyond the pond for any signs of the rabbit.

Emma held the carrot like a sword. "I'd like to call him Sam," she announced. "I would like him to be Sam."

"Sam it is," Grace said, still searching for any sign of the rabbit. As they neared the shed, she noted a small shift in some of the huge leaves of the hostas along the back fence.

"Maybe Sam likes a cool spot, especially on a hot day like this," Grace said, moving closer to the large leaves. Pushing one slowly aside, she saw the rabbit crouched under the leaves, his nose sniffing the air, his eyes alert.

"There he is," Grace whispered, pointing toward the bunny that looked ready to leap away.

"Can I play with him? Will he let me hold him?" Emma asked in an exaggerated whisper as she held out the carrot.

"Probably not today," Grace said, wanting to hug Emma to her and never let go. She'd never known a moment with so much emotion in it, never imagined that this was what it felt like to love a child and to do something so simple as to search through the garden for a rabbit. She wanted many, many more moments like this.

Glancing at Aidan, seeing the adoring look on his face, she knew beyond a shadow of a doubt she couldn't let go of any of this, no matter what it took. As she stood there, waiting for the rabbit to leap away, she realized in that instant she loved this little girl with all her heart.

The rabbit darted sideways and disappeared farther into the flower bed. "He's gone!" Emma said, charging toward the spot where he'd been. "Let's go," she yelled to Grace as she scrambled through the wide, green leaves, making them sway and bend.

"You won't be able to catch Sam. He's faster than either of us."

Emma stopped. "Where did he go?"

"I have no idea. But he likes my backyard so he'll be back soon."

"Yours?" Emma asked, coming to a full stop, making the giant leaves shudder.

Grace took a deep breath, aware that Emma might not realize that this was her home, as well. Feeling she had no choice but to answer, she said, "I live here."

Emma put her thumb in her mouth, turning in a wide arc. "Where? Where do you live? In there?" she asked, pointing to the shed.

How should she handle this? Emma only knew about her dad and Lisa being in the house. What would happen if she told Emma the truth? And was it the truth? Did she intend to return to her home, regardless of Emma's response to her?

Anxiety tightening her tummy, she smiled

as she leaned closer to Emma and said, "I live in this house. This is my garden."

"No. You don't. Daddy does and Lisa. Not you." Emma scowled at her. "We live here. Not you."

Had Aidan not said anything to his daughter about her? About their life together? How could that be possible? She glanced at Aidan, who looked worried. As he walked toward her, she struggled not to cry.

"Emma, why don't you go in and get Lisa to give you some Cheerios as your snack?" Aidan asked, taking Emma's hand and leading her toward the deck door.

Grace sought the bench seat at the corner of her garden and sank unsteadily onto its cool surface. Hurt boiled up through her, betrayal ground its way into her heart.

Why hadn't Aidan mentioned to Emma that she lived here? Had he assumed she wasn't coming home again? Her stomach ached with anxiety and disappointment. She had to get out of here, away from all this. Coming here had been a huge mistake. She would go around to the front of the house, grab her purse and leave.

Out of the corner of her eye, she saw Aidan come through the deck doors and down the steps toward her. It was too late for her to escape, and as she met his gaze, she really didn't want to. She'd made a mistake, assumed too much, and now she had to face her actions because of it.

As he made his way around the perennial bed she'd planted last year, his eyes on her, she steeled herself for the inevitable confrontation. "Why doesn't Emma know who I am and that I live here?"

He stopped a couple of feet from her, his expression downcast. "Grace, I wasn't sure if you planned to come back, or if I could convince you to return. Emma has had such a confusing time these past weeks, so many things happening in her life, I felt it best to only tell her the things that mattered in her daily life."

His words stung. "Are you saying I don't matter in Emma's daily life?"

"No. It's just that things have been sort of up in the air, and I really didn't know what to tell her about you."

She fought for control. She could not cry. "I wasn't here because you wouldn't include me. It was your choice, not mine. Now your daughter is upset that this is my home as well as hers. You wanted my help, but how can I help if Emma doesn't want me here?"

Hesitating, his eyes searching hers, he said, "I had to make a decision about who was in her life when we arrived here. She was crying and upset. I'd already messed up badly where you were concerned. From what I could tell, there was no chance that you wanted to be part of our lives. It wasn't a decision meant to hurt you. It was a decision made to offer my daughter as stable a life as possible under the circumstances."

He softened his tone as he moved to the bench beside her. "For now, you're someone she likes and can play with. I didn't take it any further than that because I didn't want to disappoint her."

"Why didn't you ask me if I wanted her to know that I lived here?" Grace demanded, aware of how unreasonable she sounded but not able to stem the accusation.

"Because we aren't together anymore, Grace. We're trying to figure things out, and I really believe we will. But if you weren't coming back, then what would be the point in telling Emma who you really were? If I told her, only to have you decide not to return home, how would Emma cope with that? It's clear she likes you, but if she lost you, too…"

His words hung in the air between them.

Her heart pounding in dread, she said, "Aidan, if only we'd waited and worked out the details of taking her into our lives… All of this would have turned out so differently."

"Yeah…" He looked into her eyes, his face solemn and sad. "If I could turn back the clock…" He sighed as he reached for her hand. "What do we do now? What do we tell her? Whatever we tell her now won't be easily changed without making her upset."

As she looked at her husband, she had to admit that she was to blame here, as well. She and Aidan had to fight for their marriage. They'd never had to before this, but now everything hinged on both of them seeing what they were about to lose. "There's no point in rehashing the past where Emma is concerned. We both should have found a way to talk to each other about this."

His eyes searched her face, his gaze filled with love and longing. "All I've ever wanted is you, Grace. I can't help believing that, if we work on it, we can be happy again." He eased closer, the scent of his skin intoxicating. "We can be a family."

CHAPTER NINETEEN

AIDAN COULDN'T STOP himself from putting his arm around Grace's shoulders. He needed to touch her, to feel her close to him while he waited for her to speak. What would she say? Would she feel pressured by Emma's needs to answer him before she was ready? But she'd come here to see him, and that had to mean she wanted to work things out.

Or maybe her only reason for being here was to get her quilting fabric. They'd talked a little when she first came to the house, but she hadn't committed to anything other than that they needed to talk. Something they'd both agreed they needed to do long before she arrived at the door.

"Grace, please believe me when I tell you I've changed. This does not have to be resolved right this minute. You came over here to get your parcel. I'm the one who assumed that you might be willing to be here for Emma. I dragged you into my problem of finding someone to replace Lisa. That wasn't fair."

"With Emma in our lives, it's crucial that we face what is going on between us. I accept that you made your decision about me and my role here so as not to confuse her, but if we don't decide what we're doing, how we're going to live, we will confuse her even more."

His heart sank to his stomach. Was she saying that they couldn't fix their differences over Emma? Each time he saw Grace with Emma he was more and more certain that she was falling in love with their child. "Then what do we tell Emma when she asks who you are? Do we say you're a friend? If we aren't getting back together, will you still want to be part of Emma's life? You have to help me here, Grace. I'm lost and afraid that it's all over between us."

She stood before him, her face turned to his, a sad smile hovering on her lips. "I love you, Aidan. I came here not only for my fabric, but also to work on how to solve our issues. I was so afraid to come here."

He started to interrupt, eager to explain she needn't be afraid of him, but she put her hand over his mouth to stop him.

"Aidan, we can't let our marriage go. We've

been through a rough patch, but I have to believe we can work this out."

"Grace, the truth is this. I don't deserve your kindness and caring. But if you're willing to work on this, I will do whatever it takes to have you back here in my life."

He drew in a deep breath to ease the thundering in his chest. "We can do this, but we have to be clear what is going on in our lives where Emma is concerned. If there is one thing I've learned in the short time she's been with me, it's that she has to feel safe, to know that people love her. And we still have to get through Lisa's return to Spartanburg and how Emma will cope with that," he said, pulling Grace's hand closer to his chest in an attempt to draw her to him.

He smiled at her, holding her close as he remembered how stupidly he'd behaved. "I wish I'd listened to you. If I had, and we'd made a plan for putting our family together, none of this would have happened."

"We don't know that. I doubt very much that any child could lose their mother and not have issues that needed to be dealt with."

He was so thankful for her words. But not nearly as thankful as he felt with her beside him, talking with him, sharing her thoughts.

"Are you ready to be a full-time mom? Ready to forgive me for screwing everything up? If we are going to be with each other, we need to figure out how that will work, at least, as much as we can. I realize we won't get everything right, but if we can find a way to be happy as a family..."

He had to find out what would happen next or die trying. "What do you want to do? I really want you to tell me what you think would work out best for you, for all three of us."

She didn't say anything for so long he began to panic. What was she thinking? What would he do if she didn't feel she could be part of his life?

Steady. Trust yourself. Trust her.

Her eyes met his. He knew by her expression that she'd made a decision. His body felt drained, finished.

"Aidan, I don't want to rehash the past few weeks and what's gone on between us. You're right when you say we need to make a decision, both for us and for Emma. Especially Emma."

She looked up into his face and it was as if the sky had brightened. "What you did hurt me so much. But what you said is true. It was years ago, and I believe you when you say you didn't continue to see Deidre. I want to be with you. I want us to be a family."

He wanted to yell for joy as he wrapped his arms around her and kissed her face, her eyes, her lips, while his hands roamed over her back, down her body. Her sudden intake of breath fanned his desire. "I've missed you. Every day. Every minute of every day." He smoothed his hands over her body, feeling all the familiar spaces, her curves, the bony crest of her collarbone. He loved all of it.

"I missed you, too…so much. It's been awful being without you. It was so strange to come to my house, see things being done differently and realize that if I didn't work things out with you I would not be coming to this house, our home, ever again."

"So, what do we do now?"

"Can we think of something, some way to spend time together as a family? Away from here? Away from all the reminders of what we nearly did to each other?" Grace asked, letting her fingers play along the open neck of his shirt, her touch making him wish that there was no one in the house but them.

As his eyes met hers, he could be certain of only one thing. If they'd been alone, he would have taken her upstairs and made love to her.

"We could always spend a day with Emma at a theme park where she could play. We could watch her be happy. If she asks who you are, we can say that you and I are her family."

"How do we know what she'll ask when we go back into the house?" Grace asked.

"We don't," he said, running over the possibilities, all the while distracted by the way Grace's body fitted along his, the scent of her hair, the warmth of her skin. "Maybe we should go in now and tell her who you are. Why you're here."

"And what if she is so upset she can't be soothed? What if she can't accept me as part of her life, not to mention the idea that I would be her mother? Maybe we should wait for a little while until she's more settled?"

Aidan met Grace's anxious gaze and knew only one thing. He and Grace would once again be in the same bed tonight. Whatever needed to happen, whatever explanations were necessary, he would not live without her for another night. "I'm going to talk to Emma about this. I'm going to explain who you are, how important you are to me, how much I love you. And then I have to have faith that our daughter will be okay with it."

Grace felt a shiver of anxiety. What if what

Aidan wanted to do turned out to be a catastrophe, with Emma inconsolable and calling for her mother? "There has to be a better way. I mean we need to find a way to convince Emma that I'm not taking her mommy's place and that she can feel safe." Worried, she snuggled against Aidan, eliciting a sigh of pleasure from him.

"Wish you and I could stay like this, have nothing to think about or worry over for at least a few days." He leaned closer, kissing her lips, awakening her need for him, for all they had missed while living separately.

"Wish we could, too..." She turned to Aidan, catching the look in his eyes, a look of devotion that swept through her heart. She sat up straight, suddenly alive with an idea. "What if we took Emma to Disney World for a vacation, even just a couple days? We could do it right after Lisa leaves so that Emma has something fun to do. It might make losing Lisa a little easier for her. That way she wouldn't feel she was losing you when we talk casually about me coming home, and she sees how much fun the three of us can have as a family. If we do this right she will not feel left out or threatened by me being around."

Every ounce of Aidan's attention was focused on Grace, making her feel cherished and cared for. "You are a genius," he said enthusiastically. "That would work out perfectly. I'll book us into the Disney resort in Florida. We will have so much fun, the three of us." He grabbed her, pulled her to her feet and walked with his arm around her shoulders as they approached the patio doors. "Holding you, having you here with me feels so good," he murmured into her hair as he opened the door into the house.

Their entrance into the family room was met with a squeal of delight from Emma. "Daddy! Lisa and I need to show you something." She took his hand, pulling him into the living room. "See!"

"See what?" he asked, searching the lawn.

"Right there." Emma pointed toward the hibiscus bush near the corner of the flower bed in front of the window. The rabbit, his nose wiggling, was peering out from under the shrub. "I love him. Can he be my rabbit?" she asked, her face turned up to her father.

Love overflowed his heart. "Yes, he can be your rabbit."

"I've already named him. His name is Sam," she said, a look of mischief in her wide blue eyes.

"Sam. Sounds good to me. What do you think, Grace?" he asked as she came up behind them.

Grace was struck by the thought that at any other time in her marriage she would have reached out, put her arm around his waist and hugged him. But with Emma watching and her uncertainty about their relationship despite Aidan's profession of love, she hung back.

Standing beside him, seeing him with his daughter, Grace was struck by how much they looked alike, each with curly auburn hair and wide smiles.

She glanced around the wide foyer, the long length of window forming one wall of the living room, the dining room beyond the living room, its table set as if waiting for the fun and laughter of a dinner party.

Aidan turned his smile on her, making her tummy tingle. "Are we sure this rabbit is a boy?" he asked.

"Not sure. But the name works. If needed we can change the name to Samantha, Sam for short," she said, noting that Emma was suddenly showing a great deal of interest in her. "What do you think?" she asked, leaning down toward Emma.

"Just Sam." Emma shook her fist for emphasis. "The rabbit is mine. He looks really, really hungry. I want to get more carrot and some lettuce and see if he will eat it from my hand," she said, heading back down the hall toward the kitchen. They followed, glancing at each other.

As Grace moved toward the kitchen with Aidan, she had the sensation that she was coming home: home to a life of toys everywhere, Cheerios in the cereal cupboard and a little girl who was enthusiastic about everything.

"We're the lucky ones, aren't we?" she said, hugging Aidan close, her smile open, her heart humming. "We are in our home with our daughter."

"Life doesn't get much better than this, Mrs. Fellowes," Aidan said. "We'll get packed and take Emma away on our first family vacation to Disney World."

He pulled her into his arms, kissed the breath from her lips. "Welcome home, my love."

* * * * *

*If you enjoyed this romance,
don't miss these titles
from Stella MacLean:*

*UNEXPECTED ATTRACTION
SWEET ON PEGGY
TO PROTECT HER SON
THE DOCTOR RETURNS*

*Available now from
Harlequin Superromance.*

K